Remember, Remember

THE SHERLOCK HOLMES AND LUCY JAMES MYSTERIES

The Last Moriarty
The Wilhelm Conspiracy
The Crown Jewel Mystery

Upcoming:
The Jubilee Problem
Death at the Diogenes Club
The Return of the Ripper

The series page at Amazon:
http://amzn.to/2s9U2jW

OTHER TITLES BY ANNA ELLIOTT

The Pride and Prejudice Chronicles:
Georgiana Darcy's Diary
Pemberly to Waterloo
Kitty Bennet's Diary

Sense and Sensibility Mysteries:
Margaret Dashwood's Diary

The Twilight of Avalon Series:
Dawn of Avalon
The Witch Queen's Secret
Twilight of Avalon
Dark Moon of Avalon
Sunrise of Avalon

The Susanna and the Spy Series:
Susanna and the Spy
London Calling

OTHER TITLES BY CHARLES VELEY

Novels:
Play to Live
Night Whispers
Children of the Dark

Nonfiction:
Catching Up

REMEMBER, REMEMBER

A SHERLOCK HOLMES | LUCY JAMES STORY

BY ANNA ELLIOTT AND CHARLES VELEY

This is a work of fiction. Names, characters, organizations, places, events, and incidents are either products of the author's imagination or are used fictitiously.

Typesetting by FormattingExperts.com
Cover design by Todd A. Johnson

ISBN: 978-0-9991191-1-2

Part I

Back in Time

1. A Rude Awakening

"Miss? Miss?"

The voice filters slowly into my consciousness, as persistent and irritating as a steady drip of water from a rusted tap.

"Miss, are you alive?"

That is what one might term an excellent question.

I have to admit that my current reality: face down on some sort of cold, rock-hard surface that smells strongly of horse dung, chilled to the bone, and with a headache that feels like sharp-edged rocks are crashing around inside my skull—appears to rival even the traditional fire and brimstone on the spectrum of unpleasant outcomes for the afterlife. But I do not believe myself to be dead. Which would lead one to the conclusion that I am indeed alive.

"Miss? You can't sleep here. The museum will be opening soon."

No, I am definitely still alive.

Which I suppose on the bright side means that I am not consigned to an *eternity* of lying here with a crashing headache and a strange male voice addressing me as *Miss*.

Something awful has happened. An unnamed horror twists in my stomach. Something awful is waiting for me—ready to pounce.

I can't remember what it is, but I can feel dread pooling like a lead weight in my chest.

"Miss?"

I push myself up to sitting—at least my arms and legs still appear to function—and pry open my eyes.

"*Will* you stop saying that?"

The owner of the voice sits back, blinking in surprise at the suddenness of my resurrection.

"Saying what?"

Now that I am more fully awake, his voice sounds low and pleasant. He has an accent of some sort that I can't place.

My first glance provides me with a jumbled impression of dark hair under a domed blue helmet and thickly-lashed dark eyes.

But the feeble light of what appears to be either very early morning or very late evening is stabbing clear through to the back of my skull.

I squeeze my eyes shut again, massaging my forehead in vain hopes that some of the throbbing ache will stick to the tips of my fingers.

"*Stop saying 'Miss!'*"

"I beg pardon." The man's voice—*Policeman's* voice, a sluggish part of my brain corrects. *That's why he's wearing the helmet and the dark blue tunic. He's a police constable.*

No, actually detective constable. Risking a second glance through slitted eyes, I can make out the insignia patch on the sleeve of his jacket.

"But since we haven't been formally introduced, it seemed like *Miss* was the best I could do."

His voice is amused more than anything else. But then he clears his throat, sounding somewhere midway between disapproving and awkward.

"Look here, you'd better find a place to sleep it off. Somewhere safe. If you go down to Queen's Street you could try the St. Vincent De Paul Society. I can't promise that they won't ask you some awkward questions or want to pray for the good of your immortal soul, but—"

The dark speckles are clearing from my vision, the headache retreating from agonizing to merely sickening levels of pain.

It's enough for me to finally take in the full details of the detective constable's appearance.

He's quite young. I doubt he can be more than twenty-two or -three.

He's also quite handsome. His features are lean and sculpted, with dark, straight brows, a square jaw, and a firm, graceful curve of his mouth.

His dark eyes are intelligent, but also slightly shadowed, watchful and jaded-looking—as though young as he is, he's already seen his share of the ugly side of life.

The pale white line of a scar bisects his eyebrow on the right side, making me think that he's also seen his share of violence. But somehow it only makes him more handsome, not less—turning him from a perfect paragon into a real, living, breathing human.

He looks, not humorless, exactly—but slightly grim, with an edge of danger that makes me certain any criminal would have to be an idiot to challenge him while he walks his beat.

Beneath the regulation police tunic, his shoulders are broad and straight. I think he's tall, but at the moment, he's crouching beside me on the ground, so I can't tell exactly how tall.

He looks strong and quick—and completely self-reliant. I can't imagine him trusting easily or laughing particularly often.

All of which is interesting to a student of human nature. But also more or less irrelevant, since it in no way lessens my outrage at him.

I draw myself up. "Are you implying that I'm a"—for a moment, my mind hitches on coming up with the right word—"street walker?"

The constable blinks at me, obviously taken aback once again. Then he quirks up an eyebrow. "Maybe you'd rather be called a night flower? Or some other term?"

"I do not prefer *any* term!" I glare at him. "I'm not a—"

A wave of dizziness slams into me, as though somewhere inside my mind, I've just run straight into a brick wall. Darkness swirls across my field of view all over again.

"Miss?" The constable's voice seems to come from a long way off, flattened and distorted by the roaring in my ears. "Miss, are you all right?"

I don't even have the energy to snap at him for calling me *Miss* yet again.

"Certainly."

He doesn't sound as though he believes me; his voice softens slightly. "What's your name?"

"My name—"

I don't know.

That's what I've just realized. I can't remember anything about myself. Nothing at all.

"I'd ... rather not say." I force myself to draw in a shaky breath, then another. Don't panic.

Panicking never solves anything.

How would you know? A nasty, jeering voice in the back of my head asks. *Maybe you just don't remember*.

No, stop. Just think. I recognized the detective constable's insignia. I risk a cautious look around us, and catch a glimpse of a city street, stone row-houses marching in an orderly line behind wrought-iron fences and tiny yards.

London. The word slowly surfaces inside my mind.

I have no idea how I came to be lying on this particular patch of cobblestones here—but I know that I'm somewhere in the city of London.

Somewhere in the spinning chaos behind my eyes, I *must* have the answer to exactly who I am.

Think.

But there's *nothing*.

It's not just the headache—though that's not helping. I feel as though a giant hand has reached into my mind and scooped out all trace of who I am and what I'm doing here.

All that's left is that same overwhelming sense of dread I felt before. It hasn't gone away. I may not know who I am—but my insides feel tight and clumped together with the cold certainty that *something* horrible has happened.

The detective constable clears his throat again. "Be that as it may, you need to be moving along."

"Wait!" I hold up a hand—then notice that the sleeve of my dress appears to be covered in the source of the smell of horse dung.

Ugh. "You wouldn't happen to have a handkerchief, would you?"

The young man's expression veers between bemused and exasperated—but he digs into a pocket, producing a square of cotton. "Here."

"Thank you."

I scrub the worst of the muck away from my sleeve, then hold the handkerchief out to him.

The constable draws back. "No thanks. Consider it a gift. As I was saying, the museum will be opening soon, so you'd best get moving—"

"Say 'moving' again!"

The young man gives me a look as though he's beginning to suspect that I'm not only a lady of loose morals, but a madwoman, also.

But he evidently decides to humor me. "Moving."

"Yes!"

He gives me an even odder look, but I don't care. A tiny spark—not exactly of memory, but at least of *knowledge* is flickering to life in me.

"My voice doesn't sound like yours!"

The constable's eyebrows go up. "Yeah, well. That'd be because I'm from Cheapside right here in London, and you sound like you're—"

"American!" I finish for him.

Unfortunately my feeling of triumph doesn't last long. I'm certain that the voice I hear coming from my own lips *is* accented with the tones of America.

I don't actually remember *being* an American.

This is ridiculous. I press the back of my hands to my eyes. I have to remember *something.*

I'm a young woman. *Not* a lady of the evening. I'm originally from America—

A sudden shower of images explodes across my field of view—sharp and jagged as broken glass.

A hand—my hand?—holding a revolver.

A woman screaming, howling like a lost soul.

Blood spurting onto dirty paving stones—so much blood. No one can lose that much blood and live.

My stomach spasms, bile stinging the back of my throat. I curl over, trying not to be sick.

"Miss?" The constable's voice is laced with a shade more concern now.

"I think I may have shot someone."

That is not, of course, a sensible statement to make to a detective constable. But my lips shape the words before I'm even fully aware of what I'm saying.

"You shot someone." The constable's eyebrows are once more quirked up, and his expression is calm. "Can you tell me who?"

"No."

Maybe I was wrong. Maybe the sickening sense of dread I feel isn't because something horrible happened to me. Maybe *I'm* the one who committed a heinous crime.

"Hmmm." The constable doesn't look ready to arrest me. Instead he takes my hand.

His touch is surprisingly gentle, his fingers warm against my own half frozen ones. He bends his head, inhaling with his face close to my palm. The tickle of his breath is strangely intimate—almost enough to make me yank my hand away.

But his expression is completely impersonal as he raises his head.

"There doesn't appear to be blood anywhere on your clothes. Which itself doesn't tell us anything. But even barring where a girl of your—" he stops. "A girl such as yourself would have gotten a gun, there aren't any powder burns on your palms. Nor any smell of gunpowder."

"I could have worn gloves."

I'm not sure what I'm doing. Surely I don't wish to be arrested. But somehow I can't stop myself from pointing it out.

"True. But those right there are your gloves, aren't they?" The constable points to a small lady's handbag—which I notice is lying next to me on the ground.

The gloves are not tucked into the bag, but lying right on top, as though I pulled them off and laid them there.

The constable picks one up, turns it over in his hands, then sniffs it, also. "No smell of powder there, either."

I look at him with a rising degree of respect. "You're not stupid."

For the first time since our conversation began, he actually smiles. A dimple appears in one cheek. I blink. I thought him handsome *before* he smiled.

"They didn't make me a detective because I know how to whistle."

Then he stops, sobering. "Look, Miss, ordinarily I'd be required to charge you with being intoxicated in a public place—"

I interrupt. "You have the brains to deduce that I haven't fired any weapons recently—but you can't tell that I'm not intoxicated? Do you *see* any signs of drink about me?"

Actually, for all I know, I *could* be recovering from one too many glasses of gin.

But somehow my mind rejects that possibility without my even having to think about it.

The constable's gaze sharpens as he appears to realize the truth of what I've just said. He studies me more closely—no doubt checking my eyes for bleary redness and my breath for the smell of liquor.

"So if you're not drunk—"

I scramble to my feet—managing to sway only slightly as the movement sparks another fierce throb of my head.

Until I know exactly who I am and what's happened, the *last* thing I want is to attract the interest of a policeman—however young and however handsome.

"I beg your pardon. I must have had a dream—a nightmare, rather." I force a smile. "I'm sure that I'm entirely recovered now."

The constable is still staring at me. I can almost hear the wheels turning inside his mind, trying to come up with a likely scenario that would have brought me here.

That makes two of us.

A church bell suddenly tolls from somewhere nearby.

Five … Six ….

The constable straightens. "Come on. I'll help you find somewhere safe to stay."

That is also the very last thing I want just now.

I shake my head. "I'll be quite all right on my own."

The young man hesitates—unfortunately for me, he appears to have scruples about leaving me alone.

So I add, "You are about to go off duty, and you have someone waiting for you. Maybe a younger sister?"

The young man's head snaps up sharply at that, and he looks at me through suddenly narrowed eyes. "How do you—have we met before?"

"Not that I know of."

He has no idea how very true that is.

The young man's expression moves from startled, to wary.

I feel slightly better about having been mistaken for a prostitute. I get the feeling that he does not often allow anyone or anything to catch him by surprise.

"But I can tell that you set aside a somewhat wild and dangerous youth in order to serve on the side of the law."

Both the constable's eyebrows go up this time. "Oh I did, did I?"

I should probably stop talking. But this conversation is making me feel steadier. "I admit that last is largely surmise—but I believe it is logical."

The constable looks at me. "What are you, some kind of Sherlock Holmes?"

"Sherlock Holmes." Something tugs in the back of my mind, like ripples moving on the surface of a cloudy pond. "I *know* that name."

The constable gives me another odd look. "Yeah, you and the entire British Empire."

I hesitate—but I need to leave. Now, before he remembers his earlier determination to find me a safe charity house.

"Well, good-bye, then."

Without waiting for an answer, I turn and stride off with as convincing an air of determination and confidence as I can muster.

The street is growing crowded with traffic—carriages rattling past, wagons loaded with vegetables rumbling by on their way to the market. I'm surrounded by vendors with baskets of purple flowers, and laborers with shovels and other tools slung over their shoulders.

I manage to keep up the act of determined confidence until I've turned the first corner I come to.

Then I duck into a covered doorway of a shop that's not yet opened, lean against the cold brick wall and shut my eyes.

I have no idea who I am, where I am going, how I came by the headache that at this moment is rattling the inside of my skull … or what crimes I may have committed.

I blow out a breath. *Being a lady of the evening would have been so much simpler.*

2. An Expert Diagnosis

I open my eyes, staring up at the lowering gray sky. Sadly, though, no answers appear written in the clouds. No clue falls conveniently out of the heavens.

I need to think about my situation logically. I slow down my breathing, trying to quell the rising panic inside my chest.

For a start, I can take stock of everything I know about myself, and try to deduce what I can. If my powers of deduction worked on the constable, they surely ought to work on me.

The headache appears to be concentrated in the back of my head, a few inches behind my ear.

Gingerly, I put up a hand to touch the area. Yes, there's a definite swollen lump there that throbs fiercely at even a slight brush of my fingertips.

Either I fell and hit my head—which seems unlikely, given the lump's placement—or else someone attacked me.

Excellent.

My situation seems to get better and better all the time. Now not only may I have shot someone, it appears that some nameless enemy wants me incapacitated or dead.

Well, better to keep going.

My clothes are of good quality. My high-button black leather boots are a little worn at the soles, but highly polished and still quite serviceable.

It would appear that I do not make a habit of sleeping on street corners. Therefore, presumably, I must have a home *somewhere.* Perhaps even a family who are missing me?

No.

I'm not even sure how, but again something inside me seems to reject that idea—just the same way that I rejected the possibility of being drunk before.

Whoever I am—wherever I come from—I have a bone-deep certainty that I'm not part of any jolly, loving family who are even now frantic at my absence.

My memory is still a blank, black wall—but at the same time, some small, inner gauge inside me is certain that I'm very, very accustomed to being on my own.

I open the purse that the constable pointed out to me. In addition to the gloves—good quality white kidskin, I notice mechanically, and fairly new—the purse appears to contain nothing but a handful of coins and a torn scrap of newspaper.

I blow out a breath. I was not *really* expecting the purse to contain anything helpful like a calling card with my own name and address on it. But it would certainly have been a pleasant surprise if it had.

I carefully unfold the newspaper—but it's only an advertisement for tooth powder. *Rollo's Best Tooth Cleansing Agent.*

I stare at the words blankly for several seconds, trying to decide whether they conjure up anything in the way of memory.

Assuming that this purse is mine, I must have placed the scrap of paper in here for a reason. But I don't feel even a flicker of a hint of recognition.

There's nothing else inside the purse, either—nor in any of the pockets of my coat. I search carefully once and then again, but find nothing at all to give me a clue as to who I am and how I came to be here—wherever exactly I am.

But wherever this is, I cannot stay here all day. If nothing else, the owners of the shop will eventually be arriving to open the doors.

I push myself off from the wall behind me.

At least the handsome constable is nowhere in sight when I return to the bustle of the street.

At the end of the street is a huge stone building, fronted by a white marble colonnade.

My mind slowly puts the sight together with the constable's remark. *The museum will be opening soon.*

That building up ahead must be the museum he spoke of.

I cannot remember having ever seen it before. But maybe this was where I was coming, when I—

What?

When I was assaulted?

When I shot someone?

Even exhausted, with a vile taste in the back of my mouth and a blinding headache, I can hear how absurd that sounds. *I was on my way to visit the new display at the museum when I happened to commit a murder.*

Certainly. That is undoubtedly what occurred.

Still, the museum at least gives me a starting point, a possible objective. At the very least, it might be somewhere for me to take shelter, out of the cold.

From what I can see of my surroundings, it must presently be sometime in autumn. The air feels damp, raw and chill, though not yet cold enough for it to be winter. The occasional scraggly trees that grace the fenced-in gardens I've passed are still clinging to brown and yellow leaves.

A glance down at my own attire, though, puts an end to the thought of taking shelter in the museum. I only vaguely processed the state of my clothes when I was taking stock of myself a moment ago—I was more focused on trying to decide whether I recognized the gray walking suit with black braid on the sleeves and the hem.

But now in the growing morning light I can see that my skirt is fairly plastered with mud—and doubtless other noxious substances, too. My hair is straggling down into my face, and there's a long tear in the bodice of my jacket.

In short, I look as though I've either been the victim of a carriage accident or highway robbery. I suppose either of those is possible.

It is also possible that despite my disheveled appearance, the museum officials would take pity on me and allow me inside. But it seems equally likely that they will make the same assumptions about my virtue that the constable did.

If I do seek shelter there—or anywhere—covered in horse dung, I will be remembered.

I cannot afford to be memorable. Not when whoever struck me on the head is presumably out there, still searching for me.

I rub my forehead, trying my hardest to conjure up some other fragment of recollection—*anything*.

Part of me is afraid to make the effort. What if I remember that I really did commit a murder?

But the larger part of me is convinced that nothing could be worse than this awful uncertainty. Slowly, something does rise to the surface of my mind. Not a memory, exactly, nor even an image.

It's a smell: a muddy, fish smell. Though what that means, I have no idea.

Without really being aware, I've been continuing to walk down the street facing the museum. Now I come to a corner and stop, glancing around me.

I have come to the corner of Montague Street, according to the sign. I wait, trying to decide whether I feel any spark of recognition.

But no. Nothing at all.

"You vile, unspeakable little brat, be off with you!"

The shrill voice pierces my ears, even above the rumble of traffic and the tramping and noise made by the other pedestrians.

I glance up and see that there is some sort of altercation taking place on the pavement just outside one of the houses on Montague Street—a tall, red-brick town home with something staid and stuffy-looking about its heavily curtained windows and immaculately polished brass railings.

The woman doing the shrieking is every bit as stuffy-looking as the house. Short and extremely plump, she's swathed in a thick fur-collared cape, and wears a bonnet trimmed with jet-black beads.

In between the fur collar and the bonnet, her face is red, bad-tempered, hook-nosed—and with a truly astonishing number of double chins that wobble with outraged dignity when she goes on, speaking in no less piercing tones.

"Be off this instant, or I shall call the police!"

The object of her ire is a small and extremely dirty boy who's cringing before her, looking miserable and cold and thoroughly cowed.

"But ma'am, I only asked if I could polish yer shoes."

The lady gives a sniff that rattles all the beads on her bonnet. "Polish my shoes? As though I would entrust such an important task to the likes of you! Now be gone!"

Pointing dramatically with one finger, she dismisses the child. Then turning, she takes the hand of a footman, who I now see is standing ready to assist her into a carriage waiting at the curb.

She does not thank the footman. But she does lean out of the carriage window and snap, "Oh, and Jenkins, tell Sarah that the state of the front stoop was absolutely *disgraceful* this morning. If she wishes to remain in my employ, she will have to scrub it again."

The footman—Jenkins, presumably—mutters, "Yes, ma'am."

The red-faced lady's head withdraws and the carriage rattles off.

The small boy is still standing dejectedly on the pavement a short distance away. He's really incredibly dirty. By comparison, my own attire looks almost clean. His face is smeared black with soot, and the rest of him is in scarcely better condition. Despite the cold, he wears only a pair of ragged trousers and a thin cotton shirt at least two sizes two small.

His bony wrists and hands stick out from the cuffs, the skin red and chapped-looking.

"Excuse me."

He whirls around at my addressing him, his face instantly set in a look of narrow-eyed suspicion and his whole body tensing. He's ready to run in an instant, should I appear as any threat.

But he evidently decides that I'm not dangerous, because his gaze travels over me, and then his eyes widen.

His face, like the rest of him, is bony and much too thin. But his eyes are a clear hazel-brown.

"Whatcha want?" After the first second, he drops his gaze, muttering the words at my shoes.

"Do you live around here?"

The boy's head snaps up and he gives a snort that rivals the disagreeable woman's.

"If I did, would I be beggin' for the job of polishing that old bat's shoes for 'er?" He gives me a scornful glance—followed by a harder stare.

"Whatsa matter with you?"

I was counting my small store of coins as one of the very, very few advantages to my present situation.

But now, with a sigh, I dig into the purse and hand over nearly the whole handful, keeping back only the half-shilling piece.

The boy looks as though he hasn't had a decent meal in his entire life. And if I really did shoot someone in the early hours of this morning, I presumably have enough on my conscience without adding cruelty to children to the list of my sins.

"Here. For you," I add, as the boy gives me a blank, wide-eyed stare.

"Now, can you tell me whether—" I stop, and start over. "Have you ever seen me going into one of these houses before?"

The street may not feel familiar—but it is as likely that I live somewhere around here as anywhere else.

The boy gapes at me for another second. "What? No, of course not."

I suppress a sigh. "What about this house here?" I gesture to the home of the disagreeable woman. "Do you know who lives here?"

The beginning glimmers of a plan are just starting to take shape in my mind, but I need to know more.

The boy shrugs. "Besides the old bat? No idea."

I rub my forehead. This is turning out to be a waste of good money. At least the boy should be able to buy a decent meal for himself today.

His hand has closed over the coins, and he regards me with an odd intensity. "I'd see the doctor if I were you, miss."

It's my turn to be startled.

The child's wide, hazel-brown gaze is thoughtful, filled with a look of almost adult appraisal. "You should see the doctor, miss."

He enunciates the words clearly, lending them an odd kind of emphasis. "You really, really should."

3. A BIT OF THEATER

The back of the plump woman's house is every bit as stolid and officiously respectable as the front. Even the steps leading down to the coal cellar look as though they've been scrubbed to within an inch of their lives.

But there *is* a stack of empty wooden packing crates leaning against the side of the house, and it's affording me enough cover to watch the kitchen entrance.

My head still spins occasionally, and my thoughts feel disturbingly sluggish and slow. It may be that the street urchin was not entirely wrong about my need for medical attention—but I am not thinking about that for now.

So far, the fishmonger's boy has been to deliver a parcel of fish—which afforded me a modicum of information about the household.

The door was answered by a young maidservant in a black uniform and starched white apron, who handed over a few coins to the boy and took the parcel of fish.

Through the briefly opened doorway, I could catch a glimpse of a kitchen—a huge, old-fashioned black iron cooking range, and a stout woman who must surely be the cook stirring something in a large pot.

So, a cook, a young maid, and the manservant, Jenkins, who handed his mistress into the carriage a short while ago.

Are they the only servants in the house? More to the point, does the disagreeable lady reside here with any other family members?

My memory of how the world works seems to be patchy: sharp and bright in the case of some details, and hazy on others.

Unfortunately, one of those patches of haziness appears to cover the question of how many servants a household like this would be likely to employ.

I had the vague impression that the lady of the house was a widow—and she is certainly well past the age when one would expect her to have small children at home.

But there could always be a companion, a widowed sister—even an adult daughter living here with her. And I'm so far coming up with disturbingly little basis for logic that would lead me to favor one conclusion over another.

I blink, as a fragment flashes through my mind. It doesn't feel like an entirely new thought—more like something I've heard before:

Well, faint heart never won fair lady.

But when I try to catch hold of the memory, it slithers through my fingers and vanishes.

I stiffen, pressing myself further into the shadows as the gate of the yard creaks again. Footsteps on the cobblestones announce another delivery.

This time, it's the baker's boy—delivering two loaves of bread.

I step forward, plastering my most winning smile on my face. "Hello. I was sent out here to pay you for today's loaves."

The boy is perhaps fourteen years old, with bright, carrot-orange hair, a snub nose.

He gives me a narrow-eyed look. "Never seen you here before."

I keep my smile firmly fixed in place. "I'm new, aren't I?"

Some instinct makes my voice slide into an approximation of the boy's accent.

It happens so naturally that I *know* I must have done this before: made my voice sound other than American.

"I was just'ired on yesterday." I wish I'd been able to hear the disagreeable woman's name. That would probably lend artistic verisimilitude to an otherwise bald and unconvincing narrative.

Now *those* words sound familiar, too. I blink, trying to bat the impression away. No time for chasing down errant memories now.

The boy looks me up and down, his green eyes keen. "Dirty, aren't you?"

Drat. Anyone would think that after the morning I've had, I would be owed at least *one* measly stroke of luck.

But apparently the fates couldn't do me the favor of providing me with a *dullard* of a baker's boy.

I laugh. "Don't I know it. It was supposed to be my half-day out—but since I'm new, guess who gets the job of cleaning out the facilities?"

I point towards the odoriferous little out-building at the back of the yard. Even the lady of the house's rampant cleanliness hasn't extended there.

The baker's boy barks a laugh.

Uneasiness prickles across my skin, my stomach tightening with a renewed sense of dread. If anyone questions him, he'll almost certainly remember me.

It can't be helped.

I hold out the half-shilling piece that comprises my sole remaining fortune. "'ere's the money. Jenkins"—at least I know his name—"said to keep the change today."

The boy's eyebrows go up. "'e did, did'e? That's gotter be a first, the stingy old bugger."

He pockets the coin with a shrug, hands me the loaves, and turns away.

I do my best not to sink to the ground with sheer relief as he slouches his way out of the yard and back towards the alleyway outside. Step one of my plan is accomplished—but that is only step one.

Clutching the loaves of bread, I walk as quietly as I can up the path towards the kitchen entrance.

When I'm about ten feet away from the door, I deposit both loaves on the ground. Not without a pang. The smell of freshly-baked bread has made me suddenly realize that I am incredibly hungry.

But I leave the bread, dart up to the door, knock soundly—and then step to the side, flattening myself against the side of the house, where I'll be concealed by the opening door.

There is a pause that seems to last a small eternity—and then *finally* I hear the sound of the latch lifting from the inside.

The door swings open. I can't see, of course, but the mutter of, "blasted boy gets more lazy every day" sounds like the stout, elderly cook rather than the young maid.

Perfect.

I hold my breath, wishing that I could convince my pulse to remain silent as she stumps forwards to retrieve the bread. The blood is hammering so loudly in my temples and my fingertips that it seems as though it must be overheard.

The cook—it *is* the cook—waddles ponderously down the path, still muttering imprecations against the baker's boy.

I don't wait. Darting around the edge of the door, I plunge into the kitchen.

It's empty.

Perhaps luck is with me after all. There's no sign of the younger maidservant or anyone else. Just a pot of something that smells strongly of cabbage bubbling on the stove.

The cook will be picking up the bread and turning around at any second.

Without stopping, I dart through the kitchen towards a doorway I can see at the back of the room. It opens on a set of stairs—the back stairs, clearly, the ones used by the servants—and I take them two at a time, not stopping until I reach what must be the second floor landing.

Then I stop, fighting—above the noise of my own breath—to listen for any sounds of alarm.

Everything is quiet. From downstairs in the kitchen, I can hear the occasional clank and rattle of pots and pans, but nothing else.

Slowly, cautiously, I push the door to the stairwell open and peer out into a plushly carpeted hallway. The contrast is instant and shocking, between the areas of the house reserved for the servants and those frequented by the mistress. The servants' stairwell is rickety, the floor bare except for some matting on the landing, the space unlighted.

Outside in the lady of the house's living space, the walls are papered with a heavy gold brocade pattern. Gas lights are set at intervals along the walls, interspersed with paintings in elaborate gilded frames.

I wait for a count of ten before emerging from the stairwell, but the hallway remains empty.

Picking up my skirts and moving as quickly and as softly as I can, I step to the first doorway I can see on the left and turn the knob.

It opens easily—but peering inside, all I see are neat stacks of household linens and a single, straight-backed chair. The chair is surrounded by baskets of thread and needles and piles of mending.

As a hiding place, it might suffice—but it doesn't provide the rest of what I need.

I step on to the second doorway along the hall, pausing for a moment to listen at the keyhole for any sounds from inside.

If the theoretical elderly companion is a resident here, she's going to get quite a shock when I come barging in.

All *sounds* silent and uninhabited beyond the door. I turn the knob, bracing myself—but this room is unoccupied, as well. It has to be the disagreeable woman's own bedroom.

I have no definite proof, of course—but the deep burgundy walls and heavily curtained bed; the smell of cloying perfume intermixed with what I think must be camphor; the fussy array of china figurines on the mantle, and even fussier lace antimacassars covering every available surface; the windows shut tight against even the hint of a *suggestion* of any draft of fresher air—

It all so perfectly matches what I glimpsed of the woman's personality that the room *must* be hers.

I slip inside, easing the door shut behind me and making straight for the washstand, which sits to the side of the four-poster bed.

Another stroke of luck: the water jug is full.

I've dampened the towel, scrubbed it across my face and hands, and am in the process of unbuttoning my jacket when the fates decree that I have had all the luck I am owed for one morning.

The bedroom door swings open.

For a sluggish second, the young maidservant and I stare at one another in more or less equal measures of astonishment. Her hair is pale blond and her face is round, fresh and rosy-cheeked under her white cap. Her blue eyes are flared wide, and her mouth is set in a perfect round O of surprise.

Then she takes a breath—I'm certain in preparation for screaming the house down.

"Please!" I drop the dampened towel and hold out both hands to her. "*Please*, don't give me away. Are you"—I try desperately to remember what the plump woman said just before driving off.

Tell Sarah that the state of the front stoop is disgraceful. That was it.

"Are you Sarah?"

That makes the girls' eyes widen even further, but she gives me a scared-looking half nod.

At least she is not screaming—yet.

Think.

"You're worried that you won't be able to clean the candle wax out of your mistress's carpet here, and that she'll be angry with you."

Sarah's mouth drops open again.

"What did you ... how do you ..."

"You're carrying a hot iron," I go on, nodding to the article that seconds ago I had no memory of in Sarah's hands. "And a towel—though plainly there are no linens to be ironed in here. I can also see a great blob of wax over on the carpet beside the bed. Your mistress must have dropped her candle as she was getting into bed last night."

Sarah still stares at me, her expression torn between alarm and bemusement. "That's right. Dripped wax all over the floor, she did. And then shouts at me for it—as if it was my fault!"

Indignation at the injustice replaces Sarah's surprise at seeing me. "She said she'll take the expense out of my wages if I can't get the wax out."

Another of those vague wisps of memory is flickering at the edges of my mind.

"You'll have better luck using a sheet of blotting paper with the iron than a towel," I tell her.

It is not exactly life-saving advice—but the best that I can do under the circumstances.

Sarah blinks at me. "Really? I never heard that."

"I used to stay up reading late at night and drip wax onto the sheets and blankets."

I can remember that—I think. What I can*not* remember is who I was afraid would find out about my late-night reading habits. A parent? A schoolmistress?

Sarah's eyes narrow with a look of sudden appraisal. "Look here, *who* are you?"

I put my hands together. "Please." I don't even have to work to put a convincingly pathetic wobble in my voice. "I won't hurt you and I'm not here to steal anything, I promise. It's just that I've been attacked"—that much is true, even if I don't remember it—"and I needed someplace safe."

If Sarah's eyes widen any further, they will be as large as teacup saucers. But she casts a quick glance over her shoulder, then takes a few steps into the room, shutting the door behind her.

"Was it white slavers, miss?"

"Was it *what*?"

"White slavers, miss. Cook's always warning me about them when I go for my afternoon out. She says there's immoral men out there who'd snatch up a girl like me as soon as look at me."

"Well—" I put a hand up to the throbbing lump on my head.

I suppose it *could* have been white slavers—whatever those are.

My memory of the world may be patched with haziness, but I'm fairly certain that the city of London contains more than enough ugliness to turn the cook's immoral men from the theoretical to the all-too real.

If I shot one of them, at least I wouldn't have to feel so guilty.

"I don't know who they were," I temporize. "It was nighttime—dark."

Since I only woke up at dawn this morning, that must be true.

"Ooh, miss how frightful!" Sarah's expression is both horrified and a little admiring. "How ever did you get away?"

How *did* I?

That is an excellent question, and one I had not fully considered before. I was knocked unconscious. Did whoever struck the blow assume I was dead? But if they wanted to kill me that badly, why not stay to make sure the job was truly done?

Did some casual passer-by happen along and frighten them away?

That's possible.

Sarah is waiting expectantly. She's still wide-eyed—but there's a faint flicker of enjoyment, or at least excitement, in her gaze.

I can't blame her. My arrival is probably the most exciting thing to happen in this household in the last month.

I don't have the heart to disappoint her.

"I fought them off," I say. "There were only two of them. I kicked the big one's ankle—he was the one who'd grabbed me—so that he let me go."

Is any part of this true? I would love to think that I'm somehow remembering, but I don't think so, I'm just inventing freely, with the same ease with which I forged a false accent with the baker's boy outside.

Whoever I am, I seem to be an accomplished liar.

"Then I hit the smaller one over the head with my"—what might a lady be expected to be carrying?—"with my umbrella. And then I ran."

"Ooh, miss," Sarah breathes. "How thrilling!"

The note of enjoyment is *definitely* present now—but it's impossible to dislike her.

I manage a small smile. "I suppose that is one way of putting it."

A frown furrows Sarah's brows. "Why not go home, though? I'd have thought you'd want to be in your own place after a fright like that."

I hesitate. Shall I tell her the truth? I may be *good* at lying, but the effort of spinning untruths to this girl is making me feel even more sick to my stomach.

If I involve her too much, though—or give her too many details about myself—I could unwittingly put her in danger or get her into trouble.

What if the police somehow find out that I've been here? She needs to be able to honestly state that she knows nothing about me at all—definitely not the fact that I may be a murderess.

"I'm afraid to go home," I tell her. "What if those men know where I live and are somehow waiting for me?"

It's a possibility that hadn't occurred to me until now—but as I say it, I can hear how horribly likely the idea really is.

Even if I eventually remember where I belong, it may not be safe for me to go anywhere near there.

Panic begins to creep up the back of my throat again, but I quash it down.

One step at a time.

"I came in here because I was hoping to wash and maybe change my clothes," I add. "In case they're out there, searching for me."

I wave my hand at the window, indicating the street outside.

Sarah continues to stare at me—but then she gives me a quick, decisive nod.

"You just leave it to me, miss. We'll get you properly fixed up." She gestures with her free hand towards the washstand. "Finish up your washing there, and I'll go and see what I can find for you."

I smile with relief. "Try the blotting paper on the wax stain first," I tell her. "Before your iron goes completely cold."

4. Costume Change

The blotting paper—taken from the room's writing desk—and hot iron work like magic, removing the ugly blob of wax without a trace. Which is a relief. At least one of my returning memories has been proven accurate.

Still smiling her thanks, Sarah leaves me, pausing at the doorway to say, "You go ahead and enjoy your bath, now."

I do as she says. Though it cannot be said that I *enjoy* it. My heart pounds sickeningly as I strip down to my chemise and take what I imagine must be the hastiest sponge bath of my life.

I want to trust Sarah not to turn me in—but all the time she's gone, my imagination keeps painting helpful pictures of her going straight to Cook and Jenkins—or the nearest police constable—and telling them everything.

I feel horribly exposed without my clothes on, too.

I know I ought to examine the corset and petticoat I've just removed—but my hands are shaking and my fingers are too clumsy to do more than note that they appear to be of the same good quality as my outer garments.

The click of the door latch makes me whirl around, my heart trying to leap up out of my chest.

But as it turns out, my fears are unfounded.

It's Sarah—and only Sarah—who slips back into the room.

She's carrying a bundle of fabric under one arm and a steaming cup of tea in her other hand.

"Sorry it's taken me so long, but I thought maybe you could do with a cup." She hands me the tea, taking away the dirtied wash towel, and gives me a small smile. "Had to tell Cook I'd seen a mouse in the pantry so that I could get it out of the kitchen without her seeing."

I raise the cup to my lips, wrapping both hands around it for the sake of the warmth. "Bless you."

I mean it sincerely, too.

The tea is strong, made with plenty of milk and sugar, and as I swallow, I feel my exhaustion retreat a step. Even the throbbing in my head is a little better.

Sarah waves my thanks away. "It's nothing, miss."

She unrolls the bundle of fabric, revealing it to be a dress of brown poplin, sprigged with a pattern of small white flowers. "It's my Sunday best," she explains. She eyes me critically, her head on one side. "It'll be a bit too loose on you, but the length should be all right—and anyway, it's clean."

"I can't take your dress!"

Sarah waves away my protest, too. "It's all right, miss. You need it more than I do, I reckon. And anyway, I won't be getting a chance to wear it for another week, almost. Maybe by then you'll be safe and you can get it back to me."

I feel even worse about the lies I've told her, but I nod. "Thank you."

A thought occurs to me as I glance down at the gray walking suit I've just stripped off. It's dirty, but it is still considerably higher quality than the dress Sarah is offering.

At the least, maybe she can clean it and sell it for a profit.

"What if we trade?" I ask. "You can have my things if you like. Just in case I can't return your dress to you before next Sunday."

Or if I don't ever manage to return it at all.

Sarah hesitates, so I add, "Please, it's only fair."

"Well, all right then, miss." She hands the brown poplin over to me. "Here, put this on, and we'll see what can be done with your hair."

The dress does hang loosely on me, but it's serviceable, and easily slipped on over my own underthings. Sarah helps me with doing up the buttons at the back, then gestures to the dressing table and mirror that stand on the opposite side of the room.

My heart speeds up as I move to the upholstered stool.

I've been avoiding the mirror expressly because I'm afraid of what I'll see—or remember—at the sight of my own face.

But I drop onto the seat—and then I'm staring my own reflection in the eyes.

"If I looked like you, I'd be a bit happier about looking in a mirror," Sarah says behind me with a half-laugh.

Am I pretty?

I suppose, objectively speaking, that I am. My face is a smooth oval with delicate, clean-cut features and a very faint hint of an olive tone to my skin. My lips are full and rosy. My eyes are large and thickly lashed—and a striking shade of green.

What concerns me far more, however, is that the sight of my own face is not familiar at all.

Save for the dark eyebrows that draw together when I feel my own scowl deepen, I might imagine that I was looking at a portrait painting of a complete stranger.

I shake my head, trying to focus on the task at hand.

My hair is thick and dark—and as I suspected, in complete disarray, with straggling waves spilling over my shoulders. I pull out several pins, and the rest tumbles down.

"Do you want me to help, miss?" Sarah asks.

"That's all right."

I may not recognize my own reflection, but my hands seem automatically to know what to do: deftly twisting and smoothing the long thick locks into order. Working quickly, I smooth my hair straight back and coil it into a low, plain knot at the nape of my neck. Severe, but neat—and it helps to hide the swollen lump behind my ear.

I finish securing the last of my hairpins and then survey the dressing table. There are a surprising number of little gilded pots of creams and powders. Surprising, because I would have guessed the lady of the house the sort to view all cosmetics as an instrument of the devil.

I'm also surprised by how easily I recognize them; the jars of rouge for the cheeks and rice powder for the face are familiar, somehow.

"Go ahead, miss," Sarah says, following my glance. "Use whatever you like, she'll never know the difference."

My cheeks could use a touch of color. Either I'm naturally pale, or else getting hit over the head does not agree with me.

But I want to look inconspicuous, not glamorous or alluring—so I avoid the rouge altogether, instead dabbing my face with a light dusting of the powder.

Then I frown as I examine my eyes in the reflection. There's unfortunately nothing I can do that will obscure their color, but I dip into a small pot of black Kohl. Instead of using it to darken my lashes, I lightly trace it along the length of my eyebrows, making them a shade thicker and darker.

Not exactly an infallible disguise, but the best I can do.

As I sit back to study the effect, I'm hit with a sudden jarring sense of familiarity—so intense that for a moment the room seems to tilt and spin all around me.

I've done this before.

The face in the looking glass is no more familiar than it was a moment ago. Less, even, since the thicker eyebrows accomplish their goal of altering my expression.

But I'm *certain* that I've done this before: sat at a dressing table like this one and made up my face this way with quick, practiced strokes.

"That's very good, miss," Sarah says—and the faint hint of memory pops like a soap bubble.

"Thank you." I straighten up. "And now I need to leave before I get you into trouble by being discovered here."

"That's all right, miss. The mistress has gone to visit her sister in Clapham for the day. But I had best be getting on with the dusting. She'll be cross enough to bust a stay lace if I don't get it done by the time she's back. You can stay, though, if you want to rest a bit."

"No, thank you. You've been incredibly kind. But I really ought to leave."

"Well, all right, miss." Sarah looks at me, a furrow of worry marring her brow. "You'll be all right out there, on your own?"

She's frightened for me. For the first time maybe since I arrived, she's realized fully that the attack on me actually *happened*; that it's not just a thrilling story, but a real danger that I could face out there.

"Oh, yes."

Judging by my reflection, Sarah and I are the same age but right now I feel older than her by practically decades.

I don't want her to lose her faith in the world on my account.

I smile. "I shall buy another umbrella directly I leave here—and then if those men try to trifle with me again, I shall teach them a lesson they will not soon forget."

Sarah smiles in return, the worry leaving her expression. "Oh, miss. You're ever so brave."

"That's very—"

Inaccurate, considering the sick, hollow feeling I have right now. "Kind of you," I finish. "Now, should I try to get out the front or the back door?"

"Oh, the front door, miss. There won't be anyone about. Jenkins'll be in the pantry polishing the silverware at this time of day. Come on, I'll show you down."

I stare into the mirror for one moment more. My own green eyes look back at me, the color heightened, if anything, by the cosmetics.

Who are you?

My reflection doesn't answer.

Sarah and I tiptoe down the long upstairs hallway and then down a wide flight of stairs.

Sarah stops at the front door. "Well, goodbye, miss, and good luck to you." She looks slightly wistful, now, at having to see me go. "It's been ever so exciting meeting you. Just like something on the stage."

Another of those gossamer, soap-bubble memories seems to float up—but it's gone before I can even identify what part of Sarah's speech triggered the feeling of familiarity.

"Are you fond of the theater?"

"Oh, I *love* it, miss!" Sarah's whole face brightens, her blue eyes turning eager. "Not that I've been to a proper show, but I go to Covent Garden every chance I get on my half day and buy a ticket for one of the revues. I'd try for the part of a chorus girl—except my parents would die of horror to see me acting on the stage. Well, that and even my own mother would tell you I sound like a crow when I sing and have two left feet when it comes to a dance."

Sarah breaks off with a laugh—then claps her hand over her mouth, remembering that we're not supposed to be making any noise.

Impulsively, I squeeze her hand. "Thank you so much. I'll find a way to pay you back if I possibly can."

Sarah looks slightly taken aback by my effusion—but pleased, all the same. "It wasn't nothing, miss."

"Yes it was, it was a great, great deal more than nothing. I shall remember your kindness always."

I turn to the door—and rub my forehead, suddenly hearing the irony in my words. I can only *hope* that I shall continue to remember Sarah.

5. Strange Encounters

I find myself at more than a little of a loose end as I leave both the brick house and Montague Street behind.

Up until now, the necessity of confronting each immediate problem as it comes has sustained me. But now—like running headlong into a brick wall—I realize that I have no idea whatsoever as to what I ought to do next.

"Watcherself, miss!"

The voice behind me makes me jump and turn to see a couple of workmen in checkered caps and suspenders, carrying a heavy-looking crate between them.

"I'm sorry." I move over to the side of the pavement—realizing for the first time that my feet of their own accord seem to have carried me back to where I began this morning. Or nearly so.

I have circled around to the rear of the museum, to a narrow entrance that looks like it must be reserved for deliveries and cleaning crews and such.

The two workmen are trying to wrestle the massive wooden crate in through the door—but it's a tight fit, and they're struggling to keep a hold on the awkward burden.

As I watch, the lead workman—the one moving through the doorway backwards—trips over the stoop of the entrance and lets go of his share of the load.

The crate slips, smashing to the ground, the top breaks open, and a number of small articles packed in straw spill out onto the cobblestones.

"Bloody hell, now see what you've gone and done, Jack," the older of the two workmen growls.

The younger one ducks his head. "Sorry, dad."

"Bloody butterfingers," his father growls. Then he appears to realize that I'm still watching them. He tips his hat in my direction. "Beggin' yer pardon, miss."

I barely hear him. As though the crash of the wooden crate against the cobblestones were some sort of signal, a realization has struck me.

"This is The British Museum!" I can feel myself practically beaming, I'm so delighted to have recollected something so specific.

The older man gives me a curious look. He has a round, jolly-looking face, fringed by thick brown side-whiskers.

"That's right, miss. This here's The British Museum. Leastaways, I hope it is, otherwise we're making this delivery to the wrong place." He grins. "We were hired to bring this crate on up here from the docks. Antiques"—he pronounces it carefully as an-ti-cues—"or some such."

He scratches his head, looking at the mess on the ground, which appears to me to consist mainly of broken shards of some dark brown pottery. "Can't think why anyone'd pay good money for a lot of smashed crockery. But at least one good thing—they're already all broken, so no one's likely to notice if a few of them have some extra cracks."

He turns back to his son. "Come on, Jack. Don't just stand there, get them bits picked up and lets get on with it. We've got another four crates still in the cart."

He jerks his head towards the street, where I can see a fully laden cart hitched up to a small, depressed-looking donkey.

"Yes, Dad." Jack ducks his head again and bends to start scooping the straw and pottery somewhat haphazardly back in.

I keep walking, almost without being aware of what I'm doing, and finally wind up at a patch of grass and a few trees that have been planted to face the museum.

There's a bench between the trees, and I sink down onto it, staring up at the stately, classical edifice.

The British Museum.

The memories buzz like flies in my ears—annoying, but just out of my reach.

For some reason I was *here*. But why?

A rheumy cough makes me look up to see the hunched figure of an old man standing beside my bench and peering down at me through a pair of round spectacles.

"I beg your pardon."

His voice is thin and cracked with age. A straggling white beard traces the length of his chin, and yellowed skin clings to his cadaverous cheeks. Beneath an ancient-looking brown bowler hat, his hair is also white—and quite long for a man, reaching well below his ears.

"Might I share your bench for a few moments, young miss?"

"Yes, of course." He doesn't look as though he could possibly do anyone harm—and anyway, I'm a little afraid to say no. He looks so fragile and decrepit that the first strong gust of wind might knock him to the ground.

"Thank you." He limps arthritically forward and settles on the bench with a huge, gusty sigh that seems to come all the way up from his toes. "Perishing cold today, miss, isn't it?"

On my list of things that I would prefer to avoid right now, *inane talk about the weather* ranks nearly as high as *face whoever assaulted me again*.

But I nod, and offer him a smile. "Yes, indeed."

As replies go, it doesn't strike me as remotely controversial. But a look of surprise, almost instantly concealed, flashes across the old man's bearded face.

"I *said*, perishing cold, isn't it, miss?"

Perhaps he's slightly touched in his wits. "Yes, I know," I say patiently. "And I agreed with you. It is certainly quite cold today."

A look of consternation spreads across the old man's face. "Do you think, miss, that there might be any chance of *snow* falling?"

I rub my forehead. I don't wish to be unkind to him—especially if he is going slightly soft in his wits. But all I really want is to be allowed to sit here and think in peace, try to remember what I was doing here.

There's something nagging at me. Something about the museum—the broken pottery shards?

No, whatever the memory was, it's now gone again.

The old man leans closer, raising his voice. "I said, do you think there might be any chance of—"

"Snow." My patience slips slightly. "I know. I heard you. I have no idea."

I glance up at the sky, striving to gentle my tone. None of this morning's catastrophes are the old man's fault, after all. "It's cloudy enough, certainly."

There's a short silence, and then the old man clears his throat.

I shut my eyes, praying to any deity who might be listening that he doesn't ask me about the chances of rain.

But he only heaves himself up off the bench with another rheumy cough. "Well, I'll be saying good-day to you, young miss."

Raising his bowler hat, he turns and limps away. Only when he's nearly reached the corner of the museum do I realize that there's a small rectangular bit of paper lying on the bench where he sat down. It must have dropped out of one of his pockets.

"Sir!" I stand up, calling after him. "Sir, you dropped this. Sir!"

But it appears that the old man also numbers deafness among his afflictions, because he doesn't even glance behind him.

Putting on a surprising burst of speed, he vanishes around the side of the museum—back towards the wing that faces onto Montague Street.

I hesitate, trying to decide just how far good Samaritan-ship prompts me to go.

The paper scrap at first glance doesn't *look* important. It's a calling card, with a name and address embossed on one side.

But one never knows. What if the old man is expected at this address and can't find his way because he's lost the card telling him where he ought to go?

With a sigh, I dart after him.

I'm nearly run over by a passing hansom cab as I chase after him—but I reach the corner of the museum intact.

The old man has disappeared.

Montague Street looks just as it did earlier. Staid and respectable, with traffic rolling by in the road and pedestrians strolling along the pavement. But absolutely no sign of a white-haired old man.

I put a hand up to rub my forehead again. The exertion of running—in addition to making me breathless—has also brought the throbbing headache back. Dark flecks dance in front of my eyes.

Then as I debate what I ought to do now, my gaze lights on the name printed on the calling card, and I read it properly for the first time.

Dr. William Everett, MD
Specialist in Disorders of the Nerves

I stare at the words for a long moment, while the traffic noises and the hum of the city street all around me seem to fade away.

You should see the doctor, miss.

That's what the street urchin told me. Maybe through the old man's accidentally dropping this card, fate is intervening, pointing me in the direction I ought to go.

Specialist in Disorders of the Nerves

Having no recollection of who I am, save that I may—rightly or wrongly—believe myself to be a murderer? Surely that ought to qualify me for the good doctor's attention.

6. THE DOCTOR IS IN

My heart beats rapidly as I approach the first uniformed police constable I see. But he's a lank, tow-haired man in his thirties with a handlebar mustache across his upper lip. *Not* the handsome young detective constable I met with earlier.

Thank heavens.

The constable gives me a brief, disinterested glance and then points me in the direction of Harley Street.

"You want to go up Gower Street. Then turn left into Chenies Street. You'll reach Harley Street in just over a mile."

It's a long walk, according to the constable. But I'm occupied with scanning everything—the streets, the bakeries and boot shops and milliners' establishments … even the knife-grinder's stalls on the street corners—for any hint that any of this is familiar territory for me.

When at last I reach Harley Street, I draw out the calling card again, consulting the address.

According to his card, Dr. Everett operates his practice at number twenty-nine—which proves to be a handsome dwelling of white stone, with a door painted deep forest green.

A brass plaque beside the door reads, *Patients and Visitors, ring here*—and beneath is a push-button bell.

Nerves flutter through my stomach as I raise my finger. What if Dr. Everett believes me guilty of some crime and calls at once for the police?

Worse, what if he thinks me truly insane and has me locked up in an asylum?

I'm on the point of turning around and retreating, when suddenly the door pops open.

A man's face—very long and thin with a ginger goatee and a pair of very pale blue eyes—peers out at me.

"C-c-can I help you?"

I swallow down my squeak of alarm at his sudden appearance. "Doctor Everett?"

"Yes." The man bobs his head. "Th-th-that is my name."

He's thin and stoop-shouldered and appears to be somewhere in his middle forties. His ginger-red hair is beginning to turn gray at the temples.

His voice is mild to the point of timid, with a slight stutter—and his inflection seems to rise naturally at the end of each statement, so that the words become, *Yes? That is my name?*

I can understand why he would specialize in nervous disorders. Even the most hysterical patient would have difficulty in working up any terrors of him.

"I've lost my memory." The words slip out before I've consciously made up my mind whether or not to consult the doctor at all.

He blinks at me, pale blue eyes widening with slight surprise. Then he clicks his tongue. "Dear, dear. Won't you step in, Miss—" he pauses questioningly.

I suppose that I am committed now. "I can't remember. I can't even remember my name."

Again Dr. Everett's eyes widen in fractional surprise. "I see. Dear me." He steps backwards, extending a hand to usher me inside. "Pray, accompany me into my offices and we shall see what can be done for you."

Despite the doctor's mild manner, uneasiness prickles through me as I follow him across the threshold of Number 29.

My current position is already uncomfortably vulnerable—and I'm aware that the decision to follow a strange man into his place of business renders me even more so.

I am mildly relieved on entering to see a plump, gray-haired, motherly-looking woman seated behind a desk in the front room.

Dr. Everett waves a hand in her direction. He has very pale, finely manicured hands, I notice.

Lily-white hands. The phrase flashes through my mind, though I cannot remember where I heard it before.

"This is Mrs. Bartholomew," Dr. Everett says. "She keeps my appointment books in order, cooks my meals, brews my tea, and generally serves as guardian angel to my practice."

He smiles. It's an oddly winning smile, completely transforming his thin, rather solemn face.

Mrs. Bartholomew gives an almost girlish giggle, her hand on her ample chest. "There, now, doctor, I'm sure you're too kind."

Dr. Everett gestures towards a door at the back of the room. "My private consulting room. If you would care to step this way, you can explain to me more fully the details of your—ahem—condition."

The consulting room proves to be a cozy, comfortable space, with walls painted a tranquil shade of blue, an oriental rug on the floor, and a sofa and chairs upholstered in deep red velvet. A cheerful fire crackles in the hearth.

"Please." Dr. Everett extends a hand, gesturing me to a chair to the left of the fireplace.

I sit down. Just sitting is a relief—but the heat from the fire is also welcome, thawing my frozen toes and fingers.

"Thank you."

As I stretch my hands towards the fire, my eye is caught by a lovely sculpture of a human head atop the mantle. It's done in what looks like white marble, and the style is primitive, but still charming: a girl's face, with hair cut in a stiff, corded bob that falls to just beneath her chin.

Beside it rests an alabaster jar with a stoppered lid in the shape of a dog's head.

"Ah." Following my glance, Dr. Everett nods. "You have noticed my weakness for Egyptian antiquities. It is a particular hobby of mine."

He smiles. "I confess to a boy's fascination with all things Egyptological. I daydream sometimes of abandoning my staid practice and joining an archaeological dig. Spending my days in digging for long-buried treasure beneath the windswept sands."

"It sounds lovely."

A sudden tiny fragment of memory—or at least realization—slots into place in my mind. "Do you ever visit The British Museum?"

Maybe the old man didn't drop Dr. Everett's card after all. Maybe it was the doctor himself who accidentally left it behind on the bench.

"Indeed, I do." Dr. Everett's face brightens with enthusiasm. "I am proud to claim myself a patron of that fine establishment, in fact. Since I have yet to realize my own dreams of traveling to Egypt's buried cities and lost tombs, I have at least offered funds to a team of archaeologists currently exploring the tombs around Thebes." He glances at me. "You are familiar with Egyptian geography?"

Am I? It doesn't *sound* in the slightest bit familiar. I shake my head.

"No matter." Dr. Everett waves a hand.

His shy but engaging smile flashes out once more. "I am told that the discoveries will be part of an important new exhibit of Old Kingdom artifacts. But I must apologize. I am monopolizing the conversation, prattling on about my own hobbies when what is surely of far more importance is the question of what has brought you to my door."

He pauses, his hands clasped around one raised knee and his pale blue eyes mildly alert—interested, but not judgmental, and certainly not at all threatening.

I rather suspect that his talk of Egyptology was not a digression at all, but rather a practiced routine, designed to put patients at ease.

"I've lost my memory," I say.

Dr. Everett's expression sharpens momentarily, then smooths out into the same mildly curious look of before. "Yes, so you informed me outside. Have you any idea what might have caused this recent memory loss? I am assuming that it is recent, by the way?"

"Yes. Since I woke up this morning. As to what caused it, I was rather hoping that you could tell me that."

I smile to lessen the bluntness of the words.

"Quite so, quite so. Well, as to that, there are several possible causes for the condition the French psychologist Théodule-Armand Ribot has termed amnesia. However, in order to establish what lies at the root of your—"

He breaks off at a tap on the door. "Excuse me, please."

Rising, he crosses to the door—revealing Mrs. Bartholomew. She's carrying a tray on which rests a large pot of tea and a plate of buttered muffins.

"I beg pardon, doctor. But I thought the young lady looked as though she could do with a bit of refreshment." Mrs. Bartholomew nods at me. "Also, I came to tell you, sir, that that telegram you've been expecting has just arrived. I told the messenger boy to wait so that you could give him your answer."

"Certainly, certainly."

It crosses my mind to wonder whether anyone has ever compared his speaking habits to the animals on the ark. His statements seem to frequently march two-by-two.

He turns back to me. "I beg your pardon, this will take but a moment. Please, do help yourself to the refreshments that our resident domestic angel has so kindly provided, and I shall return to you directly."

Mrs. Bartholomew deposits the tray on the table beside my chair.

"There, dear. Shall I pour you out a cup, or can you manage?" She gives me a kindly smile.

"Thank you." I let her pour the tea and accept the cup she offers.

"You drink up now. You look half frozen." The older woman pats me on the shoulder, and with a click of her tongue, follows the doctor out of the room.

I sit staring at the cup of tea in my hands for several moments after the door closes behind them. Then I look down at the plate of buttered muffins.

I am more hungry than thirsty. Actually, now that I am in sight of food, my stomach feels positively hollow.

I've eaten three of the muffins by the time the door opens and Dr. Everett returns. He's smiling—a different smile than his earlier wry, self-deprecating one. Now he is beaming and looks positively jovial.

"Well, well."

Apparently, his *wells* also march in pairs.

The doctor rubs his hands together briskly. "There has been a most extraordinary—but I am sure you will agree—most welcome discovery."

I feel my eyebrows climbing towards my hairline. "Oh, really?"

"Yes, indeed." The doctor drops into the chair opposite mine once more and takes a breath—then goes on, making an obvious effort to keep his words slow, his voice as gentle as he can. "Now, this may come as quite a shock to you. But I hope and trust that it will be a pleasant one. A young man has just arrived at my doorstep. A young man I believe to be your husband."

If my eyebrows climb any higher, they will actually *disappear* into my hair. "My husband," I repeat.

"You are surprised," Doctor Everett says. He nods. "Quite understandable, I am sure. So was I surprised, when the young gentleman appeared, in search of his wife—who, he informed me, was prone to fits of amnesia in which she had no idea of who she was or where she had come from. He has been quite distracted, scouring London for the young lady in question—you in fact."

Dr. Everett beams at me again. "For I believe that we may safely assume that this man's wife and yourself are one and the same. Your appearance matches his description exactly—and I am sure you will agree that there cannot very likely be two young women with amnesia wandering this great city of ours."

He chuckles, and I smile obediently.

"It would certainly seem most unlikely," I agree.

"Quite so."

Dr. Everett rubs his hands together. By sheer power of will, I manage to refrain from adding another *quite so*.

"Now, I understand that this is a good deal for you to take in," the doctor goes on. "That is why I insisted on coming to speak with you first, to prepare the way, so to speak. But with your permission, might I bring your husband in now? He is naturally quite anxious to see you."

"Naturally." My lips feel slightly stiff and disconnected from the rest of me.

Doctor Everett gives me a worried look, followed by an encouraging smile. "I have your permission, then? All other considerations aside, in my professional opinion, the sight of a familiar and much-beloved face might do much to restore your memories."

He trails off questioningly.

I nod. "Certainly. Bring my—bring the gentleman in."

"Good, good."

He crosses to open the door and leans out, saying to someone in the exterior waiting room. "You may come in now."

I watch as a second figure appears in the doorway—then I straighten up with a jolt, staring at the new arrival.

The young man who comes into the room on Doctor Everett's summons is fair-haired, about my age—and he looks like he could have stepped straight off the page of a child's illustrated book of fairy tales.

My nameless police constable was handsome. This man's face is beautiful. Really, that is the only word to describe him.

His eyes are large and blue, his brow noble, his features finely drawn. His golden hair tumbles artistically over his forehead.

His face lights up at the sight of me. "Darling!"

He crosses the room in a few quick strides and comes to take my hands in both of his. "I have found you! Thanks be to a benevolent Providence. I cannot tell you how relieved I am."

He bends his head, pressing a kiss to the back of my hand. The warmth of his lips against my skin almost makes me jump.

"How … how did you find me?" My lips still feel stiff.

The young man raises his head. "It was not entirely by chance. We had intended to consult Doctor Everett here about your condition. So when upon waking this morning, I found you missing, I hoped that sooner or later you might find your own way here."

"I see." I swallow. "Can you tell me … that is, what is your name?"

The young man's expression turns sorrowful as he searches my face. Up close, I can see that his eyes are slightly red-rimmed.

"You do not remember me, dearest? Not at all?"

"I—" I press a hand to my forehead. "I cannot—that is—"

The young man's expression turns penitent. "It's all right, darling. Do not distress yourself. We have overcome these spells of yours before—and will again, I am sure."

He presses my hands more tightly. "My name is Frances. Frances Ferrars. And you are my wife, Eleanor."

"Eleanor," I repeat. Not so much as a flicker of recognition stirs in me at the name. I moisten my lips. "And how long have we been married?"

"Just over three years."

I look down at our joined hands. His fingers are slightly calloused, but warm and firm around mine.

"Where do we live?"

"We have a home in Arlington Street. My family's ancestral home." He squeezes my hands again. "I will take you back there directly—if the doctor thinks it advisable?"

He gives Dr. Everett a questioning glance.

Dr. Everett beams paternally at us both. "I believe that is the best treatment that I can provide. The therapeutic effect of being in familiar surroundings will, I am certain, restore the memories you have temporarily lost. Although if you should suffer from any lingering ill-effects, I beg you to come and visit me again, and I will prescribe a tonic for the nerves."

"A tonic," I repeat. I raise my hand, pressing it again to my eyes. "Yes. Thank you. I—I beg your pardon. I seem to be feeling quite dizzy and faint."

"Perfectly natural, perfectly natural," the doctor says. His voice is reassuring. "You are exhausted, and your nerves have sustained quite a shock. However, I am sure that with rest and sleep, you will feel entirely restored."

He transfers the genial smile. "Mr. Ferrars, I leave her in your capable and caring hands. I am sure you will see to it that she gets all the tender concern and loving kindness required to effect a full recovery."

"Yes, indeed." Ferrars puts a solicitous arm around my shoulders. "Come along, darling. I have the carriage waiting just outside. We will be safely home before you know it."

I tilt my head to look up at him. "Thank you." I turn to Doctor Everett. "And thank you, doctor."

"Not at all, not at all." Doctor Everett moves to open the door for us. "I am only thankful to have been able to facilitate such a happy ending to your most distressing trials."

7. Deductions and Revelations

I stumble twice on the way down Dr. Everett's front steps. Ferrars keeps his arm solicitously around my waist until we reach the pavement.

"Nearly there, darling."

He stops, gesturing to a Landau carriage waiting for us at the curb. It's a big, black affair, drawn by a team of four beautifully matched gray horses. The door is open, and I can see that the interior is upholstered in tufted blue satin.

"Just climb in, dearest," Ferrars tells me, "and we shall soon have you home."

I stop, stepping out of his grasp.

"Do you know, I believe anyone who would prefer to do that would be much stupider than I am."

The expression on Ferrars's face is almost comical. His jaw drops open, and he stares as though he cannot believe what he has just heard me say.

Then he clears his throat, trying again for a soothing, jocular tone, "Now, darling, I know this is all quite overwhelming for you. But if you will just get into the carriage—"

I cut him off. "I am afraid that I shall have to decline your kind offer."

Ferrars is not nearly so pleasing to look at when he is stunned speechless. His blue eyes take on a glassy, vacuous expression, and his mouth opens and closes like a fish on the end of a fisherman's line.

"You and Dr. Everett seem to believe that just because I have lost my memory, I have also lost all powers of rational thought."

Anger warms me—as much at the insult to my intelligence as at the thought of what they were planning to do to me once they got me into the waiting carriage.

"In the first place, there was no knock or sound of a bell before the supposed telegram arrived for the good doctor. Therefore, there was none. Therefore, Doctor Everett merely wished to consult with someone out of my sight."

Ferrars's mouth opens and closes again, but no words emerge.

I cross my arms. "I am sure that if I had actually drunk the tea that Mrs. Bartholomew so kindly provided, I would be a very great deal more credulous and easier to manipulate. It was drugged, was it not?"

"I—" Ferrars's voice has a strangled quality. His eyes continue to goggle.

"Not that it really matters," I interrupt. "Though you can tell Mrs. Bartholomew from me that for a supposed angel of the home and hearth, her muffins are a day or two past their prime. Also, you may inform Dr. Everett that the next time he tries to persuade a lady that she is married, he would be better advised to check whether the lady is actually wearing a wedding ring."

I extend my bare hands. "As I am *not*."

Ferrars tugs at his collar as though he suddenly finds it too tight—but at last manages to regain his voice. "I should have mentioned before. That is ... you...er...misplaced the ring. That is, it was lost—"

"Good heavens." I look at him. "If that was the best effort I could make at lying, I would give up telling lies altogether, I really would. Which brings me to *you*."

I fix Ferrars with my hardest stare. "There wasn't time to go searching for someone to deceive me. You must be some sort of associate of Doctor Everett. But your hands are that of a man who works for his living. Definitely not those of the man who owns this very handsome carriage. Also, you seem to have overlooked the fact that the owner of such a carriage as this would also be equipped with a coachman."

We both gaze up at the empty driver's box. "How exactly were you planning on explaining a man in your position doing his own driving? Or was I supposed to be drugged unconscious by that point, so that no explanations would be needed?"

I turn to look at Ferrars, but he doesn't answer.

"You are used to trading on your good looks and charm. You very likely have older women eating out of your hand—right up until the point when you rob them blind. And, whoever you are, you do not have an ancestral home in Arlington Street. That is one of the most exclusive neighborhoods in all of London."

I'm not sure how I know that. But as the words leave my mouth, a sudden flicker of memory—real memory—flashes through my mind, like a lighted scene appearing on a stage.

Myself, standing over a table on which is spread out a map of all of London and its environs.

A voice, speaking beside me. "*If you wish to make your home in the great cesspool known as our fair city, it would be wise to make a study of its neighborhoods and byways. I flatter myself that I am familiar with every street and alleyway—and I assure you, that knowledge has saved my life more than once.*"

For an instant, the memory is so vivid that it is more real than Ferrars and the sights and sounds of Harley Street all around me.

But I cannot recall *who* the speaker was. The voice seems momentarily even more familiar than my own. But when I try to concentrate on the memory enough to search out a face to match the voice, the recollection goes dark, the curtain rung down.

Ferrars—though that is almost certainly not his real name—is leering at me, an ugly, calculating gleam in his blue eyes. His lips are drawn back, baring his teeth.

"You've got it all worked out, haven't you?" He puts his hands together in mocking applause. "But it's not going to do you any good. You're coming with me all the same."

He seizes hold of my arm, trying to drag me towards the carriage.

I plant my feet. "Let go of me! Let go, or I shall scream!"

There's not much traffic in the road; it must be approaching the dinner hour. But there are a few passers by on the opposite pavement.

Ferrars gives a laugh that seems to scrape up the entire length of my spine.

"Go ahead and scream yerself silly. I'm yer husband—or so the good doctor in there will swear." He gestures towards

Dr. Everett's door, his cultured accent slipping away, revealing the cockney underneath. "We can also both swear that you're mad as a 'atter. We could have you locked up in Bedlam before you can say Bob's yer uncle. So get in the bleedin' carriage."

He puts his arm around me, giving me a shove from behind. "We can do this the 'ard way or the easy way—but either way, it ends with you inside."

Ice stabs through me, turning my insides into a hard, freezing knot.

I may not remember everything about the workings of the world. But I suspect he is all too correct in his assessment of my position.

Nearly correct.

"In that case, I believe that I shall have to choose the hard way."

On the last word, I bring my foot up and stamp as hard as I can on Ferrars's instep.

He gives a surprised yell of pain and lets go of me, doubling over.

Just as my fingers seemed to remember of their own knowledge how to arrange my hair and make up my face, now my body seems to act of its own accord.

Joining both of my hands together in a combined fist, I strike sharply at the back of the young man's neck.

It's so easy that it is frightening. Who *am* I?

The thought flashes through my mind as, with a grunt, Ferrars collapses onto the ground. He is not unconscious. That would take more strength than I have. But he *is* momentarily dazed.

I don't wait. I can't let him catch me. And Dr. Everett could come out of the house at any second.

Whirling, I turn and run as fast as I can, pelting blindly down the street, back the way I came.

8. THE LONG ARM OF THE LAW

With my heart pounding hard enough to blur my vision, I risk a quick glance over my shoulder.

The street behind me is crowded. I am on a busy thoroughfare, bustling with pedestrians from all walks of life—from flower vendors hawking wilted wares to elegant ladies out for an afternoon's shopping.

But I cannot see any sign of either the young man who called himself Frances Ferrars or Dr. Everett. I'm safe—for now.

I am also completely, entirely lost. My headlong flight from the doctor's establishment took so many twists and turns that I have absolutely no idea where I am or how far relative to Harley Street I have come.

I force myself to slow my pace, so as to match better with the other pedestrians. I'm already attracting some odd looks from passers-by—and an indignant snort from a very stout gentleman whose foot I nearly stepped on.

I should look about for a street sign or some other way of finding out exactly where I am.

But now that I'm no longer running, the reality of my current predicament suddenly hits me—like a ton of bricks dumped off the back of a cart.

What kind of evil business am I mixed up in?

There's a milliner's shop on my right. I stop walking and stare blindly into the window filled with ribbons and gloves and hats adorned with improbable combinations of fruits and flowers.

Do Dr. Everett and his handsome friend try to kidnap every young woman who comes to the doctor's practice—or have I done something to make them single me out in particular?

I'm not sure which possibility is more frightening.

I have blood-soaked memories of gunshots and a woman screaming. I know that someone struck me on the head and left me lying on the street outside The British Museum. I know that either by fate or malicious chance, I happened to find Dr. Everett's card.

But try as I may, I can't arrange those disjointed fragments into any kind of pattern that makes sense.

Given the fact that he attempted to drug and abduct me, it's patently ridiculous to wish that Dr. Everett had not been interrupted right in the middle of his diagnosis. But I find myself wishing that he had given me more details about the condition he called amnesia.

I would love to know how long amnesia can be expected to last.

Unless possibly it is irreversible?

The thought of spending the rest of my life this way, wandering blindly around London, makes me feel as though a noose is tightening about my throat.

I force down a deep, steadying breath.

It could be worse. I could actually *be* Eleanor Ferrars, shackled by marriage to the young man who called himself Frances.

I shudder.

The reflection of another face appears in the glass window beside mine. I note it mechanically—then, with a jolt of pure horror in the pit of my stomach, with *recognition*.

It is the old man. The white-bearded ancient who sat down next to me at The British Museum and babbled about the weather.

Panic catapults me into motion, acting before I've even had time to fully register the shock.

Lashing out, I kick one of the old man's legs from under him, following the blow with a strike to the chest that knocks him back by a foot or two.

For a second, his startled eyes meet mine. His lips shape a word.

But I'm already running—as blindly and without thought for direction as before. My feet slap the pavement, fear hammering inside me like a steam piston.

If the old man somehow found me—and it absolutely, positively cannot be a coincidence that he appeared behind me when he did—then who *else* may be able to track and find me?

I dart down an alleyway filled with cans of ashes and barrels of reeking trash, emerge into another street, and keep going—barely drawing up in time to keep from being run over by a hansom cab.

"Bloomin' imbecile!" The driver shakes his fist at me. "Yer got eyes in yer head—why not use 'em?"

I press my hand to my ribcage in an effort to stop the hectic pounding of my heart.

Come to think of it, it was probably the old man who dropped Dr. Everett's card—just as I assumed in the first place.

Except that now it would appear that he dropped it on purpose—in an effort to deliberately drive me into visiting Harley Street and the doctor's practice.

A large, solid form dressed in blue appears directly in front of me—but I'm going too fast to stop. I plow straight into a broad, uniformed chest.

Strong hands seize me by the shoulders—probably just an effort to prevent me from falling. But I'm so panicked that I lash out instinctively.

My fist connects solidly with the police constable's nose before I realize that I've just added *assault of a police officer* to my list of other possible crimes.

This is obviously *not* my day.

The policeman clamps one hand over the lower part of his face—though he keeps firm hold of me with the other.

Looking up, my eyes meet his—which are very dark brown, set under slightly tilted dark brows.

No.

Even as realization jolts through me, another sudden fragment of memory flashes through my mind's eye.

This time, it's an odd recollection of sitting in what I think must be a music hall.

A man in a green bowler hat and green checked trousers was on the stage—and every time he said something humorous, the accompanying musicians would play a particular rhythm on the cymbals and drums. Two syncopated taps on the drums, then a smash on the cymbals.

Ba-dump-crash.

The constable takes his hand away from his face and stands, scowling down at me.

Yes, just as I suspected, some divine hand ought at this very moment to be playing out its own *ba-dump-crash* rhythm. The better to emphasize the extremely nasty sense of humor with which fate is treating me.

"You again," he says.

It's the *same* man. The same young detective constable who found me unconscious in the street this morning.

He is back in uniform, though he still looks tired, with faint shadows beneath his eyes.

Understandably, I suppose. If he is on duty again already, he can't have had very many hours of rest.

He raises one eyebrow at me. "Committed any more murders you'd like to tell me about?"

I grind my teeth together, cutting off a most impolite retort. But then, happening to glance past the constable's shoulder, my gaze lights on something that turns my veins to ice.

The white-haired old man is limping determinedly towards us like an avenging fury. He's still perhaps half a block away, but I recognize him instantly.

I catch hold of the constable's arm. "That man is following me!"

The detective constable looks at me. "Murder and now persecution. Anything else you'd like to share? Maybe a plot to steal the crown jewels?"

I gnash my teeth harder, stamping my foot. "Constable—" I stop. "What is your name?"

The young man gives me a flat look. "My name?"

I resist the urge to stamp my foot again. "I have just punched you in the face. Surely that puts us on a familiar enough basis that I ought to know your name."

The constable's mouth twitches just briefly in what might be a hint of a smile. "I'm not entirely sure I follow your line of reasoning. But the name's Kelly. D.C. John Kelly."

"Very well, then, Constable Kelly, I am not making any part of this up!"

The old man is nearer, now—near enough for me to see the monstrous scowl that twists his features.

I'm not a coward—or am I? I suppose I don't really know the answer to that.

But I have a difficult time in keeping my voice from trembling as I go on.

"Unless you think that I enjoy being assaulted, nearly drugged and kidnapped—*and* almost persuaded that I am married to a man who looks like a grown-up version of Little Lord Fauntleroy!"

The detective constable just looks at me, his face completely blank of expression.

For the brief space of silence between us, I can hear the echo of my own words—and how utterly insane they sound.

I can't even remember *reading* Little Lord Fauntleroy. The name of the character just appeared in my mind.

Constable Kelly opens his mouth. He's going to tell me that I'm a candidate for a madhouse. Or prison. I tense, ready to run if he tries to arrest me or drag me off to the asylum.

"Which man?"

I've been so absolutely certain he won't believe me that for a second I can't even take in the meaning of his words. "What?"

"Which man is it that's following you?"

"That one." I point over Constable Kelly's shoulder.

"The old timer?" I can hear the surprise in the constable's voice. I suppose it does rather strain credulity that the limping, white-haired old gentleman moving towards us might be a threat to anyone.

"Yes."

Constable Kelly seems to struggle with my assertion for a moment. But then he raises one hand and strides a few paces nearer towards the old man—who has come to an abrupt halt maybe a dozen yards away.

"You there," the constable calls out. "Stop."

The old man's gaze flashes rapidly from me to Constable Kelly and then back again.

Then he whirls around and bolts, racing away down the street with the speed of a much younger man.

Constable Kelly gives chase for a few strides. But then the old man—who has suddenly also developed the grace of a trained acrobat—leaps onto the back of a coach that is rumbling by.

For a second, I am certain that he's going to fall. His hat slips off, rolling into the street. But the old man grips tightly onto the coach's boot, and the coach itself rolls obliviously on, the driver no doubt completely unaware that he has taken on another passenger.

In another moment, they have vanished around the corner and are out of sight.

Constable Kelly gives up what is obviously a futile pursuit and stands staring after them. Then, slowly, he turns around.

His brows are drawn so tightly together that they form an almost perfect V over the bridge of his nose. But I have no idea what he's going to say—whether he's going to denounce me for a liar or ask me again whether I've been drinking.

Instead, though, he comes straight up to me to stand staring down into my face for another long moment.

The earlier rain has given way to a weak and watery glimpse of sun. Constable Kelly's face is focused, sharp and slightly grim in the pale light.

I tense, ready to run—or possibly punch him again—if the words *hysterical, drunken*, or *imaginary* cross his lips.

But he finally exhales a long breath. "I think you'd better tell me everything from the beginning."

9. Tea

Detective Constable Kelly leads the way to what appears to be a small restaurant on the opposite side of the road. I start to follow—then stop short as we reach the doors.

"Is something wrong?" Constable Kelly is frowning again.

I arch an eyebrow at him. "*Ladies Own Tea Association*?" I ask, reading the name of the establishment, as it appears printed in gold letters over the door. "Is this a favorite of yours?"

Constable Kelly gives me a quelling look. "I was trying to find a place where you'd feel at ease. But if you'd rather go to the beer hall in the next street over—"

"No, no," I assure him. "The Tea Association will be perfectly acceptable."

Acceptable to me, at least; Constable Kelly's entrance causes quite a stir among the rest of the patrons as we push through the doorway.

The tea room is filled with ladies taking a refreshing cup of tea after their morning shopping—and at sight of the constable's broad-shouldered and uniformed figure, they startle and murmur amongst themselves like a flock of birds at sight of a hawk.

A middle-aged hostess with quantities of fluffy blond hair hurries over to us—her eyes wide with alarm.

"May I help you ... that is ... would you like ..." Her hands flutter as she trails off ineffectually.

Her manner rather suggests that Constable Kelly is the first male patron to grace the shop since its opening.

Constable Kelly doesn't look in the slightest bit embarrassed or out of place. Even after our brief acquaintance, I'm already certain that the constable has enough self-assurance to make himself at home anywhere.

He's taken off his helmet, holding it under one arm. "A table," he says. "And a pot of tea, please."

"Certainly, step right this way."

It probably doesn't hurt his case that he has such dark good looks or such melting brown eyes.

With much fluttering and twittering, the hostess escorts us to a table towards the back of the tea room. The other customers stare—but as the constable does nothing but follow behind the hostess, they by and large return to their tea and gossip and cucumber sandwiches.

"I will be back directly with your tea," the hostess promises us, with a final flutter of her hands.

The chairs and table are not made for someone of Constable Kelly's height—any more than the tea room is designed for masculine clientele.

I have to stifle a smile as—grimacing slightly—he folds himself into the delicate Queen-Anne style chair and tucks his long legs under the lacy tablecloth.

Then he looks across the table at me. "Well? What's the verdict?"

"Verdict?"

"You've been making up your mind on whether or not you can trust me. You're trying to decide right now just how much of the true story you're going to give me."

That is what I was thinking—*exactly* what I was thinking. But I'm a little surprised that Constable Kelly was able to guess it so accurately.

"You're not the only one who can read people, you know." He stops, looking at me. "How about you start there—tell me how you knew everything you said about me this morning."

That feels like a lifetime ago, but I nod. "All right. But there isn't really so much to explain. Let's see, what did I tell you?"

I frown in an effort to recall. "Oh yes—that you were about to go off duty. Anyone might have surmised that you had already finished with your nightly patrols—the layers of mud caked on your boots, for one thing, attested to the number of miles you had walked. You had also loosened the top button on your tunic, suggesting that you were on your way home for a well-earned rest. I could tell furthermore that you are not married. The state of the handkerchief that you lent me suggested that much."

Constable Kelly's eyebrows go up, but he doesn't speak.

The hostess returns with our tea, and I go on, "No wife would allow her husband to go out with a handkerchief that had been so clumsily and inexpertly hemmed. Though the fact that you were carrying it at all might mean that you are too poor to afford a better one. But clearly you are not so destitute as that, judging by the good quality and state of repair of your boots. The other option—the only logical option—is that you must have a sentimental attachment to the person who hemmed it for you. A father might carry such a token from his daughter—but you are young to have a daughter of sewing age, and as I say not married. So, I thought it more likely that you had a much younger sister at home."

The bemused, slightly quizzical look is back in the constable's expression as he looks at me.

I pick up my teacup to take a sip. "What else did I say? Oh—your misspent youth, that's right. Well, the scar in your eyebrow is clearly several years old—obviously predating the time of your service to the police. The scar is also clearly the result of a knife wound. You are by your own statement from Cheapside, so I would hypothesize you came by the scar in some sort of a street fight. You also have an obvious predisposition to assume the worst about someone—which speaks to having lived among those who have done nothing to foster your faith in human nature. However, you have applied yourself diligently to your chosen career—hence the promotion from PC to DC. As I said before, I would think it *likely* that your joining the force had to do with the younger sister I mentioned. Perhaps your parents died or were killed, leaving you with the sole responsibility of caring and providing for her?" I raise my shoulders again. "But as I admitted earlier, that last is really only guesswork."

There is a long moment's pause while Constable Kelly looks at me across the table.

"All right," he finally says. "So, does all of that tell you whether or not you want to trust me?"

I look across the table at him. I want to be able to trust him. I would love to be able to trust *anyone* right now. I would love to have an ally.

But the fragment of memory explodes through my head again: *my hands on the trigger of a gun. Blood spattering onto paving stones.*

Excellent reminders of why it would be insane for me to trust an officer of the London police force.

"Where did *you* learn to read people?" I ask.

"Let's just say you learn a lot, begging for handouts—or sizing up your next mark—on the streets of Cheapside." He stops.

It's rather remarkable, really, that he doesn't add anything more: a demand that I give him an answer, in exchange for his. Or even an assurance that I can safely trust him with my story.

He just sits, still-muscled and watchful, waiting for me to make up my own mind.

I finally come to a decision. "All right."

Maybe it's reckless. But in the absence of even my own memories, I have nothing but instinct to go on. Instinct led me to trust the young maidservant Sarah—and in the same way it warned me right from the start that I could not trust Dr. Everett.

That was why I did not drink the doctor's tea, even before Frances Ferrars put in an appearance.

Now, I do not entirely *relax* in Constable Kelly's presence—but neither do I feel the back-of-the-neck warning prickle of imminent, intangible danger that I did in Harley Street.

"I'm going to tell you everything—at least, everything that I know."

* * *

The pot of tea has nearly gone stone cold by the time I finish speaking and sit back.

Constable Kelly is silent, watching me—as he has been through the whole of the time I was talking. Then he says, "I think I'd like to speak to this Dr. Everett of yours."

My breath goes out in a rush.

"Dr. Everett is not *mine*, I assure you. But I would love for you to question him."

In the entire snarled, knotted tangle of whatever business I am mixed up in, I can see at the moment only one thread to pull on: that of the not-so-good doctor.

Whether the clue will lead me any further to discovering my own identity remains to be seen—but it is at least a place to begin.

I would also love to see the young man who called himself Frances Ferrars try to charm his way out of an arrest warrant.

"Can you give me his address?" Constable Kelly asks.

"I can do better than that." Fishing in my handbag, I find Dr. Everett's business card and hand it over.

The constable stares at it for a long second. His lips move silently. "Harley Street. That's outside my regular beat. I'll have to get permission from my sergeant to go and take a look. If you'd like to wait here—"

I hesitate. Part of me would be *delighted* never to encounter Dr. Everett and his smooth, cheese-white hands again. But that is the cowardly choice.

"No. You might need me to identify him and the other man. I shall come along with you."

10. THE BIRDS ARE FLOWN

Even if I had my memories back, I do not believe that I could recall disliking anyone so instantly as I do Constable Kelly's sergeant.

"Are you sure this is the place?" Sergeant Mallows grunts.

I accompanied Constable Kelly to his station house—a grim and cheerless building on a grim and cheerless street.

Somewhat to my surprise, the sergeant on duty not only gave his permission for the venture to Harley Street—he also insisted on coming along. Which is why he is currently stamping along at Constable Kelly's side.

Sergeant Mallows is a big, heavyset man of forty or forty-five, with a face that is almost precisely the color of a slab of undercooked beef.

Or maybe I am just prejudiced against him, since he has yet to acknowledge my presence in any way, from the time we left the station house until this moment now.

It is not even that he thinks me a criminal.

For simplicity's sake—and because I did not trust him not to throw me into the station holding cell—we did not mention to

Sergeant Mallows the details surrounding my loss of memory. He knows only that I visited Dr. Everett in hopes of finding answers to my condition—and was nearly drugged and abducted as a result.

"*I* am certain that that is the place," I tell him.

Sergeant Mallows gives me a withering glance and a second grunt that speaks volumes as to his belief in my ability to find an address again.

Without saying anything, Constable Kelly hands over the card I gave him, and Sergeant Mallows squints at it.

"Well, it looks like the address on the card all right. But—look at it." He waves a hand.

Now that we're nearer, I can see what the sergeant means.

The bay window at the front of Dr. Everett's address is uncurtained and empty. And tacked to the front door is a large, hand-lettered sign, reading, *To Let*.

I stop short, staring—feeling as though the ground I'm standing on has suddenly given way to empty air.

"But—that's not possible." My voice sounds strange, hollow in my own ears. "They were *here*—"

Sergeant Mallows spares me another disdainful glance and a huff of irritation. "Well, we're here now. May as well take a look around."

He leads the way up the front steps and puts a hand to the doorknob—which turns easily, the door swinging open under his hand.

Constable Kelly follows the sergeant inside. I can't tell what the constable is thinking at all. His face is a carefully neutral blank.

I enter through the front door last—and then stop, gaping in astonishment all over again.

Everything is gone. The chairs, the carpets, the cheerful fire, the handsome desk where Mrs. Bartholomew sat welcoming patients in ...

The door to the inner consulting room is open—and through it, I can see that the space is just as empty as the outer room. The comfortable upholstered couches, the Egyptian antiquities on the mantle—they've all vanished, as though at a wave of some stage magician's magic wand.

If I hadn't seen the number on the front door positively as we came through, I would double back in order to check that we were at the right address.

"Is this your idea of some sort of joke?" Sergeant Mallows growls at Constable Kelly.

Constable Kelly's eyes are fixed straight ahead. "No, sir."

Muscles bulge in the sergeant's jaw, his face growing an even deeper shade of red. There's an ugly look in his small, pale-blue eyes that makes me suspect that Sergeant Mallow is a dangerous man to cross.

"Because if it is, I'm warning you—"

I interrupt. I can't let Constable Kelly get into trouble on my account. "Constable Kelly is not to blame. He knows only what I've told him. He would never have come here if it weren't for me."

While I'm speaking, I have the odd impression that Sergeant Mallows's attention is fixed elsewhere—at some point behind my back, I'm almost sure. But when I glance over my shoulder, I can't see anything there.

"And *you.*" The sergeant's watery eyes fix on me and he heaves his bulk more fully upright. "I don't know what game you're playing at, if you're mad or just no better than you should be. But the next time you want to go spinning wild stories, I'll thank you not to waste my officer's time with them."

He dismisses me with another snort of disgust and then turns back to Constable Kelly. "And you ought to know better than to believe such wild tarradiddles." Sergeant Mallows shakes his head, making the jowls on his cheeks tremble. "I took a chance on you, Kelly. There aren't a lot of men would hire someone with your background. But I told the Superintendent you were a good man and deserved a chance to make something of yourself." The sergeant leans forwards, lowering his voice. "Prove me wrong, and you won't like what follows. Do we understand each other?"

Constable Kelly's eyes are still fixed straight ahead, his face still impassive. "Yes, sir."

"Good." Sergeant Mallows jerks his chin at the door. "Get this baggage out of here while I see to closing up."

By *baggage*, he means me. I open my mouth—but then close it again.

I can see in Sergeant Mallows's face that absolutely nothing is to be gained by arguing with him or trying to persuade him that I'm not out of my mind.

I'm not even sure that I'm not out of my mind.

The doubt slices into me, keen as a knife-blade between my ribs. I was absolutely certain that everything happened here just as I told Constable Kelly—my meeting with Dr. Everett, Frances Ferrars, and everything else.

But the wards of Bedlam are probably full of patients equally convinced that their own delusions are real—and I am not exactly in a position to boast of my own clear-headedness, considering I still do not even know my own name.

Numbly, I turn to follow Constable Kelly out of the door and down the front steps. The constable stops there, and I draw to a halt beside him.

"What do you think?" I'm almost afraid to ask.

Constable Kelly is frowning—but not at me. He's staring back up at the doorway of number twenty-nine. His face is grimmer than I've yet seen, his dark eyes hard.

"I think I'd like to know what caught the sergeant's attention in there—and why he was so anxious to hustle us out of the door just now."

For the second time today, I feel nearly faint with relief.

"You noticed that, too? I thought he was staring at something. But I couldn't be sure."

"I noticed." Still watching the front door, Constable Kelly dips his head. "I'd give a lot to know what exactly he's doing in there right now."

"You could ask him."

Constable Kelly exhales a humorless laugh. "Right, I'll ask him. How far do you think *that'd* get me?"

"Probably thrown out of the station—and possibly off the police force completely." I remember the ugly, threatening look in the sergeant's eyes.

I look up at Constable Kelly. "You don't like Sergeant Mallows?"

Constable Kelly's eyebrows quirk up. "You've known him for what—a good half an hour, now? How do you feel about him?"

I suppose he has a point. "I thought maybe he improved on further acquaintance?"

I break off as I see a shadow moving behind the front window. "I think he's coming out."

Constable Kelly and I seem to have the same instincts. Without even needing to talk about it, we both dive towards the mouth of the nearest alley.

It is late afternoon—which means that since it is autumn, evening is already starting to fall. The sky is darkening to a dusky gray, and shadows cloak the alleyway.

Sergeant Mallows does not even glance in our direction as he stalks past on the opposite side of the road. He is absorbed in studying something that he holds in one hand. A coin? A medallion?

He slips whatever it is into his pocket before I can get a good enough look to be sure.

I wait until the sergeant has marched past and is well out of earshot before I ask, "Should we follow him?"

Constable Kelly considers for a second. "The sergeant's not stupid. There's too much risk he'd spot us. And he's probably just heading back to the station house."

The sergeant is turning back in the direction we came from.

"Now what?" I ask.

Constable Kelly looks at me—then he glances around at the thickly falling shadows. A lamp lighter is making his way down the street, bringing the row of gaslights to life.

"Do you want to come home with me?"

I feel my mouth drop open. Maybe the cautious trust I placed in Constable Kelly was misguided after all.

It's almost frightening how much that thought makes my stomach clench up.

I don't want to depend on John Kelly's chivalry. I don't think I can afford to depend on anyone, except for myself.

But before I can manage to say a word in reply, the constable himself appears to hear how his own words sound.

"I don't—sorry. I'm not very good at this kind of thing." He rubs the back of his neck. "I didn't mean anything improper, I swear."

He's almost flustered—which for a young man so capable and self-assured is cause enough to make me stare.

"I just thought you probably don't have anywhere to go tonight." The east London accent is more pronounced in his voice—and it's too dark to be certain, but I think there might be a flush of embarrassment on his cheeks.

It's oddly endearing.

"You can try a church's aid society, of course. I'll help you find one, if that's what you want. But they get a rough lot in there, and I don't know that you'll be safe. If you want—and if you don't mind sharing a room with my sister—we can offer you a place to sleep, anyway. I don't think there's a lot more we're going to do for tonight."

I hesitate, studying him. "For *tonight*?" I emphasize. "Do you mean that you *are* going to do something more at a later time?"

Constable Kelly's eyes narrow as he looks past me towards the street where Sergeant Mallows vanished from sight.

The twilight deepens the shadows around his eyes, making him look grim and almost dangerous. He may not bluster or storm like the sergeant—but I don't think that John Kelly is a man I'd want to cross, either.

"I don't have any idea what this is all about. But I don't like being lied to," he says. His voice is quiet, but laced with enough steely determination that I almost shiver. "So yes, I'm going to do something. Even if right now I don't know what."

He stops. Just as before in the tea shop, he doesn't say anything to try to influence my decision one way or the other. He just stands quiet, watching me, while the silence rests between us for a second.

"So, I was right about your sister?" I finally ask. It should not perhaps be high up on my list of worries right now—but there is a small satisfaction in knowing that my deductions about the constable were correct.

"You were right about a lot of things."

I hesitate for another second. I am suddenly, overwhelmingly aware of my own exhaustion. All I want is to sit down somewhere quiet and rest. No, that is not quite true. All I want is to sit down somewhere I know I'll be *safe*.

Rightly or wrongly, I do feel safe with Constable Kelly.

"Won't your neighbors—or your landlady—think it peculiar, your bringing me home?" I ask.

Or scandalous. Even with only the most proper of intentions, a young unmarried man bringing a young unmarried woman home to his place of residence for the night is simply not done.

I may not have all my memories, but I do recall that much.

"Trust me." Constable Kelly looks tired for a second, and then his lips curve in an expression that's half grimace, half smile. "Where Becky and I live, no one's going to bat an eyelash."

11. Introductions

I try to stay alert, but I am weary enough—and my head is aching enough—that the majority of our journey passes in something of a blur.

But then we turn onto Great Russell Street, and from there onto Dyott Street—and from there, we enter what feels like a maze of narrow, crumbling lanes and alleyways, all crowded with buildings so dilapidated that they look like rows of jagged broken teeth against the night sky.

The warm yellow light from a nearby chestnut seller's fire illuminates the grimace that crosses John Kelly's face.

"Welcome to the holy land," he says. "Otherwise known as Saint Giles."

Have I heard of Saint Giles before? I feel as though the name might possibly be familiar—but I can't chase the memory down.

I follow Constable Kelly down streets so narrow I could reach out my two hands and touch the buildings on either side.

There is trash—and worse, no doubt—everywhere, clogging the gutters, running in a foul river through the middle of the streets. If there are cobblestones here, they're too deeply buried in muck for anyone to see them.

At first, the smell is so overpoweringly vile that it feels as though the very air is trying to claw its way down the back of my throat. Then my nose simply goes numb.

I haven't said a single word, but Constable Kelly gives me a brief glance. "Unmarried officers are supposed to live in the divisional section house. But since I have Becky living with me, I have special permission to rent a place here. Which is all I can afford and still be close enough to the station house."

I can tell by the taut, braced set of his shoulders and the way his eyes are constantly scanning the road up ahead that he thinks it possible that we will be attacked. I cannot discount the possibility myself.

At one point, we pass by a pair of teenage boys, snarling and pummeling each other and rolling on the ground like wild dogs.

"I'm hoping in a year or so we can move to better—"

The constable breaks off abruptly at sight of a commotion in the street up ahead. There is some sort of public house on the corner, and in the light of the lantern hanging over its door, I can see a small boy in tattered trousers and a cloth cap racing towards us, running for all that he is worth.

The reason for his flight is instantly obvious: on the boy's heels is a huge, bald-headed man with a fiery red mustache.

The bald man is keeping up remarkably well considering his bulk—and he is waving what looks like a meat cleaver over his head.

Putting on a burst of speed, the boy closes the last few feet between us and dives behind Constable Kelly with a terrified gasp.

Constable Kelly stops walking and faces the other man. "You're Reg, from The Old Mitre, isn't that right?"

He looks amazingly calm, considering that the bald man is even taller than he is—and still holding the cleaver.

"Is there a problem?"

Reg bares his teeth at the small boy, who's still cowering behind Constable Kelly's legs.

"The problem is this young devil's been sneaking into my bar room and trying to monkey around with my piano," Reg growls. "Could damage a valuable instrument."

Constable Kelly keeps his expression affable. Neutral, but polite. "Sorry about that. Here. This should cover any damage done."

He digs into the pocket of his uniform trousers and comes out with a few sixpenny pieces.

Instead of looking mollified by the offering, though, Reg's scowl deepens. He takes a step forwards, slapping the flat side of the cleaver against his palm.

"Think you're better than all the rest of us, don't you? Now that you're a bloody blue bottle."

Constable Kelly's expression doesn't change—but his posture shifts, slightly, falling into a loose, easy stance that tells me as clearly as words that he is expecting trouble.

I feel my own muscles stiffen. For the first time since I came back to consciousness this morning, I'm *glad* that I seem to be accustomed to violence and know how to defend myself.

The small boy behind him looks as if he's going to say something, but Constable Kelly shushes him with a firm hand on his shoulder.

"I wouldn't say that." His voice is still pleasant, but he never takes his eyes off of Reg.

The big man's face twists in a sneer as he looks Constable Kelly up and down. "They say you used to run with the Sloggers."

Constable Kelly doesn't move. He doesn't even tense—but he somehow goes completely, utterly still, in a way that's almost eerily peaceful.

"I did." He spares a brief glance at me—clearly checking on where I am—and then asks, "You want to know what I learned while I was with them?"

Reg's gaze fixes on John Kelly's blue uniform. "Some rubbish about how it's better to be on the side of the law?"

Constable Kelly smiles. "Yeah, not exactly."

And then finally, he steps forwards—so fast that he's almost a blur of motion. I don't even see what exactly he does—but when he is finished, Reg is sitting on the ground, clutching his throat and wheezing for breath.

Constable Kelly doesn't even look at the tavern owner. Instead, he scowls down at the small boy, his expression fierce and at the same time almost resigned.

"Well? What have you got to say for yourself?"

The boy looks as though he's trying to make up his mind whether to be defiant or tearfully repentant. His chin is quivering, but his eyes—they're very bright blue in the lantern light—are hard.

"I didn't do his rotten piano any harm! I was just bored, and I thought maybe I could pick out a tune—"

Constable Kelly's scowl deepens. "What have I told you about going out on your own at night?"

The boy's eyes drop to the ground. "I had a plan," he mutters.

"I see. And this plan of yours—did it include *not* getting yourself hacked apart with a meat cleaver?"

He glances back at Reg, who's still wheezing and fighting for air on the ground, his face an unhealthy grayish purple color.

The boy doesn't answer, except with a sniffle.

Constable Kelly sighs and puts an arm around the boy's shoulders. "Look, I'm just trying to keep you from getting hurt. You didn't even bring Prince with you."

"I know. I'm sorry!" The boy suddenly bursts into a torrent of sobs. "I'm sorry, Jack, really I am."

He throws his arms around the constable's waist, burying his face against Constable Kelly's blue uniform. The dirty cloth cap is knocked off, revealing two long blond braids that flop down over the boy's—*girl's*, rather—thin shoulders.

With another sigh, Constable Kelly gently turns her around to face me. "Sorry. I didn't introduce you yet. This"—he glances down at the small, woebegone figure beside him—"is my sister, Becky."

12. Buy a Flower?

Becky stares up at me with wide, red-rimmed eyes. She appears to be about eight or nine years old, I would guess—and looks absolutely nothing like her brother. She is as fair as her brother is dark, with a scattering of freckles across the bridge of her upturned nose. Her mouth is too wide to be strictly-speaking pretty now—but I think she will be quite lovely when she's older.

More importantly, she looks both intelligent and spirited.

"Who are you?" she asks in a small, tear-clogged voice.

She's not just putting on an act of penitence, hoping to avoid punishment; she really is sorry for the trouble she caused.

I open my mouth. I don't want to lie, but I am also not sure how to answer her.

"She's a friend," Constable Kelly says. "She's had some trouble, so she's coming to stay with us for tonight."

"Oh." Becky gives me another serious inspection. "Do you like music?"

Do I? "I'm not sure."

"I do."

In the background, Reg finally manages to stop wheezing for air and heaves himself to his feet. He gives Constable Kelly a brief, lowering glance—but apparently decides that he would rather be able to walk in the morning, because he reverses direction and trundles away towards the tavern's swinging double doors as fast as his bulk will allow.

"Do you think he's going to give us trouble?" Becky asks her brother.

"I don't know." Constable Kelly rubs his forehead and then looks down at her. "But I'm a police officer, Beck. I can't be punching citizens just because my little sister has annoyed them."

"I know." Becky's shoulders droop.

"Do you?" I can tell from John Kelly's expression that he doesn't *want* to make her feel any worse. His hand twitches as though he's on the verge of patting her shoulder again and telling her that everything is all right.

But instead he crouches down so that his eyes are on a level with the girl's. "Then maybe next time you can remember it before you go sneaking out on your own after dark and getting into some hare-brained scheme. What happens if I lose my job?"

"We can't pay Mr. Ludwell." Becky's voice is so small I can barely hear it. "We won't have anyplace to live."

Her head snaps up and she looks at him in sudden panic. "You're not going to leave me, are you? Or send me to a workhouse?"

"Don't talk crazy. Who said anything about a workhouse?" Constable Kelly pulls her into a hug. "We're family, you and me." His voice is steady, firm and reassuring. "And I promised you I'd look after you, didn't I? When have you ever heard me make a promise I didn't mean to keep?"

"Never." Becky sniffs, but looks mildly comforted.

"All right then." Constable Kelly ruffles her blond braids and stands up. "Let's get on home. We'll have to put some extra water in the soup on account of our guest here."

He nods to me, and Becky giggles.

Something aching and hollow seems to open up inside me as I watch the two of them—the complete, trusting adoration in Becky's small face as she looks up at her older brother. The way he keeps one hand protectively on her shoulder.

The feeling isn't a memory, nothing as definite as that. More just a feeling that once upon a time *I* was Becky's age—and I would have given absolutely anything in the world to hear someone say those words to me: *we're family*.

"Buy a flower, miss?"

I look round with a start to see that an elderly flower vendor has sidled up to me while I was absorbed in watching Becky and her brother.

The old woman has to be one of the ugliest I've ever seen—hook-nosed, stoop-shouldered, and with a mouthful of rotting teeth. She has a wart the size of a ha'pence on her chin—and her straggling gray hair looks as though it's been cut with hedge clippers.

She also doesn't appear to be having much luck in selling her wares tonight: the tray of wilted bunches of violets she's carrying is completely packed full.

"Flower, miss?" she asks again. She shakes the tray of nosegays fiercely in my face. "Come along, help a fellow creature in need."

The gust of gin on her breath is strong enough that I feel I ought to be growing tipsy just breathing in the same vicinity.

"No thank you." I do my best not to recoil. "I'm sorry, I haven't any mon—"

"You, then." Without even waiting for me to finish, the old woman transfers her attentions to Constable Kelly. "Come along, young sir. Buy a flower for your sweetheart here."

The flower vendor staggers over to him, attempting a drunken wink as she taps the side of her nose and lowers her voice to a hoarse whisper. "Maybe she'll thank you with a kiss."

The look of mingled embarrassment and consternation on Constable Kelly's face is enough to make me bite my lip. I trample my urge to laugh. After the day I have spent—and now the altercation with Reg—this is just too much.

"She's not my sweetheart."

"Oh, come now." The flower vendor waggles her head at him. "A pretty girl like her? Buy her a flower, and maybe she could be."

As the old woman brandishes her tray of wares at Constable Kelly, I suddenly stiffen, staring at her.

I've seen the old flower vendor before. The impression is so overwhelming that I miss whatever Constable Kelly says in reply.

I *know* I have seen the elderly woman somewhere before.

But that is surely absurd. And even if it is true, how can it possibly matter? Maybe I ran across the old woman elsewhere in London. But it's not as though she's likely to have names and addresses for everyone to whom she has ever tried to sell her sorry-looking bouquets.

"Look." I can hear the striving for patience in Constable Kelly's tone. "I'll take one bunch for my sister here." He nods to Becky. "As for the lady—" he glances up at me with an odd expression, followed by a quirk of a wry smile. "I'll leave it up to her. Here's a loan."

Before I realize what he's doing, he hands me a penny coin. "She can decide whether she wants to buy her own flowers or not."

The old woman seems to be satisfied with that arrangement. She hands one bunch of flowers over to Becky, then turns expectantly to me.

"I really don't need flowers." I hand her the coin. "But see if you can find a bed somewhere for tonight. It's going to be dreadfully cold."

Now that the night has fully fallen, the raw chill in the air is turning bitter.

"Hmmph." The old woman takes the penny—but then she looks from me to Constable Kelly, seeming reluctant to leave.

Where have I seen her before? *Where*?

I lean forward a little, trying to search her face beneath the curtain of shaggy gray hair.

But before I can even recapture the feeling of familiarity, the old woman turns abruptly away and with a final *hmmph*, stamps away up the street.

Constable Kelly lets out what sounds like a breath of relief. "And now that that's all taken care of, let's go home."

13. THE HOUND—AND THE HOME—OF THE KELLYS

Constable Kelly and Becky live in the next street over—which is marginally less bleak and depressing than the rest of what I have seen so far in Saint Giles.

"This is us." Constable Kelly points towards the corner house in a group of buildings set around a central paved square with a pump in the middle.

This is *much* better than the rest of Saint Giles, if they actually have shared running water.

Constable Kelly opens the door to a set of rooms on the ground floor of the building—and we are instantly greeted by a huge, tawny brown, frantically baying and barking dog. The term *mastiff* springs to my mind, though I'm not sure from where.

The dog is not attacking—as is my first panicked thought. The barks and howls are merely evidence of the huge animal's ecstasy on our arrival.

With the ease of long practice, the constable catches the dog before it can plow one of us over with its leaps.

"And this," he says, raising his voice to be heard over the cacophony, "is the last member of the family. Prince."

Prince finally settles—though he snuffles at me inquisitively as we make our way inside.

"He's our watch dog," Becky puts in, beside me. "Jack got him for me for when he's on duty. So that I won't be on my own."

I can well believe that even the most hardened criminal would think twice about breaking into a house containing the huge mastiff.

His tongue is lolling out in a doggy grin at the moment. But the teeth in his mouth are the size of my littlest finger.

The Kellys' lodgings are small—just two rooms—and sparsely furnished, but very neat and clean. There's an outer room that seems to serve as both a parlor, dining room, and kitchen combined. It's probably Constable Kelly's bedroom, as well, to judge by the blanket I can see folded on the arm of the well-worn sofa.

A pot of something bubbles over the fire in the hearth.

"Becky can show you where you can wash, if you like," Constable Kelly says.

Becky seems to have been struck by a sudden fit of shyness. Her eyes are huge as she studies me—but she doesn't say a word as she opens a door and shows me to the inner chamber.

"Is this your room?" I ask her.

A narrow wooden bed, a washstand, and a rickety wooden chair are the room's only furniture—but the walls are papered with dozens of scraps cut from sales circulars and advertisements: flowers, ladies in extravagant hats, butterflies ... plainly anything that Becky found pretty has been snipped out and used for decoration.

She ducks her head and then hurries out, closing the door behind her.

There's a jug of water in the washstand. I rinse my hands and face, and then glance quickly in the small, cracked mirror.

At least this time my own features and the wide green eyes staring back at me are familiar.

There are no cosmetics here for me to pilfer, so I merely check to be sure that my hair is tidy and go back to rejoin Constable Kelly and his sister in the outer room.

Prince has ceased barking and taken up an observatory post by the fire. And Constable Kelly and Becky are talking quietly.

"All right," I hear Constable Kelly say. "So, tell me what you were thinking, trying to sneak in to play the piano in a public house."

Judging by the expression on Becky's face, she was very much hoping that her brother might have forgotten the subject.

But she sighs, digging in the pocket of her tattered jacket. "I got it from the sheet-music vendor's cart in the market," she says in a small voice. "He let me have it for half price because it was torn, see?"

She holds up a grubby piece of paper on which are printed the lines of the treble and bass clefs.

"A bargain." Constable Kelly's voice is torn between exasperation and something like amusement.

"I just wanted to hear what the tune sounded like," Becky adds.

"May I see it?" I ask.

Both brother and sister look at me, startled. I've startled *myself* with the request—which seemed to come out of my lips completely on its own.

Becky passes the paper over to me. Which is lucky, because my fingers twitch with the strangest urge to snatch it straight out of her hands.

I can't explain or understand that, but something about the lines and the printed notes on the page seems to almost *call* to me.

I glance over the sheet of music. I don't think the words and notes are familiar. And yet I can feel my lips start to move.

The day is done, and the darkness
Falls from the wings of Night,

My voice rings out, clear and true and soaring on the melody.

I do not know how I'm singing the music on the page. It just seems to happen by instinct—the same instinct that led me to defend myself from Frances Ferrars and the elderly man.

But this is so, so much better, because it feels right. *I* feel right.

For the first time since I regained consciousness this morning, I feel as though I am doing exactly what I want to be doing—exactly as I am meant to be doing. The music just seems to flow from me, as effortlessly as breathing.

As a feather is wafted downward
From an eagle in his flight.

I finish the song and then stop—realizing abruptly that both the Kellys are staring at me. They may look nothing alike, but right now their mouths are both dropped open in identical expressions of astonishment.

Even Prince is sitting up in his place, staring at me with his ears pricked up and his head on one side.

"It goes something like that." Suddenly self-conscious, I hand the sheet of paper back to Becky.

"Well. I think that answers the question of whether or not you like music."

14. A Bump in the Night

"Her mother taught her to play the piano a little," Constable Kelly says.

He keeps his voice low, so as not to wake Becky—who is now asleep in the inner room.

She held out as long as possible after our dinner of stew. But she finally fell asleep with her head resting on the arm of the couch, and a short while ago Constable Kelly carried her in to her own bed.

"Her mother?"

What I really want to ask is whether that lady was Constable Kelly's mother, too. I am dying to know more about the brother's and sister's respective stories.

But I cannot think of a way to phrase the question without seeming either abominably curious or simply rude.

Constable Kelly shrugs and does not answer directly. He has taken off his blue uniform tunic and is in his trousers and a plain white cotton shirt with the sleeves rolled to his elbows.

He's sitting on the room's only chair, watching the leaping flames of the fire.

I'm perched on the couch. I should be exhausted after the day I've had, but somehow instead I feel wide awake.

"It's not much fun for her, being on her own when I have to be on duty," Constable Kelly goes on. "I try to angle for patrolling at night whenever I can, but it doesn't always work out."

"You don't know anyone who could look after her for you?"

Constable Kelly gives me a sidelong look. "Yeah, my old mates from the Sloggers are just lining up at the door, hoping for work as a nanny."

I can see his difficulty. Since he's the one who brought it up, I ask, "The Sloggers?"

"It's a street gang in Cheapside. I used to run with them, just like Reg said. Lucky for me, I was never arrested, or I'd have had a lot harder time getting work on the Force."

It is almost impossible for me to imagine what that transition must have been like. "Why the police force?"

Constable Kelly raises one shoulder. "It paid enough to feed both me and Becky and keep a roof over our heads. And it seemed like it would give me at least halfway decent odds of staying alive long enough to see her grow up. Cheapside Sloggers mostly wind up dead or in jail—or both."

He rubs his forehead. "Of course, maybe Becky's the one I should be worrying about keeping alive."

I smile slightly. "I don't know. I used to dress up as a boy and sneak out to fight clubs when I wasn't much older than she is. And I lived to tell about it."

Constable Kelly's head snaps up and he stares at me. I stare back, suddenly realizing what I have just said.

"How did I *know* that?"

"Do you remember it, then?"

I shake my head in frustration. "No. I mean, I *think* I did a second ago—but now I'm just ... remembering that I remembered it. I can't remember actually *being* there. Except—"

Fight clubs. I suppose that would explain a great deal about my survival skills.

I draw my feet up under the hem of my gown, hugging my knees.

"Except that I have a ... a kind of feeling that I was on my own a lot of the time. I didn't have any family or any home to go to. I knew I couldn't depend on anyone else to keep me safe. So, I had to learn to take care of myself."

A little of the hollow, lonely feeling puddles around my heart, and I add, "Not that you need me to say it, but Becky is lucky to have you."

Constable Kelly is quiet for a second, still looking into the fire. Then he says, "She's only lived with me for a bit under two years. Since her mother died. Well, she was my mother, too. Not that I called her that. I never knew who my father was. And when I was six or seven she took up with a new man who didn't want me hanging around. So, she kicked me out onto the streets and left with him to go up to Liverpool."

"She just *left* you?" I stare, incredulous.

Constable Kelly shrugs. "She was just a kid herself. Only fourteen when she had me. And I could walk out of that door and find a dozen, girls and boys both, who'd make me look like one of the lucky ones. I knocked around, but I survived."

No wonder he fell in with a gang. To a scared seven-year-old living alone on the street, it would have meant family of a sort—or at the least protection.

"And Becky?" I ask.

Constable Kelly glances at me. "Three years ago, my mother turned up again, out of a blue sky—with Becky in tow. Seems her new husband had been arrested. He'd owned a tavern—but he'd been found to be selling smuggled liquor, so he was thrown in jail and had all his property seized. All she and Becky had were the clothes they stood up in. Their money'd run out, and they'd had to beg and hitch rides all the way back from Liverpool."

He stops, his eyes shadowed with the memory. "I gave her some money—enough to rent them a room in a lodgings house and feed them for awhile. But she was sick—dying of consumption. She begged me before she died to look after Becky."

"And you did as she asked?" I can't help but be amazed that he would *care* about his mother's dying wishes, after she abandoned him without so much as a backward glance.

But Constable Kelly only shrugs again. "It's not like any of the whole mess was Becky's fault. And I wasn't going to let her be carted off to the workhouse or put in some children's home."

No, of course he wouldn't. I don't know Constable John Kelly well—but I am sure that he wouldn't throw his half-sister unto the cruel mercies of the world.

Prince snuffles in his sleep at Constable Kelly's feet, his paws twitching in some canine dream.

I take a breath. "*I* could stay with Becky for you."

Constable Kelly looks at me quickly, both his eyebrows going up in surprise.

I hurry on, "Just for now, I mean. Until I can find out—well, anything—about who I am or where I belong. But in the meantime, I could look after Becky and at the least stop her from annoying any more tavern owners. Although—"

A sudden thought strikes me, and I stop short. "Maybe you would not *want* to trust me with your sister. I mean, I wouldn't blame you if you didn't. I could be anyone—any kind of criminal—"

But Constable Kelly stops me, shaking his head. "No. You couldn't."

His face is all hard planes and angles in the firelight, his dark eyes serious, intent beneath the scar on his brow.

It's strange—strictly speaking, the so-called Frances Ferrars is, I suppose, the better looking of the two. But right now, the errant thought flashes through my mind that I wouldn't even glance at Ferrars if John Kelly were in the room.

Constable Kelly's face has both strength and character, as well as good looks—where Ferrars's was a bland, empty mask.

"I know criminals," Constable Kelly goes on. "From both sides—being one and arresting them. I have no idea what to make of you. But whoever and whatever you are, you're not a murderer. If you shot someone, it was for a good reason, and because you had no other choice."

After knowing him less than a day, John Kelly's opinion shouldn't really carry such weight with me—and yet somehow at his words, I feel oddly lighter, as though an invisible weight has been suddenly lifted from my heart.

I meet his gaze and say, quietly, "Thank you."

The room is silent, save for the occasional snore from Prince, and the small crackles the fire makes. Outside, I can hear all the street noises of a London night: shouts and voices raised in drunken song, and from somewhere more distant a splintering crash of what sounds like breaking wood.

But here in this room, everything feels safe—cozy, the rest of the world held at bay.

I rub my temples. "Although I do still wish that I could remember. It's very unsettling, not even knowing my own name." My fingertips curl in frustration. "I can add up the pieces—everything I know about myself. But I can't seem to make any sense of them."

Constable Kelly shakes his head. "You're something different, that's certain."

"What?" I widen my eyes in mock surprise. "Do you mean to say that you don't run across young women with no memories on a regular basis? How shocking!"

"I didn't mean your memories being gone. Even if you remembered your whole life perfectly, I'm pretty sure I'd still have never met anyone like you."

I smile unsteadily. "That could be the nicest thing that anyone has ever said to me. Of course, my memories only go back a little over twelve hours. But it was still very nice."

Constable Kelly smiles, too. The expression completely transforms his face—making him look younger, less dangerous and hard-edged.

Our eyes meet—and for a second, time seems to slow to a mere crawl. The whole rest of the world fades away.

I don't want to move. I don't even want to *breathe*, for fear of shattering this moment. And yet there's an odd kind of pressure in my chest, too—a curiosity to know what will happen next.

Something falls with a crash outside—likely from just behind the small window at the far end of the room.

In an instant, Constable Kelly is on his feet. Prince wakes with a snuffle and a short, sharp bark, all the fur on the back of his neck rising.

My heart hammers as Constable Kelly crosses to the front door, yanks it open, and strides out into the night.

No one knows that I am here—or they shouldn't.

Unless I was somehow followed?

Unless the tavern owner Reg told someone? Or the elderly flower vendor was somehow an enemy in disguise?

Which sounds ridiculous, even inside my own mind.

I try to steady my breathing. Wildly fanciful theories are not going to help me right now.

It is barely a minute—though it feels like much longer—before Constable Kelly returns.

He shakes his head in answer to my questioning look. "Nothing there. Just an empty trash bin and a couple of crates knocked over at the side of the house—like someone plowed into them, maybe."

Or as though someone were trying to stand on them and see inside through the window.

To judge by his expression, Constable Kelly has had the same thought. But he drops the bar on the door into place, bolts the latch—he's obviously reinforced the security measures of this place—and says, "You should try to get some sleep. Prince will wake us if there's anyone out there."

I *should* try to sleep. Both of us should. But I can't help asking, "Have you thought about what you're going to do—about Sergeant Mallows, I mean?"

The line of Constable Kelly's mouth hardens. "For a start, I thought I'd see if I can have a look around the sergeant's desk tomorrow, sometime when he's not around. See if anything jumps out at me as something he might have taken away from Harley Street. Barring that—well, that and keeping an eye on him"—he shakes his head—"I doubt there's a lot I can do. I could talk to one of the station house Inspectors. But I don't have any proof that Sergeant Mallows did anything wrong. The Inspector's not going to call him onto the carpet for questioning just because I've got a feeling he knew more than he was letting on about an empty house."

He's right. "Do you think we ought to go back to the house in Harley Street? We could see whether or not there's anything else that Dr. Everett and Sergeant Mallows may have missed."

"It's a thought. We can go after I get off duty, maybe."

Since I am not anxious to face Dr. Everett—or Ferrars—on my own, I nod.

Going with a uniformed police constable will also make it less likely that I get arrested for breaking and entering.

"Anyway. Nothing more we're going to do tonight." Constable Kelly rubs a hand across his face and then indicates the sofa. "You can have the couch."

"I can't take your bed!" I protest. "Where will you sleep?"

I have a feeling that I ought to be expressing far more maidenly horror at the thought of sharing a room—if not actually a bed—with a young man for the night. But somehow, I cannot seem to work up any very great concern.

I trust Constable Kelly. And the niceties of social decorum do not feel as though they have much of a place in my life at the present.

"I can take a spare blanket and make do on the floor." He smiles briefly. "I've slept in worse places, believe me."

"So have I. Well, I assume that I have. The street outside The British Museum was certainly worse."

Constable Kelly checks the latch on the window, then pauses at the door to his sister's room, glancing in to where Becky is sprawled asleep across the narrow bed.

"What if we switch? You can have the couch for tonight, and tomorrow night we'll trade."

The mention of tomorrow night makes me feel slightly better—even with the thought of our possible peeping Tom lingering at the back of my mind.

I at least have this small, safe refuge in which to stay.

Maybe—just possibly—I am not completely alone. As if he's picked up my thought, Constable Kelly says, "You can stay as long as you'd like. And if you keep Becky company, I'll be grateful. But you've got your own place in the world, out there somewhere, too."

The fire is dying down to just embers, making it hard to see his expression. But I think there's an odd shadow of something like regret or sadness at the back of his gaze as he looks at me. But the look is gone in a blink, making me wonder if it was ever there at all.

"Wherever it is you belong, it's not in rented lodgings in Saint Giles. That much I'm sure of."

15. A Case of Identity

I wake to the soft clinks of cutlery—and realize upon opening my eyes that it is early morning. Against all odds, I slept dreamlessly through the night.

Both Constable Kelly and Becky are already awake and dressed, working at getting breakfast in the tiny area by the hearth that serves as their kitchen.

"I went out and fetched water from the pump," Becky says. She still looks at me a bit shyly, but gives me a small smile. "If you'd like a wash."

Since I haven't any change of clothes, there is very little for me to do beyond splashing my face with cold water and re-braiding my hair.

The lump behind my ear still feels painful to the touch—but the throbbing headache is at least nearly gone.

I emerge back into the outer room to find Constable Kelly ladling bowls of porridge out from the cooking pot on the hearth.

"Thank you." I accept my bowl and sit down at the small table, taking a chair beside Becky's. "Do you have to be on duty today?"

He's wearing his uniform trousers, but not the blue tunic or helmet yet. "I'll have to be off in a minute or two."

"What's all this?" I ask Becky. I gesture to a pile of papers beside her place at the table.

"Oh that—they're my Sherlock Holmes stories!" Becky's shyness seems to evaporate completely at the question. She turns to me, excitement brimming on her small face. "Have you read any of them? Oh—of course, you wouldn't remember, would you? Jack told me all about how you can't remember anything before you woke up."

I glance quickly at Constable Kelly. He shakes his head almost imperceptibly. I thought so; he hasn't told his sister *everything* about me.

For her own safety, I'm sure he wouldn't have told Becky about Sergeant Mallows, either.

"It's so exciting!" Becky bounces a little in her chair. "I thought maybe we could try to de—*deduce*"—I can hear her struggle momentarily with the word—"who you are. Just like Sherlock Holmes and Doctor Watson."

"And which one are you?" Constable Kelly quirks up an eyebrow. "Watson or Holmes?"

Becky sticks out her tongue at him. "You like the stories, too, Jack! You know you do. You always listen when I read them."

"Only because you don't give me a choice."

I barely hear their teasing.

Sherlock Holmes. I feel as though the name has snagged on some inner thread inside my mind and is tugging. Sherlock Holmes.

Constable Kelly mentioned the name yesterday, I remember—and it felt as though it were familiar to me then.

"What kind of stories are they?" I ask Becky.

"The *best* kind! Detective ones." Becky picks up the top magazine from the pile and rifles quickly through it, then sets it down in front of me when she comes to the page she wants. "Look!"

The title on the magazine page reads, *A Case of Identity*.

An illustration shows a tall man in a smoking jacket, welcoming a rather plump, plain lady into a sitting room.

I stare down at the printed page, the nagging feeling of familiarity even stronger. I feel as though I should remember … *something*.

But I banish the sensation. I am getting thoroughly sick of my memory giving me these subtle hints, and never any definite answers.

"And after we read this one, I've got all these here." Becky gestures triumphantly to the stack beside her plate.

Constable Kelly looks at his sister with a small twitch of a smile. "Well, I can see you'll be well entertained, anyway."

"I'm sure I will be."

He pushes away from the table and goes to shrug into the rest of his uniform. "I have to be going." The smile is gone as he turns back to look at me over the top of Becky's head.

"Take care."

"I will." Left to my own devices, I might try investigating on my own. But I have Becky to think about now—which means that I have no intention of doing anything more dangerous than reading through the entire stack of Sherlock Holmes stories in Becky's possession.

Constable Kelly hesitates, as though he's still reluctant to leave.

I am disturbingly reluctant to *see* him leave. So, I force a smile. "Of the two of us, I think you're a good deal more likely to run into danger than I am."

Constable Kelly finishes buttoning up his tunic and gives me an answering grin. "You say that now." He tugs on one of his sister's braids. "You haven't yet run the risk of Becky here talking your ears off."

Becky is both lively and talkative—but I welcome her chatter. It is a pleasant change from having only my own thoughts to occupy me.

We finish *A Case of Identity*, and *The Red-Headed League*, then move on to *A Scandal in Bohemia*.

"Who taught you to read?" I ask Becky, when she pauses for a moment.

She reads slowly, moving one finger along the line of text as she goes, but she is quite fluent.

"My mum had my dad hire a tutor for me. She wanted me to grow up to be a lady, she said. That's why she had me learning the piano, too."

I don't want to pry, but I say, "I'm sorry about your mother—and your father, too."

Becky shrugs her thin shoulders, her eyes on the floor. "My dad never paid much attention to me anyhow. He always said he didn't want me underfoot. I do miss the piano. And my mum—" she stops.

Her gaze is still fixed on the floor, but I can see her swallow. Then she raises cornflower blue eyes to my face.

"Maybe you're lucky you can't remember anything. Sometimes remembering just makes you sad."

I hesitate, then reach to squeeze her hand. "Maybe you're right."

Becky raises one hand to brush at her cheek. Then she straightens. "At least I've got Jack. And Prince." She strokes the big dog's neck. "And anyway, I won't need to play the piano, if I grow up to be a police constable, too."

I feel my eyebrows rise. "*Can* women be police officers?"

I can't remember whether there are any laws forbidding it—but it seems somehow highly likely, given what I've seen of the world in the past day.

"Not yet." Becky looks unconcerned. "But I think they're bound to let girls in sooner or later. Jack says if anyone can persuade them, I can."

I smile.

Becky glances down at the story on the table. But she seems to have tired of reading for the moment, because she says, "Do you think that you could teach me to sing like you—"

A knock at the door interrupts her, making her cut off in mid-word.

Prince is instantly on his feet, his hackles raised and a low growl rumbling in his throat.

My heart is hammering. "Could it be your brother back, do you think?" I whisper.

Becky shakes her head. She doesn't have any of my reasons to be frightened—but maybe some of my own nervous anxiety is communicating itself to her, because she keeps her voice to a whisper, also.

"No. He won't be back for ages, yet. And anyway, he wouldn't knock."

The knock sounds again—louder, this time, insistent. A deep, booming male voice shouts out, "Hello! Anyone at home?"

"Yes!" Becky calls back.

I clamp a hand over her mouth—but it's too late.

"Hello!" The voice shouts again.

What should I do? The question seems to hammer in time to my own pulse. Answer it? Ignore whoever it is and hope that they will go away? The knocking resumes—hard enough to rattle the front door on its hinges.

I swallow and rise, stiff-legged, from the table. I can't just sit here and wait for whoever it is to break the Kellys' front door in.

"Go into the other room," I whisper to Becky.

She looks at me with wide, suddenly alarmed eyes. "Why? Is something—"

"I'll explain later," I promise. "But for now, go into the other room. You can pretend that you're Sherlock Holmes spying on some dastardly criminal. Just shut the door and don't come out unless I tell you to. Promise?"

With a stiff, jerky nod and a final worried look over her shoulder, Becky obeys.

I wait until the latch on her bedroom clicks. Then I cross to the front door and swing it open.

I stop, staring at the figure before me with a mixture of relief and astonishment.

Standing on the doorstep is an organ grinder—one of the itinerant musicians who perform on city street corners in hopes that passers-by will grace them with a few coppers.

This man is somewhere hovering around middle age—with possibly the largest, blackest, most luxurious mustache I have ever seen. His hair is likewise shiny and black as boot-polish.

His gray eyes peer at me from behind a pair of gold-rimmed spectacles. And on his shoulder—the main source of my astonishment—is perched a tiny monkey, dressed in a small purple vest and matching cap. Behind him the door to the flat across the hall opens. Someone—Jack's neighbor, probably—is listening.

The man looks me up and down, then grunts out, in a surly, gravely tone, "Just wanted to let you know that I'll be givin' a performance in a few minutes." He jerks his head at the central paved square behind him. "Thought yer might like t' come."

He lands hard on the final word, giving it an odd emphasis.

I frown. "A performance." After being certain that disaster had found me, my mind is struggling to adjust itself to a small, fluffy monkey and its master.

"Jugglin' and such. Rollo here does tricks, too. Wonderful, he is."

The man nods to the monkey—who doesn't seem to appreciate the compliment. With a chattering screech, he lunges, attempting to bite the organ grinder on the ear.

"Thank you—" I stop short—feeling as though a bucket of freezing water has just been dumped over my head.

The monkey's attack has drawn my attention—and now I stare, transfixed, at the mustached man's ears. Or more accurately, his ear *lobes.*

A voice—I wish I could remember who the blasted owner of the voice is, but I still cannot—sounds in the back of my mind.

A man may disguise his features with putty and paint, twist his posture, don a false beard. But the lobes of the ears are practically impossible to disguise—and nearly as distinctive as a fingerprint for individual shape.

Now the three pictures align themselves in my mind, like portraits hung in a row on a gallery wall:

The old man who shared my bench and later accosted me in the street.

The elderly flower vendor from last night.

And lastly, this itinerant organ grinder standing before me now.

They're all the same person.

All three of them, one and the same.

My heart beats sickeningly. "Thank you so much. I would love to see your performance. I will be sure to come out in just a few moments."

I rattle the words off so quickly that I hardly even know what I am saying.

The organ grinder's face creases in a frown, and he opens his mouth—but I step back before he can get a word out, banging the door in his face and bolting it behind me.

I *fly* to the inner room—where I find Becky, sitting bolt upright on the bed.

"What's happen—" she starts to say.

I interrupt her. "Quickly. We need to leave now—at once!"

I'm already scanning the room, looking for any other exit. Our only option appears to be a single window, set high in the wall and covered by a gingham curtain. "Are there any bars on that?" Crossing to push the curtain aside, I answer my own question. "No. Good. It will be a tight fit, but I think we can manage. Here. You go first."

I start to boost Becky up.

"What about Prince?"

I stop, shutting my eyes. But there is no chance that I can heft the dog's weight up to the height of the window. I doubt he would fit, in any case.

"He'll be all right." I hope, hope, *hope* that that is true. At least if ever a dog looked capable of defending himself, it is Prince.

"We just need to go and find your brother—and then Prince will be here waiting for us when we all come back."

I doubt Becky believes the situation is as simple as that. But thankfully, she doesn't argue. She lets me boost her up feet first through the window, hangs briefly by her hands, then drops down out of sight.

The need for haste pounds in my veins. How long do we have before my mysterious visitor decides to come around the back and see for himself whether or not I have escaped? Surely not more than a few minutes, at best.

I follow Becky through the window—pausing only to snatch up a thick woolen shawl that I happen to see hanging over the back of Becky's chair.

"Now," I whisper, when I'm crouching next to her in a narrow, extremely dirty alleyway. "Which way do we go to find your brother's station house?"

16. Remember, Remember

The route that Becky takes me on is convoluted enough to make an entire fleet of cartographers beg for mercy.

We dodge through a network of alleyways, cross traffic-clogged streets, and once actually climb a ladder up onto the roof of a building, then back down the other side.

My headache has come back, the lump on my skull throbbing sourly with every jarring step—as though wishing to remind me that someone out there wants me dead.

Maybe it was the disguised organ grinder who struck the blow.

At the moment, that seems hideously likely.

Finally, we emerge from the mouth of a narrow side-lane and step into the bustle of Oxford Street. From there, we make our way to Great Russell Street.

"Jack's station house is that way." Becky gestures. "But he won't be there. He'll be out walking his beat by now."

She's right. I should have thought of that for myself.

I pull the shawl I took from her room more tightly around my head and shoulders. It is not much of a disguise, though—and

I feel horribly exposed out here, on the busy street. The back of my neck prickles with the expectation that a nameless attacker will come at me from behind.

"Do you know the route he walks?" I ask.

Becky shakes her head—then waits, quietly for me to decide what we're going to do now.

What *are* we going to do?

"I'd rather be Irene Adler," Becky says.

I'm focused on trying to decide our next course of action—and looking around for any sign of our many-faced visitor among the crowds of people all around.

I look at her blankly. "What?"

Becky's eyes are bright, her cheeks a healthy pink. She doesn't appear any the worse for our panicked flight.

Of course, for her this morning's exercises were probably a distinct step downwards from being threatened with a meat cleaver.

"You told me I could play that I was Sherlock Holmes," she says patiently. "But *I* said, I'd rather be Irene Adler. She was a girl—and she outsmarted Holmes."

I smile despite myself—then stop short as my eyes land on the stately bulk of a building up ahead.

The British Museum.

It is almost as though this place is a magnet, drawing me back time and time again.

I make up my mind. "Come along." I put a hand on Becky's shoulder. "We're going inside."

The British Museum should be a safe refuge. At best, maybe I will be lucky enough to find out some clue as to why Constable Kelly found me here yesterday morning.

My heart sinks as I see the large printed sign affixed to the museum's front entrance.

The Public are admitted to The British Museum on Mondays, Wednesdays, and Fridays, between the hours of 10 and 4.

We're too early. On the way here, I heard a church clock strike nine. To my surprise, though, a uniformed guard opens the doors for us with a nod and a friendly smile.

"Miss Smith. Nice to see you again."

He's a middle-aged, fatherly-looking man with dark hair turning gray at the temples and a slightly rotund figure.

I fight the urge to look behind me, to see whether he could be addressing someone else. "I—what did you say?"

The man looks taken aback. "I only said it was nice to see you again. Oh, and I have your sketchbook and pencils here, too."

He searches behind the wooden lectern he's using for a desk. "You must have accidentally left them when you were here the other night."

"When I was here—" I close my mouth, endeavoring to force my sluggish brain into some form of coherent thought.

I had hoped for some clue as to why I came to the museum. That I might actually be *known* here never occurred to me.

And what did the guard just call me?

Since I can hardly ask him my own name, I finally manage to say, "Are you sure that the sketchbook and pencils are mine?"

"Of course. Haven't I seen you working away with them every day this week? Besides, your name's written on the inside jacket of the sketch book, plain as plain."

He is still rooting behind the lectern, but now straightens with a crow of triumph. "Aha—here they are. Slipped down behind some books old Professor Peabody left. But here they are. I knew you'd be back for 'em."

He hands over a slim notepad with a brown paper cover and a tin of colored pencils.

Numbly, I take both articles and look them over. Just as the guard said, there is a name scrawled in pencil on the inside cover of the sketching book.

Ariadne Smith.

I stare at the words blankly for what must be ten or eleven echoing beats of my own heart. Then I swallow and dredge up a smile.

"Thank you so much! I was so afraid that I might have lost them. I wonder"—I manage a small laugh—"I have been so absorbed that I have quite lost track of the days. When was it that I left these here?"

If the guard sees anything odd about my inquiry, it doesn't show in his expression.

"Well, now. That would have been …" He pauses, his brow creasing in an effort of remembering. "Yes, it would have been the night before last. Don't you remember, you asked whether you could stay a bit past closing, on account of you were nearly finished with your sketching in the Fourth Egyptian Room? And I said, seeing as it was just this once and I'd be here on night duty anyway, I didn't see the harm. I said I'd let you out of the front door here when you were done. But you must have got out on your own while I was making my rounds, because I never saw you leave. Only found your pad and pencils there, like I say."

"Oh yes, of course. I do remember now; when I realized the time, I left in a hurry." My smile is feeling rather fixed, so

I exchange it for an expression of contriteness. "I am so sorry to have given you any trouble."

The guard beams at me. "That's all right, miss, no harm done." He nods genially towards Becky, still standing beside me. "And now today you've brought a young friend along with you to see the sights?"

"Yes, that's right. This is my s—" I stop myself. I have no idea how extensive my chats with the guard have been. He might know whether or not I have siblings.

"My cousin, come up from the country to spend a few days here in town with me," I finish. "I thought that I would show her"—what was it the guard said I was sketching?—"the Fourth Egyptian Room."

"A very good choice, Miss Smith." The guard nods approval. "She'll enjoy it, I'm sure. Some new installations just going in, too. Some artifacts that even you won't have seen."

"Wonderful!" I beam at him and begin to move off—but the guard calls me back almost at once.

"Miss!"

I stop. "Yes?"

The guard's face is puzzled. "*That's* the way to the Fourth Egyptian Room." He gestures. "If you go *that* way, you'll have go though the Terracotta Antiquities Room, *and* the Bronze Room, *and* the Etruscan Room and all the Vase rooms, besides."

"Yes, of course." I keep my smile firmly plastered on, putting a hand on Becky's shoulder. "My little cousin here is *passionate* about the Etruscans. She begged me to start our tour of the museum there."

Becky, to her credit, doesn't say a word.

The guard's face clears. "Ah, I see. Well, enjoy then."

He gives us a final smile—and I almost run towards the first gallery I can see through the doors to my right.

Terracotta Antiquities Room, a placard outside the door reads—just as my friend the guard said.

The room is filled with … things. Statues and ancient-looking pots standing on pedestals and inside glass cases.

I barely see any of it, though. The gallery's chief attraction for me is that at the moment it is entirely deserted, save for myself and Becky.

There is a gilded and upholstered bench halfway down the gallery, set against one wall. I walk straight to it and collapse onto the seat.

It does not *look* as though it could be part of the display—and if it is, that is just too bad.

Becky lands beside me. "Do you remember any of that?" she asks in a whisper.

I shake my head. I grip the tin of colored pencils so tightly that the edges are digging into my palms. "No. Not at all. At least—"

Is there anything familiar about the guard's story? Or am I just trying to persuade myself that there might be?

"Let's have a look through your papers, there," Becky suggests. "It might tell us something. Or make you remember something more."

She peers at the name inscribed on the flyleaf. "Ar-i-ad-ne." She sounds the name out slowly, then looks at me doubtfully. "Is that you? It doesn't seem like the sort of name you would have."

"You don't think so?" In a way, it's a relief to hear that, because the name stirs nothing in me—not a whisper, not a trace of recognition.

Ariadne. I try it out experimentally inside my own mind. *My name is Ariadne Smith.*

I should be happy ... or at the very least relieved to have a name for myself. But instead all I feel is an overwhelming sense of *wrongness*.

The guard most definitely recognized me as Ariadne Smith, though. And he doesn't seem to have any malicious intent. So, was I here using a false name?

A clenched knot inside my chest tightens as I think of Becky and of Constable Kelly. *Please let me not have been committing any crimes here.*

My inveigling the guard into allowing me to stay in the museum after hours does not seem like an especially good sign.

"Look at this!" Becky is turning pages in the notebook.

The sheets of paper are mostly covered with half-finished pencil sketches—pottery urns and jars with animal heads, of the same type that I saw in Dr. Everett's office.

But the page Becky has stopped on is more complete, and executed in color instead of only lead pencil.

The drawing shows a mask.

A funerary mask. The proper term slides smoothly into my mind.

A funerary mask, the face molded from gold. Two huge, black-outlined eyes stare hauntingly out at me from the page, and above the mask's brow rears a headdress, worked in what could be strips of enamel or inlaid stones.

"Did you draw this?" Becky asks.

"I … I suppose," I say slowly.

I *did* draw it. I know I did.

A tiny, fragile seed of memory springs to life inside my mind.

I remember it. My hands instinctively curve with the remembered sensation of holding my pencils. Working to get the shape of those eyes just right, to find the proper shade of blue for the stones in the headdress.

"Come with me." Jumping up, I stride rapidly—and almost unseeingly—through several more galleries before I finally come to a sign that reads, *Fourth Egyptian Room.*

The gallery is dusty and crowded with antiquities that appear to have been set on display in no particular order. Scrolls of papyrus jostle with carved marble statues and brilliant blue scarabs.

There are a dozen or so visitors here, wandering slowly from display to display, peering into cases containing what I *think* must be mummies.

I look at the other visitors quickly, trying to satisfy myself that none of them is the organ grinder in disguise.

Then I turn to Becky. "Help me find this—this same mask in the picture, here."

17. THE GAME'S AFOOT

We start a slow circuit of the room. I let my eyes travel over the glass cases and the statues on pedestals—but it is difficult to focus on any of them.

I was here, not long ago. I can *feel* my memories hovering just beyond my reach.

"It's a fake," a voice beside me suddenly says.

I turn with a start of surprise to find a thin, dried-up looking little man in a brown suit and bowler hat standing nearly at my elbow.

"I beg your pardon?"

A short ginger-colored beard traces the man's jaw—and for a wild second, I am tempted to yank on it to see whether it is only a false one, fixed on with spirit gum.

But no. A glance at the man's ears is enough to assure me that he is not the false organ grinder. The shape of his lobes is quite different—and he is several inches shorter than the organ grinder, as well as being at least a stone lighter.

He gives an irritable click of his tongue, gesturing to the statue of a black cat at which I have been mindlessly staring.

"I said, it's a fake!" His voice is dry, scholarly and precise. "As Mr. Budge—the Keeper of the Egyptian collections here at the museum—really ought to have known."

He peers at the paper tag affixed to the pedestal on which the cat statue rests. "Donated by Dr. William Everett, MD." He shakes his head, his face pinched with disapproval. "These dilettante collectors. They mean well, but they *will* persist in buying up any shamelessly forged article that those rascals in Egypt try to pass off as ancient."

I stop, staring at him. "Do you mean to tell me that this statue is a forgery?"

The man gives me an irritated look and a sniff. "Have I not just been saying so?"

I barely manage to restrain myself from seizing him by his coat lapels and dragging him towards me. Memories are exploding like fireworks behind my eyes.

"How certain are you?"

The small man's expression changes from annoyance to looking slightly taken aback by the intensity of my tone.

"I am as certain as I can be, without actually examining the article myself. There are certain tests ... but if you will look at the hieroglyphic inscription on the statue's base, you will see that the carving is slightly incorrect for the time period from which the state purports—"

He launches into a lengthy explanation of which I understand perhaps one word in ten. But one thing is clear: the artifact donated by none other than Dr. William Everett is a fake.

I press my fingertips to the sides of my temples, barely noticing when at last the small man's lecture runs its course and he wanders off.

The memories are more than just occasional bright flashes. Large blocks of recollection are now dropping into my head with the solidity of bricks falling from the sky. My name is *not* Ariadne Smith. And I haven't been working on a plot to rob the museum. Just the opposite—

"Are you all right?" Becky asks in concern.

"Yes, just for a change—I *am* all right."

I *remember*. I remember staying here in the museum after closing time. Descending into the basement, then hearing voices—

A shiver slides across my skin as the last painful fragments of memory slide into place. But the simple fact of actual *knowledge* instead of supposition and uncertainty makes me feel as though a leaden weight has just rolled off my shoulders. "I'm better than all right. I—"

I stop, looking down at her. But there is no time for me to explain. "I need to get down to the docks."

Please let me be in time.

Becky's eyes widen. "I can take you there. But—"

I interrupt her, fresh realization dawning. "No. No, I'm sorry, you can't. It could be dangerous. I need to find you somewhere safe to stay."

Constable Kelly would never forgive me if I knowingly brought Becky into danger. I would never forgive *myself* if I allowed harm to come to her.

"Come along," I tell her. It must be nearly mid-morning by now. "I'm sorry. I promise that I'll explain everything to you later. But for right now, we need to *hurry*."

18. 221B

Our journey through the crowded London Streets seems to last an eternity. With every hansom cab that rattles past, I more and more bitterly regret having handed the entirety of my money over to the street urchin in Montague Street.

Those coins could have purchased a ride that would have cut our transit time in half.

But finally, we turn onto the correct street—and I head straight towards a nondescript, black painted door.

Becky stops short, staring at the address.

She has been sulking slightly over my determination to keep her out of danger and has barely said a word to me throughout the journey.

Now, though, she stammers, "But—but he's *dead*. I mean, I read about it. He went over the falls with Professor—"

"I know. I mean, I know what you read. But it wasn't true. And no, I've not gone completely mad, I swear," I add, in answer to Becky's suddenly narrowed eyes. "Though I realize that it may look that way."

I reach up to rap firmly with the knocker on the door, still speaking.

"Sooner or later, maybe the rest of the world will know that he actually survived the Reichenbach—"

I cut off in mid sentence as the door opens from inside to reveal a slightly portly man with a mustache and a kindly, weathered face.

That's right. Another block of memory lurches into place. Mrs. Hudson is away for a few days, visiting her sister.

"Lucy!" The mustached man lets out an explosive breath at the sight of me, relief etched in every line of his expression. "Good heavens, where on earth have you been? We got your message about the Harley Street doctor. But then you disappeared from The British Museum. Then Wiggins spotted you in Montague Street, but he said you were acting most peculiarly. He thought perhaps you were being watched, and dared not communicate freely or acknowledge that he recognized you, for fear of giving away your true identity. But you've missed three performances at the Savoy."

I close my eyes briefly as the realization sinks in. Poor Mr. Harris, our stage manager. I've probably given him an apoplexy. And I'm about to give him another. There's no chance that I'll be there tonight, either.

"Holmes has been combing the city for you, dressed in the most extraordinary disguises."

"I know," I interrupt him. "I know, Uncle John, and I'm so sorry to have worried you. But there isn't time for me to tell you everything that's happened. Do you know where Holmes is now?"

Uncle John opens his mouth—but before he can answer, Becky opens *her* mouth for the first time.

"Holmes?" she says—squeaks, rather. She stares at the man before us, her eyes rounded. "Do you mean that *you're*—"

"Yes, Becky," I say. "Let me introduce you. This is Dr. John Watson, whose storied accounts of Sherlock Holmes you have so much enjoyed." I smile at him. "Otherwise known as my honorary Uncle John."

Uncle John still looks both slightly worried and puzzled. But he beams at Becky.

Uncle John has what is arguably the kindest and most generous heart in all of England—and he adores children.

"It's a pleasure to make your acquaintance, young lady." He bows over Becky's hand.

The back of my neck still prickles with the urgency of the situation. All of this is taking far too much time.

"Becky's brother is a detective constable on the police force," I tell Uncle John quickly. "Constable John Kelly, of the Holborn Station in Lamb's Conduit Street."

Thank heavens that I went there with Constable Kelly yesterday and remember the address.

"You need to call in the Irregulars at once and have them find him. Tell him to come here as quickly as he possibly can—and make sure that they tell him that his sister is perfectly safe, waiting for him."

"Gladly, of course." Uncle John blinks. "But Lucy—"

It's strange—both good *and* strange—to be called by my own, true name.

"I'm sorry, Uncle John," I repeat. "There isn't time. I need to get down to the docks. Do you know where … where Holmes is now?"

With the rest of my returning memories comes the recollection that I'm never entirely sure of how to refer to Sherlock Holmes—whether in his presence or out of it.

"No, I don't." Uncle John's face creases in a worried frown. "He said that he would be back as soon as he was able, but—"

"Listen, Uncle John. Holmes may not be terribly happy with me when he comes back here."

With good reason. The recollection of the past twenty-four hours makes me wince inwardly.

"Tell him that I'm dreadfully sorry and I shall explain everything when I see him—but that he needs to meet me at the docks. There is another shipment expected in this evening. If we are lucky, we can catch them while they're still unloading."

If we are *very* lucky, we may be able to learn what exactly is being shipped that the organization we have been tracking is so very anxious to hide.

"Gladly, Lucy." Besides kindness, Uncle John's other chief character trait is his utter, solid dependability. There is a reason that Sherlock Holmes has relied on him for years. "I shall enlist the help of the Irregulars in tracking down Holmes, as well. But to which docks shall I send him?"

"The—" I stop as my newly returned memory stalls for a moment.

I only glimpsed the name on a scrap of torn shipping label. Shortly before I was knocked unconscious and left for dead on the street outside The British Museum.

"The Victoria Docks," I say finally.

"You're sure?"

"Yes." At least I *hope* that I am sure.

Becky has been following our conversation, her gaze moving from me to Uncle John and back again as though watching a tennis match.

Now she stops me before I can turn to leave. "Wait. If you call him Uncle John"—she nods towards Watson—"then who does that make *you*?"

"My name is Lucy James."

To Uncle John, I'm sure that statement is nothing out of the ordinary. He's heard me introduce myself dozens of times. But to me it feels almost miraculous. For the first time in twenty-four hours, I know who I am.

And then I stop. I know it is ridiculous—but a sudden superstitious fear squeezes my chest.

I remember, now, what was only a vague, buried impression before: that I have spent nearly the whole of my twenty-one years on this earth wishing that I could have a family to whom I belong.

Now—astonishingly—I *do*.

But I am suddenly afraid that if I say it out loud, it will all turn out to be some sort of hallucination. A side effect of the head trauma, and not real after all.

"Uncle John will explain the rest," I finish quickly. "And now I really must be gone."

19. Shoes and Ships and Sealing Wax

I overlooked one crucial factor in my directions to Uncle John: When I told him to send help to the Victoria Docks, I had no idea just how immense they would be.

Some of the harbors I've passed on my way here looked familiar, but I have never gone this far into the docklands before. I think. No, I am *certain* that I have not.

Crouching in the shadows of a large brick building, I squeeze my eyes shut. My memory still seems to have a few grayish, hazy patches, wisps of cloud drifting across the sun.

I am tired and I've eaten next to nothing all day, which does not help.

The sun is setting in a fiery blaze, daylight bleeding away into the dusky purple shadows of evening.

Huge shipping vessels bob at their moorings in the river behind me. The tide is out and mudlarks—children who make a miserable living by scavenging for nails or any other small items dropped off the ships during unloading—are out in force.

Despite the cold, they are wading barefoot in the muddy river water that comes nearly to their waists.

The Royal Victoria Dock consists of a main dock and a basin that provides an entrance to the Thames on the western side of the complex.

The dock itself has four solid piers, each with a two-story warehouse—and surrounding the dock are other warehouses, granaries, sheds and storage buildings.

Including the warehouse behind which I am currently hiding.

My heart is beating too hard and too fast, and my skin crawls. I have absolutely no idea where in this sprawling complex I need to go—but neither can I stay where I am.

There are guards—a special division of the metropolitan police—patrolling the docks in order to prevent thievery. I've seen them; it is astonishing that I have managed to evade them so far.

Then there are the dockworkers: the porters and navies and others who unload the ships' imported cargoes.

There is no chance I can hope to blend in amongst them. For one thing, the majority of them seem to be going home for the day. For another, all the dockworkers I have seen are huge, barrel-chested men with bull-like shoulders and hands like hams.

I would stand out like a cat in a kennel full of bulldogs.

I lean against the brick wall at my back. *Think.*

No, not just think. I need to remember.

I've been shying away from recollecting the details surrounding my attack, but now I keep my eyes closed, trying to recall every detail of the night in question.

I had persuaded the guard at the Museum—Higgins; my memory supplies his name—to allow me to stay after hours.

I knew that more artifacts were to be arriving for the new exhibit in the Fourth Egyptian Room, and—

"What the bloody hell are *you* doing here?"

I jolt upright at the sound of the voice—and find myself staring at the blond curls and too-handsome face of none other than Frances Ferrars. Or whatever his name may really be.

My only slight advantage is that he looks every bit as astonished to see me as I am to see him. But that evaporates after the first half second as he takes a quick step forwards, seizing me by the arm.

Stupid, stupid, stupid.

I cannot believe that I was stupid enough to be so easily captured.

I force myself to draw in a steadying breath, willing the rising tide of panic down. I got away from this man once before. I can again. Though it most assuredly will not be so easy this time to catch him off his guard.

The gathering darkness hollows Ferrars's eyes with shadow, making him look less like a soapbox model and more like a grinning skull. His teeth are bared in an expression that's somewhere between a snarl and a leer.

"You just can't stop poking yer nose in where it doesn't belong, can you?" His fingers are biting painfully into the skin above my elbow, and he shakes me, hard.

I hold still, trying to make my muscles relax. If he is going to let down his guard enough for me to make a move, he needs to believe that I am defeated, too paralyzed with despair to fight.

Difficult, since my fingers are *twitching* with the urge to smack the smug smile off his face.

I force down another lungful of air.

I have stood on a stage before royalty. I can surely act thoroughly cowed before a not-terribly-intelligent audience of one.

Ferrars's smile broadens. "We're going to have to do something about this unfortunate 'abit of yours." He drags me towards him—forcing me to exercise every scrap of my will not to recoil.

His breath is hot and sour against my face. "As yer lawfully wedded 'usband—or close enough, anyway—I have some ideas—"

Now!

I bend sharply forward, smashing my forehead into his nose. The impact explodes through my skull—but I barely notice.

Howling with surprise and pain, Ferrars releases his grip on my arm. Blood is spurting from both his nostrils, and his eyes are alight with an almost crazed fury as he dives forwards, making a wild grab at me.

I leap sideways, out of his reach, my mind frantically making a catalog of my options.

I doubt that I can outrun him—not dressed in my slender-heeled, high-button boots, at least, and on unfamiliar ground.

The best of my options appears to be to stay out of his clutches long enough for someone else to see us. One of the dock's official guards might arrive—or even some of the porters. Ferrars won't dare to attack me before witnesses.

I snatch up a broken wooden slat—part of a shipping pallet or crate—that lies on the ground and bring it up in front of me, holding it like a club.

Of course, it's also possible that whoever happens upon us first will be part of Ferrars's gang. I already know that he is not working alone.

That thought makes the scream I am about to utter die on my lips.

Ferrars's eyes narrow, even as he dashes blood away from his mouth and chin. His voice is a hoarse growl. "Just wait until I get my 'ands on you, you little—"

I brace myself, straining my eyes to see through the gathering darkness so that I can be ready for the inevitable moment when he lunges at me again.

But the attack never comes.

Instead, Ferrars's whole body is yanked suddenly and violently backwards—almost as though he has been rigged with the trick wires in a stage performance.

He flails for a second, his arms wind-milling, his bloodied face a mask of helpless surprise.

Then the shadowed figure that has a hold on Ferrars's jacket spins him around and delivers a punch to the jaw that sends Ferrars sprawling. He struggles to rise—but only briefly.

The second figure delivers a sharp chop to the back of his neck. Ferrars collapses with a faint moan onto the ground and lies still.

Constable John Kelly steps forward from out of the shadows, shaking his head at me.

"Becky tells me your name's Lucy. But I think I'm going to have to go with calling you Trouble."

20. Shots Fired

For the space of perhaps a dozen pounding beats of my own heart, all I can do is stare at Constable Kelly in speechless astonishment.

I cannot remember—I *honestly* cannot remember—ever having been more shocked.

"What are you doing here?" I finally find my voice.

"I got your message that Becky'd be waiting in Baker Street." Constable Kelly steps over Ferrars's unconscious body. "Which she still is, safe and sound. But it seemed to me like you'd maybe need a hand here."

Considering my recent confrontation with the man now lying insensible at my feet, there is only one thing that I can say to that.

"Thank you."

Constable Kelly waves that aside. "Let's get him over to that building there." He points towards what looks like a small storage shed over to our right. "Less chance that he'll be seen. And then maybe you can tell me who our friend here is, and what all of this is about."

"I can tell you now."

My heart is still beating in short, staccato bursts, all the way out to the tips of my fingers. But I spare a brief second to be thankful that I am able to offer an explanation—that I no longer feel as though I am blindfolded and stumbling around in the dark.

It also occurs to me that Constable Kelly has placed an amazing degree of trust in me. He knows nothing at all about Ferrars—but still struck the man unconscious without hesitation.

Now Constable Kelly stoops to take hold of the inert Ferrars by the wrists, and I lower my voice.

"It all started with a rumor—a tip from one of Sherlock Holmes's most reliable sources for information about international dealings at the highest levels of our government. Spies, in other words."

Constable Kelly starts to tow Ferrars towards the outbuilding. Ferrars's head flops helplessly on his shoulders. He groans again, just faintly, but doesn't wake.

"These reports concerned the bribery of customs officials. Shipments were being brought into the country. And the officials at the import and exports offices were being paid to turn a blind eye and allow the shipments into the country without inspection. We didn't know anything definite about who was behind the operation—either who was sending them or who was receiving them inside this country. But rumor had it that there was a link with a recent case of my—of Sherlock Holmes's that involved the German Kaiser. And the Kaiser would certainly not be at all averse to seeing our current government topple—or our monarch deposed."

I look up to check Constable Kelly's face. This is quite a story to unleash on him, all at once this way.

He only gives a short nod, though. "All right. With you so far."

With a grunt, he heaves Ferrars's unconscious form into the shed. Ferrars lies still—looking uncomfortable in the extreme, with his head tilted at an awkward angle and his arms and legs tangled. Though I cannot bring myself to be particularly troubled by his lack of comfort.

"Holmes went to work at the docks—these and others—disguised, of course, as a common day laborer. Eventually, he learned that the shipments being smuggled in were in large part ending up at The British Museum."

Constable Kelly straightens. It has grown nearly too dark for me to see his face—but I can see his eyebrows go up.

"I know. I thought the same. The British Museum? What earthly connection could there be between The British Museum and a ring of German spies?"

I swing the door to the shed closed, shutting Ferrars inside. "That part I *still* do not know, to be honest. But that is what brought me to The British Museum. My part of the operation was to position myself at the museum—to spend time there observing the workings of the place and ingratiate myself with the guards—and see whether I could learn anything more. Which I did."

My fingertips curl, tightening into fists. "When I was attacked, I had discovered that the smuggled containers—one and all—were shipped on behalf of a Dr. Everett of Twenty-Nine Harley Street, to be delivered as donations to the museum's new exhibit of Egyptian artifacts."

Constable Kelly's head comes up with a jerk and he frowns at me. "Dr. Everett. But that's—"

"I know. I don't know what his real name is—or if he really is even a doctor. I doubt it. But he must be high up in the spy ring's chain of command, because he—"

Crack!

The explosive burst of sound shatters the stillness of the night, cutting me off and sending my heart slamming hard into my ribs.

"That was—"

"A rifle shot," John Kelly finishes for me. "It's—get down!"

With a sudden cry, he lunges for me, knocking me backwards and onto the ground.

Crack!

Another shot hammers against my eardrums. Almost in the same instant, Constable Kelly and I both roll upright and sideways, scrambling to our feet and racing for the comparative shelter of another of the small outbuildings.

"Go!" Constable Kelly shouts at me, when I glance behind to make sure that he's following. "Go!"

I lose count of the number of shots that ring out as we race for the shed's entrance and fling ourselves inside.

It appears to be a machinist's shop of some kind. An array of tools hangs on the walls, and the air smells strongly of crude oil.

Crack!

Another shot is followed by a crash as it shatters one of the narrow windows over our heads. Glass fragments rain down.

I have to fight the urge to squeeze my eyes shut—like a child hoping to hide—as I wait for the next assault to come. Or for our gunman to burst through the door in person.

Nothing happens. I can hear distant shouts—probably from the night watchmen. But no more rifle shots.

Seconds drip by. Then a minute, and then another. Nothing happens.

The only immediate noise is the pounding of my own pulse, the painful scrape of my own breathing in my ears.

"Are you all right?" Constable Kelly finally whispers.

"Yes." It seems almost unbelievable, but none of the shots struck home.

Almost none. As I turn my head to Constable Kelly, I see that he's clutching his upper arm. A dark, spreading stain bubbles up from between his fingers.

"You've been hit!"

He shakes his head, shrugging my concern away. "It's nothing much. I'm fine."

A cold fist seems to have wrapped itself around my heart and started to squeeze.

"Fine? Where I come from, *fine* is generally taken to mean a state in which one is *not* bleeding of a gunshot wound."

I'm already scanning the darkened room, looking for a rag or anything else that I might be able to use as a makeshift tourniquet. Not that I really know what to do with one, even if I find it.

Unfortunately, my returned memory offers nothing but the knowledge that nursing is not one of my areas of expertise—Sherlock Holmes's recent experience with a bullet wound notwithstanding.

Lacking anything better, I shrug off the shawl—the one I took from Becky's room—and pass it to Constable Kelly.

"Here. We can at least try to slow the bleeding."

Constable Kelly's breath hisses out through his teeth, but he makes no other noise as I press the wadded-up shawl against the bullet wound.

"You need a doctor," I breathe.

John Kelly's eyes are on the door. "Yeah, I'll worry about that after we get out of here. Which isn't happening with a gunman still outside."

"Should we try to barricade the door?"

Constable Kelly considers, but then shakes his head. "We'll just make more noise. Besides, they probably know where we are. If they start shooting us through the windows, we'll be like fish in a barrel—especially if we've gone and blocked the door."

We both fall silent a moment, and then Constable Kelly asks, "So how did you wind up on the street outside the museum?"

A shiver twists through me as I call up the memory again.

"I was inside The British Museum—hiding in the basement storage area, where they bring in new shipments and deliveries to be unpacked. I had heard that there was to be a new delivery of Dr. Everett's supposed antiquities that night. I had already told Holmes and Uncle John that I suspected the doctor might be involved in our ring of spies. But they had no idea what I intended for that night. As far as they knew, I was safe and sound in the rented lodgings I had taken in my persona of Ariadne Smith."

I stop, swallowing. It was stupid of me to be there on my own—stupid and reckless not to have brought reinforcements.

Now that I have my memories back, I can see that might have been a side effect of relying only on myself for most of my life: I am not accustomed to asking for help—and not terribly willing to, either.

"Dr. Everett was there himself," I whisper into the dark stillness all around. "He and I think three other men. Not Ferrars—I would remember if I had seen him. These men were rougher, and older. They were unpacking crates of antiques—pottery shards and statues and such. But they obviously cared nothing at all about the articles themselves. They kept dropping them on the ground helter-skelter and then tearing through the packing as though they were searching for something."

I swallow, remembering the scene: the flickering lamplight, the straw and broken fragments of the Egyptian artifacts scattered on the floor.

"I remember hearing one of them say, 'Where are they?' I inched forwards—hoping to get a glimpse of whatever it was they were searching for. But I must have kicked something accidentally—a loose pottery fragment or something else. The noise attracted their attention. I ran."

I stare straight ahead. "I don't entirely remember what happened next."

This is the part of my story where my memory grows hazy—whether from the blow to the head or just from the terror of my desperate flight.

"I remember running through the basement of the museum, searching for an exit." Praying that my panicked turns wouldn't lead me into a dead end where I would be trapped.

"I remember finally getting outside. But that's all."

"So you didn't actually shoot anyone."

"No." That may well be the biggest relief about having my memories back. *Those* haunting fragments are once more relegated to their proper place in my mind.

I will probably still have nightmares about them—as I know I have for the last months—but at least I do not have to wonder what they mean.

"That was—" I stop, wondering how exactly to explain. "That was part of another case I investigated with Holmes. Last year. Maybe I'll tell you about it sometime."

"You should wait until Becky's there." I can hear the brief flicker of a smile in Constable Kelly's voice. "A Sherlock Holmes case she's never read about before? She'll be dying to hear it, too."

I laugh under my breath. Though I know that we are both thinking the same thing: the odds of our living long enough for me to tell the full story to Becky are not particularly in our favor.

I stuff that thought down and keep going—mostly in an effort to distract myself.

"At any rate, I suppose that Dr. Everett or one of the other men must have caught me as I was fleeing from the museum and struck me down. I don't know why I'm still here—why they didn't murder me then and there. I suppose they must have been scared off by something? Maybe one of the night watchmen at the museum came along, and they had to run off?"

I shake my head, breathing to try to steady my racing heart.

I may not remember all of the details, but I do remember the terror of those few minutes. Reliving it in memory has made my hands go cold and clammy and my chest feel too tight.

I can only imagine what Dr. Everett must have thought when I walked into his office. He must have at first suspected that my presence was some sort of a trap—and then been convinced that fate had delivered me like a wrapped-up Christmas parcel.

"Have you ever thought that you were going to die?" I ask suddenly. "I mean, been absolutely, utterly convinced that a moment was going to be your last?"

"Sure." It's too dark for me to clearly make out Constable Kelly's expression, but I sense his nod. "Plenty of times."

"How do you put the memory behind you? How do you stop being afraid?"

I'm already discovering that the return of my memories is something of a two-edged sword.

Constable Kelly shifts position. I have the impression that he's about to reach out towards me. But then he seems to change his mind, his good hand dropping back to his side.

An odd pang of something almost like disappointment flashes through me.

Then he says, his voice quiet in the dark, "You can't give up, right? Otherwise you might as well have really died."

He stops abruptly.

Just outside the door to our shed comes a soft, rattling scrape.

I freeze, my insides congealing into a clump of ice. *What now?*

Beside me, Constable Kelly rises smoothly and silently to his feet.

I can hardly force him back down again. But I am determined not to let him face whatever new threat is outside there. Not when he has just been shot while trying to protect me.

Slowly, slowly, I inch my way towards the hanging rack of tools I can see dimly on the nearest wall. There has to be something that will qualify as a weapon.

My fingers have just closed around the handle of a wrench when the door swings open.

I whirl around, staring at the tall man's figure that looms in the doorway, shadowy and featureless with the comparative brightness from the outside behind him.

My hand tightens around the wrench—

And a dry, cultured voice says, "I would be most grateful if you would put the weapon down, Lucy. Having been assaulted by you once already in the last day, I find myself in no way anxious to repeat the experience. Especially since time is at the moment—"

"Holmes!" My breath goes out in a rush of relief that nearly carries me to the ground.

Before either of us can say anything more, though, Constable Kelly staggers, catching himself with one hand against the wall.

Remembrance jolts through me. "Holmes, he has been shot! And someone was out there with a rifle—"

"Yes, I am aware."

His voice and his manner are as brusquely calm as though we had met on the street and begun to discuss the likelihood of rain.

It's strange. When I was a schoolgirl, I used to pore over Watson's stories in the Strand magazine, just as Becky does.

Since then, I have met other celebrities and near-legendary figures. Some live up to their famous reputations; most fall lamentably short—but with Holmes, that is never even in question.

Every time that I see him, what strikes me most is how entirely accurate Dr. Watson's descriptions of Sherlock Holmes are.

His stories are idealized, yes. Uncle John is nothing if not a romantic at heart.

But what his stories neither romanticize nor idealize is the sheer, staggering power of intellect that blazes from Sherlock Holmes's every word and look.

His hundreds of clients trust him with their most buried secrets for good reason—and not for the sake of his sympathy. He may have human sympathy—I suspect that he does, but so far as I have seen, he keeps it buried deep.

No, the reason his clients trust him to solve their puzzles and dilemmas is the immediate feeling one gets on meeting Sherlock Holmes that you are in the presence of a mind that is as fierce and powerful as the sun's blazing rays.

It is that blazing intelligence that is staring—or rather, scowling—at me right now.

Holmes's brows are drawn together in a fierce expression, his already thin lips set in a grim line.

"I heard the shots for myself and surmised that they were being fired at you. Do you know from what direction they came?"

I try to think back, recreating the sights and sounds of our escape to this shed.

Before I can give a definite answer, John Kelly breaks in. "The shooter was stationed somewhere over there." He gestures to the right. "And high up. Maybe on top of a roof."

I recollect that he and Sherlock Holmes have never met before. "This is—" I start to say.

Holmes raises a hand.

He turns to Constable Kelly, fixing him with a keen eye. "You are certain, young man?"

I have known older—and more highly ranked—men than Jack Kelly to whither under the focused intensity of Sherlock Holmes's gaze.

Constable Kelly merely straightens his shoulders and tips his head in a brief nod. "I'm sure."

"Very well, then." Holmes steps back, satisfied. Then he suddenly stiffens, his head lifting as though scenting the air.

A moment later, I smell it, too. "Smoke!"

Holmes's eyes refocus on Constable Kelly. "You appear to be in need of medical attention, young man."

"I'm all right." Constable Kelly is pressing the shawl I gave him over his arm.

It is too dark for me to see whether the wound is bleeding through or not—I suspect that it is—but his voice is not one to brook any opposition. "Just go on, I'll be right behind you."

21. Alarum

Outside, the source of the smoke is immediately apparent. A smaller building at the farthest end of the docks is ablaze, orange and yellow flames leaping against the night sky.

From all around the docks, guards and workers and night watchmen are running and shouting out alarms.

The one advantage is that all the outcry seems to have driven away our anonymous rifleman. No shots ring out as we race towards the burning building.

I glance behind me, worried—but true to his word, Constable Kelly is keeping up with the pace that Holmes sets.

One of the dock's guards has reached the fire ahead of us. Holmes seizes him by the shoulder, spinning him around.

"What is this building?"

In the glow of the fire, I can see the guard's face. He is a young man, with a head of sandy-colored hair and freckles. He gapes at Holmes, then finally manages to answer, "S-storage."

"*Storage*!" Holmes bites off the word furiously.

"Y-yes, sir."

Holmes casts a quick glance at the building. Tattered banners of flame extend upwards from the windows and are licking at the roof.

"Go and summon the fire brigade!" He orders the guard. "Buckets—hoses—whatever measures you have to extinguish these flames!"

"Yes, sir," the young man stammers—then stares at him again. "Who exactly did you say you were, sir?"

"I am an agent of Her Majesty's government, acting in the interest of the Crown," Holmes barks. "Now do as I say!"

It is a mark of Holmes's natural authority that the young guard does not arrest us as trespassers or on suspicion of arson, but instead leaps to obey.

"Now." When the guard has vanished, Holmes raises his voice to be heard above the roar and crackle of the fire. "We must see whether anything may be salvaged. If we are lucky, perhaps we may learn what they wish so badly to conceal from our eyes."

"You think the fire was deliberately set?"

Holmes gives me a look, eyebrows raised. "You know I dislike coincidences. A conflagration of this nature—erupting at precisely the moment we trace our German spy ring here—cannot conceivably be mere chance. Our opponents clearly realized their failure to exterminate you with the rifle shots. They knew that the dock's night watchmen would be coming to investigate—and so they chose to burn their bridges, doing away with the evidence. Or so they hoped."

He starts forwards—plainly about to plunge directly through the doorway of the burning building.

"Wait!" I catch hold of him.

"What is it?" There is an edge of impatience in his tone making what I have to say all the more difficult. But I cannot help but go on.

"You can't go in there! You could be burned alive."

Holmes's expression is calm. "I estimate the likelihood of that to be less than three in ten. Though the odds will certainly increase if I delay. This young man is clearly not functioning at highest capacity"—Holmes tips his head at John Kelly. "Therefore, I am the most logical—"

"I will go," I interrupt. The words seem to come out on their own. I do not have a clear plan; I'm not thinking of anything, really—only that I cannot let Sherlock Holmes die in this fiery blaze.

"You will *what?*"

I have never seen a man in the throes of an apoplectic fit. But if I had, I imagine the victim would look something like Holmes does in this moment. His eyes bulge, his jaw muscles go rigid, and his cheeks flush an unhealthy shade of red. "You will do no such thing!"

"But why?" I demand. "I am perfectly capable—"

Holmes interrupts me. "Over the course of the past thirty-six hours, I have had little to no idea where you were or what horrors might have befallen you! Wiggins discovered you acting most peculiarly in Montague street—at which point, I hastened to make contact myself, giving you the opportunity to use the code word we had established as a sign of danger or distress—the one that would lead to your being rescued, regardless of whether or not it would damage the credibility of the persona you had cultivated."

"Snow."

I remember now. The old man—Holmes—certainly gave me every chance to say the word. Unfortunately, though, I had no recollection of having chosen it as our distress code.

"I left the card for you—the very same card which you had sent to me—as a query mark!" Holmes goes on. "A message, intending to ask whether you still suspected Dr. Everett of being a linchpin in the smuggling scheme. I expected that you would reply using the drop-spot we had arranged for the purpose in Hyde Park! I did not suspect that you would take the card and march straight into the lion's den."

At Holmes's words, another memory slips into place. We *did* arrange to leave messages for one another under a bench in the park, near the statue of Achilles.

Holmes stops, slightly breathless, then goes on, his voice rising. "I did not dare approach you overtly. If you were being watched—or had been taken prisoner—betraying your true identity might be signing your death sentence. Over the course of the last day, I have been forced to don the most outlandish and absurd of disguises in my efforts to ascertain that you were going with this young man of your own free will, rather than being abducted."

Holmes nods towards Constable Kelly. "Thank you, by the way."

Constable Kelly brushes that aside, giving Holmes an incredulous look. "The old woman selling flowers? That was *you?*"

Holmes thumps one fist against the flat of his hand. "I was nearly assaulted by a fellow flower vendor, on whose territory I had accidentally happened to infringe! Added to which, this morning in my guise of organ grinder, that accursed monkey bit me twice—once on the finger, and once on the ear!"

His gray eyes spark with outrage as he holds up his right index finger for my inspection.

I trample hard on a desire to laugh. I am fairly certain that he also has a few wisps of the Organ Grinder's luxurious black mustache still glued to his upper lip.

"I have done all of this because I wished to be sure—that is, because I wished to be assured of your safety. It was"—maybe the smoke is troubling him. "It was perhaps the most acute sense of parental concern that I have experienced in my life. So you will kindly do me the courtesy of *not* negating my efforts at keeping you safe by running headlong into a burning building!"

I blink—all urge for mirth vanished.

Before I can speak, though, Holmes plunges through the building's doorway—leaving me gaping after him, my jaw dropped open.

He seems to be gone for an eternity—long enough that Constable Kelly shifts his weight uneasily. "Maybe I should go in—"

"You have a bullet hole in your arm," I remind him. I rub the stinging smoke from my eyes, hoping desperately for any sign that Holmes is about to emerge. "If anyone is going to go in after him, it should be me!"

Coughing and choking, a tall figure dives head-first out of the flaming doorway. His face is nearly blackened with soot, and one of his sleeves has caught fire. But he is alive.

Holmes strips off the burning jacket, trampling out the flames. "I have it!"

He holds what looks like a ledger book in one hand.

I can see the pages are covered with hand-written notations and entries. "You think it will help us to hunt down whoever is responsible for bribing the customs officials?"

Holmes's voice is rough with smoke, but he nods. "I believe it is something that had best be turned over to Mycroft, who will be more adept at tracking down the ultimate source of the payments listed here. But with luck, it will perhaps bring us answers as to who our German-sympathizers are—*and* why they wish so badly to evade the inspection of the goods they are bringing into our fair city."

Despite my relief, I feel a prickle of cold at those words. Whatever reason the Kaiser's agents have for evading customs will be bad—perhaps catastrophically bad.

Holmes wipes his face with the back of his hand—and then he says, "Well done."

Any praise at all is so unaccustomed, coming from him, that for a second I stare, uncertain as to whether he is actually addressing me.

But he *is*. He is not smiling—he seldom does. But his lips are bent upwards in a softer expression than is habitual.

"I hardly did anything," I protest.

For the largest part of this investigation, I did not even recall what we were investigating.

"This ledger represents our most solid lead in months—and it is thanks to you that we were here to salvage it from the flames. If I am not mistaken, we have also the unconscious gentleman I saw back there?"

He gestures towards the shed where we left Ferrars. "Interrogating him gives us a solid place to begin our renewed investigations." The upwards bend of his lips is wry—but still more pronounced as he looks at me. "So I say again, Lucy, well done."

My throat prickles. For a second, I am absolutely convinced that I'm going to cry—which would no doubt horrify Holmes nearly into the grave.

I swallow hard, turning to Constable Kelly. "Since we are out of danger, I suppose I can introduce you now. Mr. Holmes, this is Detective Constable John Kelly. Mr. Kelly, this"—I extend my hand, blinking the sting of tears from my eyes—"is Sherlock Holmes. My father."

22. Recovery

The sun is unseasonably bright for an autumn day, painting yellow rectangles of light all along the floor and walls of the hospital ward.

Constable Kelly's bed is midway along the ward, the curtains that allow a modicum of privacy drawn back to reveal the constable sitting propped up against the pillows.

The nurse escorting us gives us a strict admonishment not to tire him—then sails away to minister to the needs of another patient.

"Well, hello there, Trouble."

Constable Kelly looks a little tired, with lines of pain bracketing the edges of his mouth. His right arm is still bandaged and in a sling—but he greets me with a shadow of a grin.

"Jack! Jack!" Beside me, Becky is nearly bouncing up and down in her excitement to see her brother. "How are you feeling?"

"Pretty well. The doctors say that I can come home in another day or so."

"Oh." Becky's eager happiness momentarily flags. "But I *like* staying with Lucy and Dr. Watson and Mr. Holmes. Lucy is teaching me to sing the way she does! And—"

"Good to know where I rank compared to singing lessons," her brother says. He reaches with his good hand to tug on his sister's braids.

"Oh, well, I want you home, too. But maybe you could ask the nurses to keep you just for another *day*," Becky begins.

"I'll still give you lessons, even after you go back home to your brother," I tell her. "*And* you're coming to the matinée performance of *The Mikado* this Sunday."

"That's true." Becky brightens. "Did you know that, Jack? That's why Lucy is such a beautiful singer. She's an actress—a real, actual, actress—and she performs with the D'Oyly Carte Opera Company."

Constable Kelly nods, his expression grave. "You might have mentioned it the last time you were here to visit. Just once or twice. Every minute or so."

Becky giggles. "Well, but if you're out of the hospital, you can come to her show, too, on Sunday. Mr. Holmes and Dr. Watson will be there."

She glances behind us at Sherlock Holmes—who has been hanging back from approaching the bed. But he nods in answer to Becky's look. "Certainly."

I've also sent matinée tickets to Sarah, the young maid from Montague Street, along with the dress she loaned me, as a token of thanks for her help.

John Kelly shifts position, grimacing slightly as the movement jars his healing wound. "Sure thing." He picks up the water glass from the table beside his bed and hands it to his sister.

"Here, Becky, do you think you could see if you can get this refilled?"

"All right." Becky nods and skips away, off down the ward.

Holmes clears his throat. "Something has happened."

I would hardly have needed Sherlock Holmes's mental powers to deduce that. Becky suspected nothing—but her brother clearly engineered the errand for the sake of getting her out of the way.

Constable Kelly nods. I can see the tension in the line of his shoulders beneath the sling.

"Yes, sir. You could say something has. But before I tell you about it—is there any news?"

"There is." My father's face tightens. The movement is almost imperceptible—but I recognize the sign. He may not be shouting or cursing, but Sherlock Holmes is monumentally angry.

"Very strangely, our prisoner—the man Lucy here knew as Frances Ferrars—was able to escape after he was taken into police custody, but before he arrived at the station for booking."

"They let him go!" I breathe.

"Reason would dictate that deduction, yes. Which leads us in turn to a still more troubling conclusion."

My mind has already made that leap. "The Kaiser's spies—they must have agents among the police force. Men whom they have either blackmailed or bribed into joining their cause."

"Even so."

Constable Kelly doesn't look in any way surprised by what we've said. His expression turns a shade grimmer, but that's all.

"That would fall in with the visitor I had this morning."

"Visitor?" Sherlock Holmes turns alert as a hound that's picked up the fox's scent. "Someone came to see you here?"

"That's right. It was a man," Constable Kelly starts to say.

"What sort of man? What did he look like? What sort of clothes did he wear?" Holmes raps the questions out with all the speed of the high-powered rifle that fired at us at the docks.

"Getting there." Constable Kelly holds up a hand. "He was middle aged. Average height, average weight. Brown eyes. I can't tell you much about his clothes—or his hair, either—because he was wearing a nurse's uniform. Veil over his hair and everything."

"A *nurse's*—" Holmes blinks, glances reflexively at the nearest white-capped nurse in the ward—then refocuses on Constable Kelly. "Someone has a sense of humor."

"Not all that funny of a one." John Kelly's voice hardens. "This man came over to my bed—pretending to adjust the pillows—and said that he'd come to let me know that Sergeant Mallows was being promoted to the rank of Inspector."

"*What?*" I cannot suppress my exclamation of outraged surprise. "A trained *monkey* would be a better choice for—"

"Yes, I'm not arguing." Constable Kelly glances down the ward to where Becky is making her way back, balancing the full glass of water in one hand. "But this man said that if I was smart, I'd forget that I'd ever heard Sergeant Mallows's name."

Holmes—not surprisingly—has recovered from the shock sooner than I. His gaze has turned both distant and frighteningly focused, his mind following some complicated inner track.

"The good sergeant must have found something in the house in Harley Street. Something he used to his advantage. But what was it he found?"

Holmes is speaking more to himself than to either Constable Kelly or me. "Documents implicating some high-up Scotland-

Yard official of treason? Some sort of personal communication from the Kaiser? This Inspectorship is likely the price Mallows demanded from our shadowy opponents—or else it is his reward, for some service rendered."

"If he blackmailed them into making him an Inspector, he had better take care—and watch behind him when he goes out alone at night."

I could—almost—feel sorry for Sergeant Mallows. I doubt he has any idea what he has gotten himself involved in.

John Kelly straightens. "There was one other thing. The man who came to see me—he didn't speak with an accent. Not an obvious one. But he was Irish."

Holmes's thoughts were clearly still on Sergeant Mallows, but at that he snaps his gaze back to Constable Kelly. *"Irish?"*

It's rare that I have seen Sherlock Holmes surprised—but he is definitely startled now.

"Not German?"

"No disrespect, sir. But I grew up in an Irish neighborhood. He was trying to sound English as Parliament and Big Ben. But he was born on Irish soil. Northern Ireland, if I had to guess."

Holmes doesn't say anything, only steps back. His expression is the fixed, aloof one that means his mind is working furiously. "Most interesting," he finally says.

Becky is almost back to us, just stepping into a patch of sunlight that gilds her freckled face and cornsilk-fair hair.

Holmes leans forwards, speaking in a rapid undertone. "I believe that we are skating around the outermost edges of a problem that has become one of the thorniest and most dangerous of my career. I believe also that I shall need allies. Particularly those in a position to investigate the rot that we believe has spread through our Metropolitan Police Force."

He stops, his eyes steady on Constable Kelly's face.

Holmes isn't applying undue pressure—but I still can't hold back the protest that springs to my lips.

"You can't ask him to spy for you! He's just been shot!"

Holmes holds up a hand. "If you please, Lucy." He glances at me. "Despite my better judgment, I have resigned myself to allowing you in on the investigation." He gives me a small, sidelong smile. "Largely because I have enough wit to realize that even my most concerted efforts would be unable to keep you from doing exactly as you choose. Let us extend the same courtesy to Constable Kelly and allow him time to make up his own mind."

John Kelly's dark eyes turn towards me. I can't at all read the expression on his lean, handsome face.

Say no!

I almost say the words out loud. I have a knife-edged memory of Becky, skipping away down the hall a few moments ago, so happy that her brother is safe.

But Mallows, Francis, and Dr. Everett—they are still at large, and they know who we are. We can't avoid this fight, which means that we will have to win it, instead.

That is Holmes's perfectly rational view, I know. But my throat closes off as I imagine Becky and me, together in some future moment after some future disaster—with me trying to find the words to tell her that her brother won't be coming back.

Say no!

John Kelly turns away from me and meets Holmes's gaze with a level look.

"I don't need time to think about it, sir. I am your man."

Part II

Forward

23. Holmes

Expecting emotional displays from Sherlock Holmes was rather like giving a cat a bath and then expecting it to thank you afterwards.

Dr. John Watson, Holmes's biographer, described Holmes's features as hawk-like, keen, and intelligent—all of which was certainly true. But no one had ever described the great detective's countenance as being overly expressive.

A look of extreme boredom generally meant interest, while a single raised left eyebrow indicated that he was shocked to the core.

Which made it all the more strange to see Sherlock Holmes looking … uncomfortable. Not just uncomfortable; Holmes currently looked as though he would like nothing more than to crawl into the Persian slipper where he kept his tobacco and refuse to come out.

His usually sallow cheeks flushed, his gray eyes bulged slightly, and his lips compressed with an expression of mingled embarrassment and outrage as he struggled for speech.

"*Why* would you ask me that?" he demanded at last.

I kept my expression calm, looking across the messy sitting room of 221B Baker Street at Holmes, who was sitting in his favorite armchair beside the hearth.

I was perched amidst the piles of newspapers on the sofa—Mrs. Hudson having made a vain effort to tidy up when I came in.

A tea tray, piled high with scones and jam and little iced cakes—Mrs. Hudson's second offering—sat at my elbow.

Experience had taught me that if I was going to carry on any kind of a relationship with Sherlock Holmes I would have to employ more or less the subtlety of a battering ram in smashing through the barriers that Holmes erected between himself and any kind of personal attachments.

Not that my father wasn't fond of me. In his own way, I believed that he was.

I *hoped* he was.

I suppressed a sigh. "My options are somewhat limited," I pointed out. "If I want male advice."

"You could have asked Watson."

"I did." I let my voice fall into a gravely approximation of the good doctor's bluff, military way of speaking. "You're a beautiful girl, Lucy, my dear—and as good and true as you are lovely. Any man who does not think so ought to come to me to have his eyes examined."

Holmes did not exactly smile, but one corner of his mouth tipped ever-so-slightly up. "That was quite a good impression."

"Thank you." I almost never got cast in comedic roles on stage—I was usually the *ingénue*—but I had a secret love for them.

I took a sip of my tea. "There are the other players at the theater, of course. But I prefer not to speak about my personal life to any of them. Besides—"

I stopped, checking myself before I could continue.

Though it was a wasted effort. Emotive Sherlock Holmes might not be, but observant, he most certainly was.

Conversing with him was not unlike sitting under the lens of a microscope: my every minute inflection and facial expression was magnified, analyzed, and rapidly used to fuel Holmes's deductions.

Now Holmes right eyebrow twitched up—indicative of sardonic amusement rather than surprise.

"Besides, a good three quarters of the gentlemen players of the D'Oyly Carte Opera Company are in love with you themselves? That is what you were about to say?"

And there went my best efforts not to sound vain. "I would put it closer to fifty percent, but yes."

It genuinely was *not* vanity that led me to believe my admirers in the opera company were so numerous. None of the men and boys who made up the choruses of Gilbert and Sullivan's famous operettas were at all reticent about voicing their affection. I almost counted the week lost that did not include a marriage proposal or at the least an expression of undying passion.

I put my hands together, wondering how I might explain that world to Holmes—a world that was as different from this cozy, untidy sitting room as a brown wren was to a peacock.

I loved the theater, and had from the moment I first set foot on stage.

Actually, I had loved it considerably before that. Before I was ten, I could remember sneaking away from my boarding school and buying tickets to vaudeville shows. My greatest wish was to one day be a performer and to sing on a stage.

But that did not alter my awareness that the world of the theater was an odd blend of fantasy and reality—and the lines between them sometimes blurred.

I doubted that half of the young men who declared their desperate love for me would in actual fact be willing to get their expensive suede gaiters wet on my behalf.

Or step in front of a high-powered rifle in order to protect me.

Holmes's eyes met mine—and I thought I saw a flicker of understanding cross their cool gray depths.

He cleared his throat, reaching for his pipe and stuffing tobacco into the bowl with the little tool he kept for the purpose.

"To be clear"—Holmes kept his eyes firmly fixed on the match he was working at lighting—"you wish my considered opinion as to why Constable John Kelly has made no romantic overtures to you since you and he became acquainted?"

I sat up straighter, feeling my cheeks growing warm.

This conversation was entirely my own doing. The rain would have fallen upwards before Holmes ever broached the subject of John Kelly with me himself. Except—possibly—to discuss Jack's acumen and intelligence as an aspiring officer in the Metropolitan Police.

Still, something about hearing my own question voiced in Holmes's detached, clinical tones made my insides squirm.

"Yes."

My only consolation was that Holmes appeared every bit as embarrassed as I. I had never known him to make such a lengthy production of getting his pipe lighted.

"Has it occurred to you that he may in fact not harbor any feelings of a romantic nature for you?" Holmes asked at last.

I curled my fingertips towards my palms. I did let myself in for this.

"Of course." I willed my voice to sound as calm as Holmes's. "It is a possibility."

One that if I were completely honest had kept me awake for far too many nights in the last weeks. "It's just that I wish to be *certain*."

Holmes regarded me for a moment above the rim of his pipe bowl.

"Very well. Setting aside my own lack of qualification to give any advice whatsoever on matters of the heart, logic would suggest a second possibility. You and the constable have known each other only a short while. What has it been?"

"Just over six weeks." Holmes made an open-handed gesture, scattering ash across the carpet. "Perhaps the young man does not wish to rush into any declarations of affection before you have had time to become more thoroughly acquainted."

"We *are* thoroughly acquainted. Besides, Johnny Rockefeller proposed to me on the second day after we met."

Holmes's gray eyes regarded me once again. "Forgive me for stating the obvious, but Constable John Kelly is not Johnny Rockefeller."

That was entirely true. Jack—a detective constable on the London police force making roughly one guinea a week—was socially and financially as far from the heir to the great Rockefeller fortune as it was possible to get.

Johnny Rockefeller's proposal to me hadn't been entirely serious, either. He was involved with another girl back in America, though I had the impression that he would have broken it off if I had given him more encouragement.

Holmes took a puff of his pipe, still watching me.

"Overlooking for a moment the constable's feelings—whatever they may or not be—do you wish to receive a proposal of marriage from him?"

I felt my cheeks flush even more brightly. Did I?

I liked and admired Jack more than any other young man I had ever met. He was brave and intelligent and *real* in a way that the young men of the theater with their pretty speeches and impassioned murmurings were not.

But marriage?

"Marriage would be safer—as well as more respectable—than an illicit dalliance, at least," I said. "My own mere *existence* is proof of the unintended consequences that those can have."

A tendency to speak without thinking is one of my besetting sins. Another being the impulse to say shocking things just to see what will happen.

I regretted my words almost as soon as I heard them leave my mouth—and not only because of Holmes's expression of horrified disbelief.

I had the distinct impression that if he were even a shade less dignified and self-possessed, he might have clamped his hands over his ears in the effort not to hear anything more.

"I'm sorry." I jumped to my feet, crossing quickly to kiss Holmes on the cheek. Which he probably enjoyed about as much as my thoughtless speech. "I must get to the Savoy. I'll be late for tonight's performance if I don't leave right away."

"*The Mikado*," Holmes said.

"Yes." The D'Oyly Carte Opera Company had been performing a revival of the operetta since August.

"And how are you getting on as one of the three little maids?" Holmes asked.

I looked at him, startled.

I was a relative newcomer to the opera company. Aside from a few performances less than a year ago when I had first arrived in England, I had been only an understudy to the principal sopranos, on a few occasions taking a lead part only when the company was touring. This was the first time I had been actually *cast* as one of the leads for performances here in London, at the Savoy Theater.

It was a great opportunity, and I had been working harder and practicing more than I ever had in my life, playing the part of Pitti-Sing, one of the "Three Little Maids from school."

What surprised me now, though, was that *Holmes* knew of my promotion. I had only been cast in the part two weeks ago.

"You have been to see the show in the last fortnight?"

Holmes looked mildly surprised. "Naturally."

On impulse, I hugged him—and as usual, his tall, lean frame went entirely rigid. I could not be sure, but any time I embraced him, I imagined him counting off the seconds inside his head, waiting for the whole messy, overly emotional experience to be over.

This time, though, his hand did come up to deliver a quick pat—so quick I might almost have imagined it—on my shoulder.

"Take care. And, Lucy?"

"Yes?"

Discomfort once again etched Sherlock Holmes's face as I drew apart from him—but he kept on, with something of the air of a man determined to see a duty through to the bitter end.

"About the other matter ... I have as a general rule very little use for Ancient Greek. But their motto of *Know Thyself* seems to me apropos to your situation. I trust you understand?"

I did. Rather than worrying about what Constable Jack Kelly felt for me, I ought rather to be deciding exactly what *I* felt for *him*.

Solid—even good—advice. Though as I bid Holmes a final farewell and turned to go, I felt oddly discouraged, almost sad.

I had so much more than I had ever dreamed I might, back in the days when I was a lonely boarding school student without any family that I knew of in the whole world.

I had now come to know both of my parents. And despite what I said to Holmes, I could not in any way regret their brief, youthful liaison. How could I be sorry to have been born? I enjoyed living a great deal.

For nearly the whole of my life, Sherlock Holmes had no more idea of my existence than I had of his. Less, actually; I at least read Dr. Watson's stories, even if I had no idea of my own connection to the great detective he described.

Holmes had coped remarkably well with the revelation that he had an unknown daughter—especially considering he had never expressed the least desire for a family. However, *coping well*, as I was acutely aware every time I visited Baker Street, was not exactly the same as *enjoying*.

Mrs. Hudson was in the kitchen as I went downstairs, so I let myself out. Afternoon shadows were giving way to the deep purples and grays of late autumn twilight. Lamplighters were busy going from gaslight to gaslight up and down the street, while day laborers and other pedestrians hurried on their way.

I drew my cloak more tightly around my shoulders, suppressing a shiver as the raw, chill air of a London November tried to crawl inside my clothes.

Today was November third. Another two days, and the bonfires for Guy Fawkes Night would be lighted in every public square.

As I started down the street, I glanced back just once at 221B—but the curtains of the upstairs rooms where Holmes and Watson lodged were drawn tight.

I turned away.

I did not *mind* waging a campaign to bash and batter my way past Holmes's defenses and forcibly insert myself into my father's life.

But I *did* wish that I could be certain that he was genuinely glad to have me there.

24. MIDNIGHT VISITOR

"And did you *see* the way that that Lila Evans pushed her way right in front of me during 'Comes a Train of Little Ladies'?" Mary demanded. "It was outrageous!"

I murmured noncommittally. I had not in fact seen the supposed offense—but my saying so would only give rise to further outrage.

The evening's performance of *The Mikado* was finished, and Mary Mulloy and I were walking back to the rooms that we shared in Exeter Street.

Occasionally shared.

The location of my mother's former residence was ideal, barely a five minutes' walk from the Savoy. But lately I had been dividing my time between Exeter Street and Baker Street, where thanks to Mrs. Hudson's kindness I could stay in flat number 221A whenever I chose.

Mary was at that very moment demonstrating the reason that I chose the longer commute to Baker Street more often than not.

"And then Peter nearly *dropped* me during the finale! He is so clumsy! It was all I could *do* to keep my *footing*."

Mary's lightly Irish-accented voice had a trick of hopping from emphasized word to emphasized word in a way that made me feel as though I were conversing with an India-rubber ball.

She was twenty-three or twenty-four—a year or two older than I was—with blue eyes and black hair. She was quite pretty, or at least she would have been, if her small mouth had not been set in a habitual expression of discontent.

"I told him that he was *lucky* I hadn't boxed his *ears* for him, the butterfingers—"

Mary's voice rattled on, sharp with aggrievement.

Every night after we left the theater, I would make a bet with myself as to whether or not she would have run out of complaints by the time we reached Exeter Street.

Tonight, we were climbing the stairs that led to the flat—and Mary showed absolutely no sign of running out of grievances.

"You said you wanted to talk to me?" I interrupted.

In fairness, I had only myself to blame that I was stuck with Mary for a flat mate. Sharing the Exeter Street lodgings had been my own idea.

She had joined the opera company only a few months before, and, having recently been a newcomer myself, I had helped her learn the inner workings of the stage productions. I thought that sharing the flat would provide company for us both—a little like the dormitory rooms I had shared at Miss Porter's school with my fellow students.

Now Mary seemed to hesitate, giving me a sideways glance as she reached into her evening bag for a front door key.

"Well, yes. But I *am* talking. I mean, there was nothing in particular I wanted to discuss." Mary shrugged. "It's just that I've scarcely seen you this last week."

"I was here the night before last."

Sometimes—as tonight—I was simply too tired to make my way all the way back to Baker Street. Besides which, a wish to collect my mail and see whether I had any messages waiting for me in Exeter Street might have played into my decision.

"Oh, well." Mary shrugged her shoulders again, unlocked the door, and pushed it open. "Did you *hear* what Mr. Harris told me tonight? He said I ought to walk with more *dignity*. According to him, I race across the stage like a dipsomaniac in search of a last glass of gin before closing time."

Mr. Charles Harris was the opera company's stage manager—a stout, middle-aged man with a blunt tongue and an extremely keen eye for what would make for effective theater.

"I wouldn't feel badly," I told Mary. "I remember in my first week, Mr. Harris told me something similar. It's so easy to want to rush madly to your mark when you first come out from the wings."

Mary only sniffed, turning aside to flip through the pile of letters that our landlady had left on the table beside the door.

I studied Mary's profile. Everything about her complaints tonight had been entirely typical. If I had a half crown for all of all of the times I had heard her make similar complaints, I would probably be wealthy enough to buy not just our flat but the entire building.

And yet, watching her, I could not shake the impression that something was wrong—something more than just Lila Evans pushing past her or Mr. Harris criticizing the way she walked.

That was the other part of my reason for asking Mary to share a flat with me.

For someone who talked about herself nearly incessantly, Mary was surprisingly secretive when it came to her past and family background. Beyond knowing that she came from Ireland, from Dublin, I knew next to nothing about her.

"Are you sure there's nothing wrong?" I asked.

Beneath the stage makeup that we both still wore, her face looked pale, with deep purple shadows like bruises beneath her eyes.

"Have you been having nightmares again?"

Mary slept on a pull-out trundle in the outer room, while I slept in the bedroom—but that didn't stop me from being awakened by her shouting and crying out when she had a bad dream.

She always muttered sullenly that she didn't remember what the nightmare had been about when I asked—but Holmes would have completely disowned me as a daughter if I had not been able to identify that assertion as an outright lie.

Now Mary gave a noncommittal shrug and another sniff. "I'm *perfectly* well."

Her hands trembled briefly on the letter she was holding—then she cast it aside into the pile of mail that she had already looked through.

"There's nothing for *you*," Mary went on. "Well, nothing *important*. No message from your tame *policeman. If* you were wondering."

And that was Mary's character in a nutshell. The moment I started feeling sympathetic towards her, she managed to set that small scrap of sympathy on fire and then trample it into ashes.

"He is not my tame policeman," I said. I kept my voice calm. "I've been giving his sister lessons in singing, that's all. I was worried because they didn't come for Becky's usual session yesterday afternoon."

With Jack's having to be on beat duty most nights, it was difficult to find a time when he could bring Becky from their rented rooms in St. Giles to Exeter Street. But for the last weeks we had been meeting on Tuesday evenings at four o'clock, before I had to leave for the Savoy.

Yesterday had been Tuesday, though, and Jack and Becky had never come.

"Oh, yes, the little girl." Mary turned away from the mail and headed towards the washroom, where she began to apply cream to her face in fussy little strokes.

She kept the door open so that she could keep talking. "I don't know *why* you *bother* with giving her singing lessons. It's not as if she's even *paying* you anything, is she? Of course"—Mary's eyes met mine in the mirror and she gave a small smirk of a smile—"if you didn't give the child lessons, you wouldn't have an excuse to keep seeing her *brother*, would you?"

I ground my teeth together. Arguing or getting angry would only add fuel to Mary's fire.

Not that I actually did give Becky lessons only for the sake of seeing her brother. I had, though, found myself looking forward to Tuesday evenings for more than just the sake of our lessons.

Jack would sit on the sofa watching while Becky and I sang scales together, his lean, darkly handsome face uncharacteristically at peace, and—

I snapped the thought off, facing Mary with a calm smile.

I was an *actress*. I would have to hand in my resignation to Mr. Harris if I could not hide my own feelings any better than this.

"Becky is a talented girl," I said. "Her voice is untrained, true, but she shows a great deal of promise. And after all, someone saw talent in both of us and gave us encouragement, otherwise we would never—"

I broke off as a loud hammering came on the flat's front door.

I turned, starting with surprise.

Mary gasped, one hand flying to her throat. "Who in the name of the saints can that be, at this time of night?"

I shook my head, reaching for the doorknob—but before I could even touch it, the door flew open on its own. We had been home such a short while that I had not even had the chance to lock and latch the door for the night.

A small, sobbing girl came bursting into the room, her eyes swollen and tear-stained with crying and her long blond hair tangled into an unkempt mess.

"Becky!"

Despite the cold outside, she was barefoot, and wearing only a thin white nightgown.

"I'm sorry!" She was crying so hard that I could hardly make out the words at first. "I'm sorry, I'm sorry, but I didn't know where else to go!"

"It's all right." I crouched down so that I could put my arm around her, holding her against me. "But Becky, what's wrong? Did someone hurt you or—"

"No." Gulping and dragging the edge of her sleeve across her swollen eyes, Becky finally managed to stop crying enough to answer. "No, it's not me. At least, not exactly. It's *Jack*."

"Jack?" A huge, unfriendly hand seemed to wrap itself around my heart and begin to squeeze. "Something has happened to your brother? Is he hurt, or—"

I stopped.

I was not much in the habit of praying—God helping those who help themselves and all of that. But in that moment, I sent the plea up to anyone or anything who might have been willing to listen.

Please let Jack not have been killed in the line of duty. Please don't let him be dead.

It seemed to take forever before Becky drew a hiccupping breath, dragging her gaze up to meet mine. Her blue eyes still swam with tears, and her shoulders slumped.

"He's not hurt. Not exactly. But he's been arrested."

25. A PORT IN A STORM

"Now." I handed Becky the cup of hot cocoa I had just warmed over the fire on the hearth. "Tell me exactly what happened—everything that you can remember."

Becky and I were alone. At my insistence, Mary had taken over the bedroom and retired for the night, leaving Becky and me on the living room sofa.

To my surprise, Mary had been quite kind to Becky. The cocoa was hers, and she'd also produced a tin of iced chocolate biscuits and handed them over with permission for Becky to eat as many as she pleased.

We kept little food in the flat as a rule, but Mary had a perpetual weakness for sweets.

So far, Becky had eaten three of the biscuits and was looking calmer, though still frightened and pale. I had given her my spare dressing gown and wrapped her in a blanket, besides.

She swallowed her mouthful and took a sip of the cocoa.

"All right." She frowned. "I don't know very much. Only what I overheard the other police officers saying—and that wasn't a lot, because they knew I was listening, and they thought I was just a stupid *kid*."

Becky's mouth twisted on the last word, her face working as though she were about to start crying again.

I felt cold all the way through, but I squeezed her hand. "Just start at the beginning," I told her. "When did this all happen?"

"Tonight." Becky took a shuddering breath. "I had already gone to bed—except I wasn't asleep yet. I was waiting to hear Jack leave to go on duty."

Becky scrubbed at her eyes. "But before I heard him go out, all of a sudden the door burst open. I heard it crash. I jumped up. I thought it might be—you know, neighborhood trouble." Her throat contracted as she swallowed. "But it was the *police*. There must have been five or six of them. They grabbed hold of Jack and said he was under arrest."

Becky's small face was white and strained, the freckles on her nose standing out like splotches of paint against her pale skin.

"They grabbed Prince and shut him up in the bedroom. Then one of them saw me, and he tried to grab me, too. I heard him say that I'd have to be taken to an orphanage—or a workhouse—since Jack was going to prison. He took hold of me—but I bit him. The rest of them were already dragging Jack away. I knew I couldn't follow. They'd just have caught me again. So I ran all the way here."

Becky stopped, looking up at me. Her hands twisted in a fold of her nightgown. "You'll help him, won't you? You and Mr. Holmes?"

"Of course."

Holmes *would* lend his considerable talents to helping Jack, even if I had to strongarm him into it.

"But Becky, I don't understand—what is your brother supposed to have done?"

"Jack asked that." Becky swallowed again, her eyes shadowed by the memory. "He was angry—but at the same time, staying calm, you know?"

I nodded. Jack had a temper, but he kept it under firm control.

"He asked the police who came to arrest him what the charges were," Becky went on. "And they said it was murder." Her voice wavered on the last word before going on, obviously quoting the words she had overheard. "They said he was being arrested on suspicion of having killed Inspector Mallows."

I stared at Becky. The tick of the clock on the mantle seemed unnaturally loud in the night silence.

"*Mallows*?" I finally said. "You're positive that was the name?"

Becky bobbed her head. "I'm sure. Jack's told me about him once or twice. He's the sergeant Jack reports to at the station house. Or he used to be. He was made an inspector not long ago. But why would anyone think that Jack had killed him?"

"I don't know."

A growing dread was pooling inside me, but I forced myself not to show it. Becky was already frightened enough.

"I don't know why they suspect your brother, but I promise you that I'm going to find out. Listen to me, Becky." I leaned forward. "We both know that Jack is innocent."

Not that Jack Kelly was incapable of killing. If he had to, I was fairly certain that he would kill to protect Becky, or in defense of his own life.

But I also knew enough about Sergeant—or rather *Inspector*—Mallows to be certain that, whoever killed him, it wasn't Jack.

I had a horrible certainty that I already knew who was responsible for his death—though unfortunately, if my suspicions proved true, that made it even less likely that we would ever be able to prove it.

"You can stay here for tonight," I told Becky. "Then in the morning, we'll go to Baker Street and plan out our campaign."

Becky looked exhausted, but she gave a small nod. "Thank you."

"You're welcome." I leaned forward and hugged her.

Becky stiffened for a second, but then clung to me tightly. Her voice came out muffled, buried against my shoulder.

"What if you and Mr. Holmes can't save him? What if they hang him? That's what they do to murderers, isn't it?" Becky's whole body shook. "Jack's all I have. If he's gone, what will happen to me? I wouldn't have anyone—"

"Yes, you would," I interrupted her firmly.

For a second, as I smoothed Becky's hair, I thought of the little girl I had been at her age.

From a physical standpoint, I had lacked nothing. I had always been sent to the best boarding schools, and was well fed and dressed in all the best clothes.

But I had no family, no one to speak up for me or fight battles on my behalf, no one to send letters to me on my birthday or a home to visit at the holidays.

I did not even know whether anyone in the entire world cared whether I lived or died.

"You're not alone, Becky. Holmes and I aren't going to let Jack hang for a crime that he didn't commit. But even if something happens to him, you will always have a place here with me, and with Uncle John and Holmes. I *promise*."

I hugged her tighter, resting my chin on top of her tangled blond hair. "Eventually, you'll be able to take care of yourself, because you're smart and capable and very, very strong. But you don't have to worry about that for right now. You're safe here with me, and I'm *happy* to have you."

I would love to see Sherlock Holmes's face if I wound up foisting an eight-year-old girl on him during those times I had to be at the theater. But I knew he also would never turn Becky away. Even the self-described thinking machine was not so heartless as that.

And at least Uncle John would be pleased. He and Becky were already well on the way to becoming fast friends.

Becky's breath went out in a shuddery rush and she slumped against me, limp.

"Now then." I hugged her again, then sat back. "Dry your eyes, and then we'd better get some sleep so that we'll be able to think clearly in the morning. We're going to need your help to prove Jack's innocence, you know. What happened to being Irene Adler?"

Becky rewarded me with a watery smile, and I patted her hand.

"Tomorrow morning first thing we'll go to Baker Street, and then we can find out where Jack is being held."

26. A PESTILENTIAL PRISON

There were, I was discovering, advantages to being the daughter of Sherlock Holmes.

As a rule, Holmes was less than enthusiastic about my involvement in his criminal investigations. However, in this case, he had very little choice but to lend both his full aid and the full weight of his influence with the London police force.

Inspector Mallows's murder concerned Holmes every bit as much as it did me—albeit for different reasons.

Now I was following a uniformed constable along a narrow hallway of the Holborn Police Station in Lamb's Conduit Street.

Holmes had arranged for me to be brought to see Jack. Not that he had actually introduced me as his daughter. He was adamant that if our relationship was widely known, his enemies might make me a target—so only a select handful of people were aware.

Holmes had merely told the desk sergeant on duty that I was an associate here to see Constable Kelly—and everyone had leapt to comply with his orders.

Holmes himself had stayed behind to ask questions of the station's superintendent and the inspectors.

Part of Holmes's purpose was a quest for any information he could learn about Inspector Mallows's death. The other part was distraction—while they were speaking to the great detective Sherlock Holmes, the officers in charge here would be unlikely to bother with listening in on my conversation with Jack Kelly.

"Right this way, miss." The constable up ahead of me cast a quick, curious glance at me over his shoulder. A young man with fair hair, round blue eyes, and a round, pink face, he looked a little like an overgrown baby. But he was huge—over six feet tall, and solidly built, which presumably saved him from being laughed at when he went about his duties.

"Friend of Jack's, are you?" he asked me.

"I'm a friend of his sister's."

The hallway was unlighted, the only illumination coming from a barred and grimy window set high in the wall behind us. I had never been to the holding cells in a police station before, but everything about this place seemed to fairly ooze desperation and despair.

It did not help at all that my mind had disobligingly called up a section of libretto from the Mikado and was playing it over, again and again, inside my head.

To sit in solemn silence on a dull, dark dock, in a pestilential prison with a life-long lock, awaiting the sensation of a short, sharp shock from a cheap and chippy chopper on a big, black block.

After performing the show nightly for the past several months, I knew every line of every song by heart. But I doubted that I would ever again be able to listen to that particular section without flinching.

"I just came so that I could tell Jack that his sister is staying with me, and that she's quite safe," I finished.

For the moment, Becky was in fact in Baker Street with Uncle John. She had been extremely unwilling to let us come on this errand without her. She only agreed to stay behind when Holmes and I pointed out that firstly, as a child, she would never be allowed in to see her brother—and secondly that if any of the police saw her, they might still insist she go to an orphanage.

Now the blond-haired constable gave me another appraising look before turning back to face away from me as we marched down the narrow hall.

Drawing a jangling bunch of keys from a loop on his belt, he unlocked a heavy gate that ran from floor to ceiling and was constructed of iron bars.

Beyond were a row of cells, little more than square, barred boxes, each outfitted with a rough wooden cot for a bed and nothing more.

I counted three other occupants of the cells we passed: two men and one woman, all slumped over on the floor, too drunk or exhausted to bother with moving to the beds.

"He'll be transferred to Holloway tomorrow," the constable told me over his shoulder. "But for now he's right here. Oy, Kelly!"

Drawing to a halt outside of the last cell in the row, the constable rapped on the bars at the front.

"Visitor to see you!"

As I moved up behind the young constable, I could see into the cell. Jack Kelly was sitting on the edge of the narrow bed, his elbows resting on his knees and his dark head bowed.

He looked up, though, at the other constable's summons. Surprise crossed his face at the sight of me, followed by a brief, wan smile.

"Hello there, Trouble."

My heart seemed to cramp.

Jack's lean, sculpted face was shadowed by a stubble of beard on his jaw. A darkening bruise blossomed on one of his cheekbones.

He wore regulation blue trousers and a plain white cotton shirt, rolled to the elbows—and the fabric on the right shoulder was torn, and marked with a spatter of what looked like blood.

My twenty-one years on earth had taught me that real life was frequently both unjust and unfair—despite virtue generally triumphing in plays. But this was just too much.

I raised my eyebrows. "You're the one in prison, and *I'm* Trouble?"

I turned back to the young constable. "Do you think you might let us talk privately?"

I added my most winning smile—the one I reserved only for emergencies, because I knew its effect—and I did not in fact enjoy having to turn down marriage proposals.

The pink-faced constable, though, proved unfortunately far more difficult to sway than the average male member of the opera company. He blinked at me, looking uncomfortable—but also undecided.

Jack cleared his throat. "Give us a minute, Will?"

The constable—Will—looked even more uncomfortable as he turned to look at Jack inside the cell. His face flushed a darker pink, and he ran a finger around the collar of his tunic.

But finally he jerked his head in a short, uneasy nod. "Fine."

Watching him, it occurred to me that Jack was probably well liked among his fellow officers at the station house. And Inspector Mallows—if the glimpse I had had of him six weeks ago was anything to go by—was almost certainly not liked or respected at all.

"I'll wait over by the door," Will muttered, jerking his head back the way we had come in. "Five minutes, only, though," he added.

When he had stumped off, Jack and I looked at each other in silence.

My eyes felt hot and prickly. Which was ridiculous. Jack didn't need me to sit here and weep over this miscarriage of justice. He needed me to find a way of getting him *out* of here.

"Becky is quite safe," I said at last. "She came straight to me last night. She's with Uncle John—Dr. Watson—now. They're going back to St. Giles to collect Prince and bring him to Baker Street."

Jack's whole body seemed to relax as he let out a breath. He must have been eaten up with worry for his sister, all through last night.

"Thanks for that. I was hoping she'd have found her way to you."

"She did. She's a very bright girl. Not that you need me to tell you." I paused, looking through the bars. "What happened?"

Something seemed to shift in Jack's gaze. His expression hardened, the line of his mouth turning a shade more grim. "I don't think—"

I interrupted. "Don't bother."

"What?"

I gestured with impatience. "You are about to say that this is a dangerous entanglement and that for the sake of my own safety I should stay out of it, abandoning all efforts to prove you innocent. To which *I* will say that you are wasting time—something we can ill afford, since your friend only gave us five minutes."

Jack glared at me, his straight dark brows forming an almost perfectly horizontal line. "It *is* dangerous, and you *should* stay out of—"

I interrupted him again. "*Dangerous*? What?" I gave him a look of exaggerated astonishment.

"The organization we have been tracking is a network of German spies, dedicated to assassinating our regent and overthrowing the British government. Their agents attempted to kill me six weeks ago—twice in fact! But I had no idea that they might be considered *dangerous*. It's so lucky that I have you to point that out. Perhaps you would also like to tell me that we are in London and the earth is round."

Jack's jaw muscles clenched. "They did try to kill you—twice. Did you ever think that they might be third time lucky?" He leaned forward, his dark eyes shadowed with intensity. "If something happened to you, I'd—"

But then he stopped.

I waited, but he did not go on.

This was exactly why I had sought Holmes's advice the day before: I had no idea, really, how Jack Kelly felt about me.

Sometimes—as now—I thought that he *looked* as though he might care for me as more than a comrade and friend.

But *speak to me only with thine eyes* was also hardly a reason to start shopping for wedding clothes and selecting patterns of china.

"Have *you* stopped to consider what would happen to Becky if she lost you?" I demanded. "She's already lost both her parents—she doesn't need anyone else taken away from her."

Jack opened his mouth, but I kept going.

"Besides, our enemies—whoever they are—already know who I am. They may not know of the nature of my connection to Holmes—but they certainly know that Holmes and I have committed ourselves to tracking them down. Which means that it makes no difference whether or not I turn around and walk straight out of this prison now. I would still be in danger. The only way that I—that any of us—will be safe is if we round the entire organization up. Not to mention that I have no intention of allowing the Kaiser to succeed in his plans to overtake our nation. So."

I folded my arms, matching Jack glare for glare. "You might as well tell me what I need to know to get you out of here."

Jack stared at me for a long moment of silence. Then, finally, he blew out a breath, tugging both hands through his unruly dark hair.

"I don't know how much I can tell you. No one will tell me anything. I know Mallows is dead. But they won't give me any details about how he died, or when or where. I don't even know why they're so sure that I did it."

"Never mind all of that." I waved one hand. "Holmes will have found out the details from the station superintendent. He's here—interviewing the inspectors and everyone else right now. No, what I need you to tell me is anything you learned about

Inspector Mallows in the last few weeks. You have been watching him?"

"Of course." Jack glanced up towards the end of the room where I could see the young constable Will standing beside the door.

Then in an abrupt movement Jack got up off the bed, coming to stand facing me at the bars of his cell. He lowered his voice as he went on. "I've been watching Mallows—just as we agreed. I followed him from here, after he went off duty. I couldn't get too close, since he'd have recognized me if he ever spotted me. But I can tell you that he goes to a pub in Covent Garden most nights—the White Hart. Stays there drinking till closing time. Or he *did*."

Jack stopped, plainly struck by the necessity of referring to his former sergeant in the past tense.

"We'll have to go to the public house and see whether we can find out whether he was meeting with anyone in particular. Anything else?"

"Nothing definite. But I can tell you that he seemed to be flush with money all of a sudden. I saw stubs of racing tickets in his desk drawer, when I got a look in it the other day. And he'd bought himself a fancy new gold pocket watch."

I drew in a breath. "He was blackmailing them."

I stared straight ahead, picturing the sergeant's red, beefy face and doughy body. I had disliked Inspector Mallows almost on sight—but I would not have wished him killed purely on account of his own greed and stupidity.

"He was blackmailing them, demanding payment to ensure his silence, and they killed him for it."

"Looks like," Jack agreed. He stopped, looking down at me for a moment. Then he said, in a different voice. "Look. I'll give up on trying to talk you into staying out of this. But will you at least promise me that you'll be careful? These are a nasty bunch we're dealing with."

"I know." Already they had shot Holmes, and Jack, too. The bullet wound in Jack's shoulder was only just barely healed.

Without fully realizing it, I had wrapped one hand around the bars of Jack's prison cell. Now he folded his fingers around mine.

"You never asked whether I did it." His voice was quiet.

I tilted my head back to look up at him, ready to make light of the question, turn it into some sort of joke. But as my eyes met Jack's, even the attempt at humor seemed to die.

His hand covered mine, his palm warm and a little calloused. His eyes were dark, shadowed and frustrated and yet oddly *wondering*, all at the same time.

He was looking at me as though he were trying to decide whether I was real or only some sort of fantasy.

"No," I agreed. "I didn't have to ask." I swallowed.

The thought ghosted through my mind that this would be the perfect moment to say something heartfelt.

I was an educated, independent, modern young woman—and I didn't *have* to wait for Jack to be the one to first declare himself.

"Time's up."

Behind me, Will, the young constable, spoke in a gruff voice—and the moment broke. Jack let go of my hand and stepped back, and I blinked hard. "I'll come back to see you as soon as I have anything to report," I said.

Not for the first time in my life, I was grateful for the stage training that let me keep my voice steady.

Jack dropped back onto the edge of the bed, favoring me with a brief twist of a smile. "Yeah, well. I'll be pretty busy here, as you can see. But I'll see if I find a spare minute to see you when you come."

27. CASE FOR THE PROSECUTION

"Now then." Holmes leaned back in the hansom cab on the seat beside mine. "Tell me what you have learned."

I scowled at the shiny wet hindquarters of the black horse that plodded before us.

The weather was chill and drizzly, with rain spattering down from a sullen sky and thick curls of mist wreathing the London streets.

Actually, it matched my mood far better than bright sunlight would have done—but the inclement weather was also grinding all traffic on the roads to a virtual standstill. I had the irritable feeling that I could have walked back to Baker Street by now.

"Not very much," I said. "Jack has been kept ignorant of all details about the sergeant's murder. But he did tell me that Inspector Mallows had been spending money more freely in these last few weeks before he died. Gambling and drinking—*and* showing off a very handsome new pocket watch."

"Ah, greed." Holmes spoke in a musing tone, his eyes half-lidded, with the look that meant he was concentrating intently. "You would be surprised how many—rich and poor, intelligent and simple alike—fall prey to its lures. Or how few people will stop to think that their newly-gotten wealth might have been too easy to come by, or too good to be true. Most people possess the happy certainty that they *deserve* every stroke of good fortune that might come their way. It is the guiding principle of many a confidence trickster in duping their marks—just as it seems to have lulled the unfortunate Mallows into a false sense of security."

"You agree that he was blackmailing our unknown opponents?"

Holmes twitched his index and middle fingers in a gesture that meant *obviously*. His gaze remained fixed on the streaming gutters of the butcher's shop we were passing.

"Did you learn anything more?"

"Just that Inspector Mallows was in the habit of frequenting a pub in Covent Garden called the White Hart."

"I know the establishment." Holmes's eyes unfocused, his thoughts clearly following some complicated inner track. "An unsavory place—even for a pub in Covent Garden."

As a general rule, Sherlock Holmes's voice was as unchanging as his facial expressions. His speech was cool, academic, and slightly sardonic—whether he was discussing a particularly grisly murder or the likelihood of rain.

Now, though, I thought that his tone altered slightly as he went on, "Constable Kelly did not … that is, he did not express any sentiments … He did not make any declarations of—"

"He did not propose marriage to me through the bars of his prison cell, if that is what you are trying to ask."

"Ah." Holmes sat back—looking as though he were profoundly wishing that he could occupy himself only with lighting his pipe.

I stared out the window, wondering what on earth had ever possessed me to confide in Sherlock Holmes.

Actually, I had been hoping that my revealing my innermost thoughts and wishes to Holmes would lead to his being more comfortable with sharing his own.

I should have tried squeezing lemonade from a rock. I would probably have been blessed with greater success.

"It has occurred to me that I owe you something of an apology for the way I responded to your earlier request for advice. I have had little practice at fulfilling the duties of a parent—"

"I don't want to be a *duty* of yours!" I interrupted. I blinked hard against the sudden stinging in my eyes. This was ridiculous. I *never* cried. Not when I was ten, and my entire class at school had someplace to go for the holidays, while I remained wandering the dormitory on my own. Not when I said goodbye to my mother in Italy, having only barely become acquainted with her. Not a few months ago, when Holmes was shot, and I was afraid that he was going to die.

Crying accomplished nothing. Yet here I sat, fighting tears for the second time in a single morning.

If I cried, Holmes would very likely leap straight out of the carriage.

"Quite so. I misspoke. I did not mean to imply that I felt it a duty to … What I wished to say was that—though I have little practice in these sorts of familial relations—I am sensible of the honor you had done me, by trusting me with your confidences."

I blinked again, managing a small smile as I turned back to Holmes.

"I haven't had much practice, either."

I hadn't had much practice in caring for *anyone*, family or otherwise. I had had school friends, growing up—but never anyone to whom I was deeply attached. The last close friend I had *thought* I had proved in the end to be a member of the same German spy ring we were tracking now.

Maybe that was why I was finding it so hard to admit how I felt about Jack.

"What did you find out?" I asked Holmes. "Were you able to learn the details of Mallows's death?"

"I was." Holmes's already thin lips compressed. "The facts are few—and ugly enough. But they can be easily summarized. On the morning of the third—that is to say, yesterday morning—the body of Inspector Mallows was discovered in an alleyway three blocks away from the police station. The amount of blood pooled beneath his body made it clear that he had died where he fell, as opposed to having been attacked elsewhere and dragged to the alley."

"Even the limited capacities of the investigating inspectors were able to determine that much."

"The cause of death?" I asked.

I braced myself—but still felt my stomach clench when Holmes answered: "He was bludgeoned to death. With a truncheon belonging to Constable Kelly."

"How did they know it was Jack's?"

"His initials were stamped on the handle. Also, his fingerprints were discovered on the weapon." Holmes's breath hissed with annoyance. "All the efforts I have made to persuade the police force to adopt the technology of fingerprinting—and they employ it in a case like this."

"But that makes it still more idiotic! No one could possibly believe that Jack—a police constable himself—would bludgeon someone to death with his own weapon and then helpfully leave the truncheon behind to be found? Anyone with the intelligence God gave to geese ought to be able to see that it's a completely ridiculous theory!"

"They are claiming that Constable Kelly must have killed Inspector Mallows in a fit of rage. Then, panicking, he ran away—never thinking about the incriminating evidence he had left behind."

Holmes's upper lip curled slightly back.

"But surely—"

Holmes did not let me finish. "Unfortunately for us and for Constable Kelly, it makes no difference whether or not the case against him is solid or has more holes than a leaking sieve."

He fairly bit the words off. It was rare that I saw Sherlock Holmes lose his temper—but he was on the verge of it now.

"What matters is that they have evidence—however shoddy, however scanty—with which to shore up their case and give them an excuse to proceed."

I felt as though I had been hit in the chest with a sandbag. "You mean that others in the police force besides Inspector Mallows are employed by our ring of spies?"

"We suspected it before, did we not? This would appear to confirm it. The commanding officer of the station—Superintendent Weddeburn—was plainly not happy with the case against Constable Kelly. But neither was he in any way planning to protest the constable's innocence or prevent him from being tried for the crime."

The heavy feeling on my chest intensified.

"Do you think Superintendent Weddeburn is in the Kaiser's employ?"

Holmes made a noncommittal motion with one hand. "It is possible, of course—but I do not believe that he is. To me, he bore the look of a man who had received his marching orders from on high, and was dutifully—some might say fearfully—resigned to carrying them out."

"You mean that some higher-up police official is putting pressure on him to see that Jack is arrested and tried?"

"That is what I mean, yes. Though I doubt that Constable Kelly will ever come to trial."

I should have thought that I would have reached a saturation point for worry by now. But apparently not. At Holmes's words, ice shot down the entire length of my spine.

"What do you mean?"

Holmes gave me a sideways glance as—with a lurch and a jolt—the cab finally began to pick up speed. Whatever obstruction had been causing the delay in the road up ahead must have cleared.

"You do not seriously imagine that our nameless opponents will *allow* Constable Kelly's case to come to trial, do you? Their survival and the success of their aims depends on their maintaining anonymity. On attracting no notice to themselves. A trial for the murder of one of London's own police force would undoubtedly attract the interest of both the public and the press—precisely what our enemies wish at all costs to avoid. Should

Constable Kelly face his day in a court of law, other eyes than ours would be sure to spy the flaws in the case against him."

Holmes stopped, his long, thin fingers drumming a restless tattoo against the cracked leather edge of the hansom cab's seat.

"If I were to place myself in our enemies' shoes, I should arrange for an unfortunate accident to occur. Perhaps an assault, or a prison yard brawl—some unpleasant outbreak of violence, apparently random, but having one crucial consequence: Constable Kelly's death."

"They're going to kill him." I tightened my hands so hard that I would not have been surprised to see the material of my gloves split down all the seams.

I knew Holmes was neither as calm nor as detached as he sounded. Yet it was taking every ounce of my own self-control not to grab him by the shoulders and demand what he was going to do to keep Jack alive.

"Sometime after his transfer to Holloway."

"But that's tomorrow!"

Holmes pursed his lips. "I doubt the attack will come in the first day or two of his residence there. That might look odd, when he would have had so little time to make enemies among the other prisoners. No, I imagine that the attack, when it comes, will happen after he has been at Holloway for at least three or four days. Long enough for them to trump up some fictitious account of his having fallen foul of one of the resident prison toughs."

Three or four days. I stared out the rain-spattered window at an apple vendor in the street outside, and a group of children huddled around a chestnut seller's fire.

"All right." I spoke only when I was certain that I could match Holmes's precise, even tones. "How are we going to get him out of prison before then?"

Holmes did not answer at once.

Until that moment—when I sat with the silence feeling like an actual physical weight in the carriage between us—I had not realized how much I was counting on Holmes to have some miraculous solution. How much I wanted him to proclaim this a knotty little problem, smoke his famous three pipes—and then offer up an answer that would save Jack's life, prove his innocence, and net our German-sympathizing opponents all in one fell swoop.

Stupid.

If I had learned one thing in my life, it was that nothing in this world came freely or without fighting for it. And trying to outmaneuver our enemies was like whacking at a mosquito while blindfolded in the dark. Without knowing more about their organization, we had small chance of success.

"Without wishing to belabor a subject we have already discussed—has it occurred to you that there may be another reason for Constable Kelly's failure to broach with you the subject of marriage or personal attachments? One that may not in fact imply any lack of interest on his part."

"What?" At even the best of times, following Holmes's style of elocution could be tantamount to deciphering the Modern Major General's song in *The Pirates of Penzance.*

Now my thoughts were having trouble in making a jump from prison yards and assassinations to marriage proposals.

"Another reason? What do you mean?"

Holmes gave me an odd glance. "You and Constable Kelly come from vastly different worlds. You grew up in exclusive boarding schools, rubbing shoulders with the daughters of the wealthiest and most elite families in Europe and America. You have performed before royalty, you count the young Rockefeller heir as an admirer—and you have attracted the notice of the Prince Regent himself."

I could not suppress a grimace. "Oh yes, I was *terribly* tempted to become the latest in the long parade of Prince Edward's mistresses. That dissipated, indulgent lifestyle of his—and those rolls of fat around his middle—are so very alluring."

"Be that as it may, Constable Kelly is still a young man from Cheapside without family—living in two-room lodgings on a pound a week. I believe it quite likely that he cannot even—"

He stopped, pursing his lips as though debating whether to say any more.

"Read." I looked down at my own hands, rubbing at a spot of soot that had fallen onto the back of my glove. "I already know that."

Holmes's eyebrows went up. "He told you as much?"

"No."

And I would have bitten out my own tongue before ever bringing the subject up myself.

"I deduced it on my own. He can read—at least a little. Just not well. It's amazing that he can read at all, really, considering that there was no one to teach him anything while he was growing up. His mother abandoned him, and he grew up on the streets with no one." I straightened. "But just because he can't read well doesn't mean that he's dull-witted! He's *very* intelligent and observant and—"

Holmes held up a hand to stop me. "I am not questioning the young man's intellectual abilities—which are quite good, even remarkably so for any member of the police constabulary. I am simply pointing out that although you may not view it in this same light, from Constable Kelly's perspective, a young man such as himself has very little to offer a girl in your position."

I opened my mouth, then closed it again. Was Holmes right? Possibly. But it was hardly the most important issue right now.

"Quite so."

I looked up to find Holmes's keen gray eyes fixed on my face. He nodded, as though he had correctly interpreted exactly what I was thinking—which, knowing him, he probably had.

Holmes rubbed his hands together briskly.

"As I have always said, it is a mistake to allow matters of the heart to cloud one's judgment or obscure one's ability to think clearly. I bring up the issue merely so that, once acknowledged, it can be set aside."

I rubbed my forehead. I wondered whether other girls felt this way in conversing with their own parents: as though they were trying in vain to keep up with a racing steam engine that kept making violently sharp turns.

Holmes leaned forward. "Our focus now must be on saving Constable Kelly's life. Which means apprehending the true perpetrator behind Inspector Mallows's death."

His face was still grim, but I thought there was a faint undercurrent of excitement in his tone. He couldn't help it; he was simply built to relish a challenge.

"In short, Lucy, we have a great deal of work to do."

28. MATTERS EGYPTOLOGICAL

"So, Mr. Holmes is going to the White Hart, to see if he can find anything out about Inspector Mallows?"

Becky took a few little skipping steps to keep up with me, and I tried to slow down my pace to match hers. Though it was difficult.

Three or four days, Holmes had said, that Jack would likely be safe at Holloway Prison.

But what if Holmes was wrong? Uncle John would probably call it rank blasphemy to think so. But even Sherlock Holmes was not entirely infallible.

"Yes. Holmes thought that he would have better luck in questioning the regulars of the White Hart than I would."

I had not argued with him. I might chaff with irritation at the ways of the world—but the fact remained that a young lady could not sashay her way into a low-class public house, announce that she had a few questions, and ask the petty thieves, ladies of the evening, and procurers who frequented the place to please be honest about their answers.

And I—I had my own plans.

"And we're going to The British Museum?" Becky asked, beside me. She skipped again to catch up.

"That's right."

That was what I had proposed as the most promising line of investigation for me to take. Holmes had agreed, and so our plans were formed.

Now, walking through the London streets with Becky beside me, something was nagging at me about my conversation with Holmes. A feeling that there was something in our discussion aboard the hansom cab that I ought to realize … or remember …

I blew out a frustrated breath. It was no use. Whenever I tried to pin the feeling down, it slipped away from me like wet soap in the bathtub.

Becky and I were just turning onto Great Russell Street, and I could already see the museum's stately white-columned edifice up ahead.

Becky tilted her head to look at me. A morning with Uncle John and Prince—both of whom we had left behind in the Baker Street lodgings—had left her considerably more cheerful.

Uncle John was one of the kindest men on earth—and he had such perfect faith in Holmes's abilities that it was difficult not to have some of that confidence rub off when one was in his presence.

"What are we looking for?" Becky asked.

"We've been watching the museum," I said. "Waiting to see whether or not Dr. Everett will surface again with more of his forged donations. There might be something more we can learn about him—or one of his co-conspirators—here. The man who called himself Everett was in and out, talking to museum officials and scholars, ingratiating himself with the guards. Someone might be able to tell us more about him."

Becky looked doubtful.

I did not blame her. This was what gamblers would call a long shot. A *very* long shot. But I did not know what else to do.

"We need a trail of bread crumbs to follow," I said. "Like in the Hansel and Gretel story, remember?"

Becky, wide-eyed, shook her head—and I remembered belatedly that her growing up first in a criminal's den in Liverpool and then in St. Giles probably had not included very many fairy-tales.

"Well, I'll tell it to you sometime, I promise. For now, we're just looking for some clue—a bread crumb—that will give us a starting point to begin our search for Dr. Everett or—"

I broke off abruptly as Becky and I reached the foot of the museum steps.

A sandwich board sign was propped up at the head of the wide stairway, just outside the museum's main entrance.

Tomorrow Night, Annual Guy Fawkes Ball, dinner with dancing to follow.

And below that announcement, in large letters:

Guest of honor Sir Edward Bradford, 1st Baronet, Commissioner of the Metropolitan Police.

I stared at the sign for so long that Becky tugged on my hand.

I shook my head to clear it. "I'm sorry." But instead of going up the museum steps, I turned around—back towards Great Russell Street.

"Where are we going now?" Becky wanted to know.

"A change in plans," I told her. "Instead of starting our investigations at the museum, we are going to the Savoy Theater, to talk to Mr. Harris."

29. WHEELS WITHIN WHEELS

Mr. Charles Harris, our stage manager, did not in the slightest resemble Sherlock Holmes. He was as short as Holmes was tall, and as portly as Holmes was lean.

However, he did share *one* important trait with my father: he was fully capable of carrying on a conversation while attending to at least three other simultaneous tasks—and very often did his most intense listening when his attention seemed to be entirely somewhere else.

Today he was listening to me while at the same time checking the lighting on the stage and also barking orders at a group of new chorus members who had been called in for extra rehearsals to bring them up to performance level on *The Mikado*.

The house lights were extinguished, just as they would be for an actual performance, and the empty rows of velvet-upholstered seats had an almost ghostly look in the dim ambient glow from the lights on stage.

"Small steps, ladies!" Mr. Harris shouted above the noise of some painted scenery being dragged across the stage in the background. "*Small* steps! You're preparing for a royal wedding, not running to fetch your father his nightly beer!"

The chorus girls broke apart, whispering nervously, then reset themselves in their positions for the opening part of the scene.

"Again!" Mr. Harris barked.

Then, proving that against all appearances, he had been listening to me all along, his head swiveled back in my direction.

"No."

My heart plummeted.

Becky was with Louisa Trevelyan and Imogen Styles, two friends of mine from the opera company. Louisa was in the chorus, and Imogen worked for the wardrobe mistress.

They had both gladly offered to give Becky a grand tour of the theater's premises, and Becky had skipped off with them—looking happier than I had seen her since her brother's arrest.

The Savoy was a magical place, with its rows of tiered balconies and plasterwork that looked like the icing on a wedding cake. The backstage areas were darker and more cramped, but no less fascinating, with whole rooms full of scenery and props that would transform the stage area into anything from a castle to fairyland to old Japan.

At the moment, though, the theater's atmospheric beauty was somewhat wasted on me.

"No?" Rash and impetuous I might be—I was sure that Jack would say that I was. And probably Holmes as well. But I was *not* so rash that I wished to talk myself out of my position in the opera company. Still, I couldn't keep from asking, "Why not? If you don't mind my asking. Sir," I added.

Mr. Harris's bushy gray eyebrows quirked up—probably at my having called him 'sir.'

He had acquired the habit—probably from years of trying to get actors to properly project their lines—of speaking habitually as though he were on stage.

I had never met anyone else who rolled his 'r's' in casual conversation.

Now he fixed me with a keen eye—for once giving me his full attention and ignoring the squawks and flutters of two ladies who had just managed to trip over each other out on the stage.

"You are suggesting that the D'Oyly Carte Opera Company ought to volunteer to provide the evening's entertainment at the Guy Fawkes ball, to be held at The British Museum tomorrow night?"

"Yes."

I had—if I did say so myself—made a very convincing case for why we ought to put on a free performance at the ball and banquet. My reasons had included everything from showing our civic appreciation for the museum to the undoubtedly good exposure the opera company would gain with an endorsement from so eminent a person as the Commissioner of Police.

"We cannot volunteer to give a *frrree* performance." Mr. Harris emphasized the word. "For the simple reason that we have already been invited to give a *paid* one. Tomorrow night, a select group of our players will be performing scenes from our most popular operettas—*The Mikado*, of course. But I had also thought to include something from *Iolanthe*. And *The Yeoman of the Guard* might be appropriate, given the audience."

I stared at him, managing at last to snap my mouth closed.

"We have already been invited to perform at the policeman's ball?"

I felt rather as though I had just scaled a rocky cliff face with my bare hands—only to look down the other side and realize that I could just have easily have taken the stairs.

"Quite so. I was going to ask for volunteers to make up the group who will go to The British Museum. Am I to understand that you would like to be included amongst those same volunteers? That works out well, since I believe there was a special request for you to perform."

The shocked feeling inside me consolidated into a solid lump of ice. "They asked for me? By name?"

Mr. Harris, apparently noticing nothing odd, glanced at the players on the stage. "Probably came to the show one night recently and heard you sing. Well, if you're willing to go and perform at the museum, I suppose that girl Louisa can play Pitti-Sing here at the Savoy for the night."

"Yes."

I managed to make my lips form the word.

Mr. Harris would have no difficulty in assembling a troupe of performers to sing at the policeman's ball. At any given time, there were somewhere around five hundred actors and actresses on his books.

I could hear Jack's voice inside my head, making me promise to be careful—but I ignored it.

Walking into a snare with one's eyes open wasn't necessarily the same thing as blundering into one.

I took a breath. "I mean, yes, I am quite willing to do the performance at the museum, and yes, Louisa will be fine singing my part."

"Hasn't your range, but she's decent enough on the whole," Mr. Harris grunted.

I could see his attention beginning to wander to the probably half dozen other places all around the theater that he still needed to visit before tonight's show.

I hurried on quickly, before I could lose him entirely. "If I might ask, who was it who invited us to perform?"

"Eh?" Mr. Harris looked away from the young stagehand who was frantically waving for his attention over in the black-curtained wings. "What's that? Oh, the museum director. Sir Edmund Maunde Thompson."

"The museum director actually *came* here?"

Mr. Harris gave me a startled look, then shook his head. "No, not in person. His secretary. Came to speak with me along with that friend of yours. What's-her-name. The one who's always bobbing up to the front of the stage like some kind of blasted cork." He snapped his fingers. "Mary, that's the one."

"*Mary*? Mary *Mulloy*?"

If Mr. Harris had informed me that Guy Fawkes himself had risen from the dead and made the invitation, I could not have been more surprised.

"That's right." Mr. Harris shrugged. "Well, the fee they were offering was handsome—payment in advance, too. And as you say, the exposure can only boost ticket sales."

I couldn't risk asking Mr. Harris for a detailed description of the museum secretary who had made the invitation. Not without rousing his suspicions.

I watched as Mr. Harris moved on to answer the agitated young stagehand's summons.

I knew what Holmes would say about this development. He was adamant—and eloquent—on the subject of coincidence in criminal investigations.

I was just as disinclined to chalk this latest development up to coincidence, or fate.

A quotation floated through my head, learned during our morning devotionals at boarding school.

Their appearance and their work was as it were a wheel in the middle of a wheel.

In other words, some unseen, unknown force was at work, like a great fat spider sitting in the midst of a web, pulling a string here, a string there.

I did not yet know who the unseen spider was, or exactly what their aim might be, but one thing was clear: they wanted me there at the Policeman's Ball on the following night.

30. Through a Glass, Darkly

Holmes took his steepled fingers away from his upper lip and opened his eyes.

"And this flat mate of yours—Mary Mulloy—she said that it was Sir Edmund's secretary who came to speak with her?"

"Yes. Sir Edmund really is the director of the British Museum—I was able to learn that much. But I haven't yet found out his secretary's name. Though we can make inquiries, of course."

I had just begun to fill Holmes in on today's happenings, keeping my voice low, in consideration of Becky, who was fast asleep in the next room.

I barely remembered a single moment of that night's performance of *The Mikado.*

I had made all my entrances and exits and sung my parts—all completely by rote, the story barely skimming the surface of my mind.

When the show had ended, Becky and I had come back here to Baker Street for the night rather than returning to my flat, much as I would have liked the chance to interrogate Mary.

Becky would be safer here, with both Holmes and Uncle John to keep a guard.

As it was, I had rejected the first three cabs that drew up outside the Savoy in answer to my summons—thoroughly confusing our poor old doorman.

Becky and I had finally climbed into the fourth cab that offered to drive us to Baker Street, and even then, I found myself continually looking back behind us for any signs that we were being pursued.

Rationally, I knew that an attack tonight was unlikely. If I were kidnapped or murdered tonight, I would not be able to perform at the gala tomorrow, which our opponents seemed to want.

However, rational thought was not having much luck with persuading away the cold, prickling feeling of unease that covered my skin.

"The *really* interesting part of the story is that the Commissioner of Police is actually scheduled to—"

"To appear at the Guy Fawkes banquet and ball," Holmes finished for me. "Yes, I know. He plans to make a donation of a rare Indian firangi—"

I was staring at Holmes, open-mouthed—but at that was momentarily diverted. "What on earth is a firangi?"

"The word is derived from the Arabic term *al-faranji*, and describes an Indian sword, typically with a blade imported by the Portuguese. Such weapons typically measure approximately thirty-six inches in the blade, and may be either two-edged or, more commonly, in single-edged, or backsword form. The blade of the firangi also often incorporates a spear-tip shaped point."

I closed my mouth with a click. "Do you know everything?"

"If I were omniscient, I would already have knowledge of both the location and the identities of our German spy ring," Holmes said calmly. "However, given the recent attempt on His Majesty Prince Edward's life, I felt it wise to make note of any forthcoming public appearances of key political figures—of which the commissioner of all of London's police force is certainly one."

"You think that an attempt may be made on his life sometime during the Guy Fawkes ball?"

"I think that if I were an assassin, such an event would offer me a prime opportunity. The security surrounding Commissioner Bradford is likely to be rather more relaxed than it would be at New Scotland Yard—or even his home. If our enemies were to choose a bomb as their means of extermination, there would be the added benefits of striking a blow at the heart of British Identity: The British Museum, home to some of our most prized national treasures. And of course, the terror that would be instilled in the general populace were such an attack to be brought off."

I could not suppress a squeak of protest. "Mr. Holmes!"

"Yes?" He looked at me inquiringly.

"You sound as though you were speculating on whether or not Mrs. Hudson will serve salt codfish for dinner on Friday night."

Holmes grimaced slightly. "*That* is a virtual certainty—not a subject for speculation. And Commissioner Bradford—as well as our majesty's government—do not need me to wring my hands in despair and proclaim how dreadful this situation may become. Our only course lies in remaining calm and attacking the problem with an unbiased, analytic mind."

I could not fault the truth of everything that he said. Although, watching him, I found it difficult to believe that we were related.

I had never in my life managed to remain so coldly analytic about even a stray puppy in the street, much less a possible attack that might claim dozens of innocent lives.

"I'm not entirely sure whether Mary was telling me the full truth or not," I said. "Though from the sound of things, I believe that we are already acquainted with the man who approached her."

"Are we indeed?"

I had cornered Mary in the ladies' dressing room during the intermission of tonight's performance and asked her for the details surrounding the invitation to perform at the Guy Fawkes ball.

Typically, Mary had been far more interested in telling me how one of the other players had stepped on the hem of her gown during the first act—and the *monstrously* unjust criticism that Mr. Harris had leveled at her, when *all* she wanted was to ensure that the audience could see her.

Finally, though, in response to my increasingly blunt demands for information, Mary had tossed her head.

"Really, Lucy, I *don't* see what you're making such a *fuss* about. You're not the only one who has admirers amongst the public, you know. As I was leaving the theater the other night, a gentleman approached me—"

"What kind of a gentleman?" I interrupted. "What did he look like?"

"Oh—young," Mary said. "And ever so handsome. Beautiful golden hair and blue eyes."

I felt a chill slither its way down my spine. That sounded suspiciously familiar.

"He said that he had admired my performance *greatly*," Mary went on. "And he very much wondered that I had not been given one of the *principal* parts, as my talent was so *vastly* superior to the *other* girls."

After which, he would have had Mary eating out of the palm of his hand. He could have asked her to walk barefoot across a bed of hot coals, and she would have done it with a smile.

"He told me that he worked for the director of the British Museum, and that part of his job was planning the ball tomorrow night—"

I interrupted her again. "He told you that he was Sir Edmund Maunde Thompson's secretary? Those were his exact words?"

Mary looked taken aback by my urgency. "Well, he said something *like* that. Really, Lucy, what does it matter?"

She tossed her head again. "At any rate, he said that he would love to have our company perform at the ball, and asked whether I could introduce him to Mr. Harris. So I did," Mary concluded.

Now, as I finished recounting the conversation to Holmes, his lips tightened a fraction.

"Ferrars."

"Yes." Our minds were apparently in complete accord—though in this case, I wished just a little that Holmes could have found some alternate theory.

But it had to have been Ferrars. Mary's description matched too exactly.

I had a sudden memory of Ferrars's hands wrapped around me: his sour breath hot in my face and his teeth bared in a snarl.

I tensed against a shiver. If I shivered, Holmes would know that I was afraid.

Actually, I would give good odds that he already did know.

"Do you think he actually does work for the director of the museum?"

"It is an interesting question. All our enquiries have failed to turn up any direct link from the museum to either of our two known suspects: Dr. Everett or Mr. Ferrars."

"True."

"However, the pseudonymous Mr. Ferrars' involvement in making arrangements for tomorrow's ball would suggest that he has some link to a museum employee, at the very least. A link which said museum employee does not wish to be publicly known."

I rubbed my eyes in the vain hope that some of my weariness would stick to my fingertips and drop away. No such luck; I was still thoroughly exhausted by the past twenty-four hours. It seemed an eternity had passed since visiting Jack this morning in the police station holding cell.

"Oh, good. We have already determined that the spy ring must have agents inside the police force. Now we must also postulate an infiltration of The British Museum."

Sarcasm was as usual wasted on Holmes.

He nodded. "It does seem the most viable theory. Miss Malloy could tell you nothing else about her conversation with the young man?"

"Couldn't—or wouldn't. I am worried about that—worried that Ferrars may have asked something else of Mary. A secret request that she's under oath not to speak about to anyone, something of that kind."

Holmes's chin was sunk on his chest, his eyes fixed on the opposite wall. "It is a possibility, certainly. From what you have said of her, your flat mate is of the precise temperament to be easily manipulated by a charming scoundrel like Ferrars."

"I know. I don't think that Mary can actually be *involved* in the scheme. She'd make very nearly the most unlikely German spy that I can imagine. But—"

"I wouldn't be too sure of that, Lucy, my dear," Uncle John interrupted me. He had been listening quietly from the depths of his favorite armchair, and I had even suspected him of having fallen asleep. "Someone like your Mary Mulloy—angry, discontented, with a chip on their shoulder and a conviction that the world owes them much better treatment than they have been given—those are the very types of people that these criminal organizations and spy rings might recruit. The angry, the disaffected—those who believe themselves justified in any acts of malice or cruelty, because they are only striking back at a cruel world—it seems to me that they would be the most easily persuaded to betray their crown and country."

Both Holmes and I were quiet for a half-second. I could not tell whether Holmes was surprised by Uncle John's speech, but I undoubtedly was.

I seldom saw Uncle John as an expert on human nature, which was perhaps unfair. In his published stories, Uncle John tended to modestly play down his own intellectual abilities, the better to allow Holmes's outstanding intelligence to shine. And in real life, anyone who habitually stood beside Holmes would look a dullard by comparison.

Still, it always came as something of a shock to me to realize that John Watson—for all his goodness and kindness—was also an intelligent, insightful man in his own right.

"Quite so," His eyes were still on the gas jet's shadows that leaped and flickered over the *VR* formed from bullet holes in the wall. "However, whether Mary Mulloy is in any degree a party to our nameless opponents is perhaps of secondary consideration now."

His head lifted, turning at last to look at me. "You are aware, of course, that this could well be a trap."

"Of course." I put my hands together.

I *had* realized it, from the moment Mr. Harris had told me that I had been asked for by name. But still, Holmes's saying it out loud made the possibility strike more sharply home.

I looked across the sitting room at Holmes. "I do not know what to do except to walk into it, though. Even after all our best efforts—even with Mycroft's assistance—we know disturbingly little about our enemies. Now we have the chance to potentially draw them into the open."

"By using you as bait," Uncle John put in. "I have to tell you that I don't like it, Lucy. I don't like it at all."

"That makes two of us." I smiled at him to soften the words. "But we are running short on time. Even if our assumption is correct that an attack on Constable Kelly will not take place until—"

Crash!

The window on the opposite side of the sitting room suddenly exploded inwards in a shower of broken glass, and a dirty white object landed with a thump on the carpet.

I bit my lip, barely managing to keep back a scream. Uncle John leapt to his feet, exclaiming, "God bless my soul!"

Becky—miraculously—must have slept through the crash, because there were no sounds from the next room. Prince, though, came tearing out from the bedroom, his fangs bared, and all the tawny brown fur around his collar standing on end.

Only Holmes seemed unfazed by the interruption. When I looked at him, I realized that he had not even moved from his chair.

"Ah yes." His expression perfectly calm, he eyed the object on the floor—which on closer inspection proved to be a sheet of torn and dirty paper, wrapped around a broken half of a brick. "I believe this must be—"

The door to the sitting room flew open, and Mrs. Hudson appeared, wrapped in a pink silk dressing gown and with her white hair done up in curl papers. Her eyes were wide and staring, and she had clearly run all the way up the stairs. She spoke between gasps for breath.

"Great merciful heavens, Mr. Holmes, what was that noise? Are we to be murdered in our beds?"

"Calm yourself, Mrs. Hudson." Rising smoothly to his feet, Holmes crossed the room to place a calming hand on the landlady's shoulder. "No one is being murdered. The noise you heard was merely the arrival of a communication I have been expecting. There is no cause for alarm. Though now that you are here, it occurs to me that I seem to have missed eating an evening meal. And possibly lunch, as well. Perhaps you would be so good—"

I interrupted him. "You cannot make Mrs. Hudson fetch us food *now*!"

An expression of honest surprise crossed my father's face. However brilliant Holmes's intellect might be, he had no awareness whatsoever that the rest of the world might not conform to his own bizarre schedules—or lack thereof.

"Oh? Why not?"

"Because it is past one o'clock in the morning! If you're hungry, I'll fetch something from the kitchen, but let poor Mrs. Hudson go back to bed."

I jumped up, crossing to give Mrs. Hudson a quick hug. Though I doubt she felt it—or that she had heard more than a word in ten of Holmes's and my exchange.

Her eyes were moving back and forth, from the paper-wrapped brick on the carpet to the shattered window and then back again. Her lips moved, as though shaping silent words, but no sound emerged.

"Mrs. Hudson?" Holmes had evidently realized something amiss, and was now regarding his landlady with an expression of mild alarm.

Mrs. Hudson's throat bobbed, and then she finally managed to speak. "A message you've been *expecting*?" The curl papers around her face quivered. "It would be too much to hope for, I suppose, that your correspondents could be asked to use the common *post*? Or write you a telegram?"

"A thousand pardons, Mrs. Hudson." When it actually occurred to him to pay attention to other peoples' feelings, Holmes could be surprisingly considerate. It was probably the reason that he had not found himself evicted from 221B long ago. "First thing tomorrow morning, I shall send for the glaziers and have the window repaired as good as new. You need do nothing at all. I will—"

"Slice yourself to ribbons trying to clean up that mess," Mrs. Hudson snorted, nodding towards the shower of broken glass on the carpet. "The day I see you've learned to use a dust-pan and broom is the day I start looking for snow in the middle of July."

She seemed somewhat mollified, though. "Ah, well. It could have been worse, I suppose. At least it wasn't a bullet this time, like when that nasty Colonel Moran was after you."

She departed, still muttering under her breath, and a moment later, I heard her footsteps descending the stairs.

"You ought to buy her some flowers," I told Holmes.

"Flowers?" Holmes thoughts were clearly elsewhere, for he looked at me with a blank, startled look. But then he nodded. "Ah, yes. An excellent suggestion. Would two dozen roses be adequate, do you suppose?"

No one could say that Sherlock Holmes was stingy. Eccentric, certainly, but never mean.

"I think Mrs. Hudson would love them. I happen to know that her favorite color is pink."

"Pink roses. Remind me tomorrow, Watson, if you would be so good." Holmes waved a hand. "Now—"

He advanced on the bundle on the floor, gingerly picking it up and unfolding the paper with just the very tips of his fingers.

He examined the brick carefully—probably identifying both the age and the location where the mud that formed it had been dug. But he must have deemed the chunk of rubble of no value, because he let it fall carelessly to the floor a second later, and turned his full attention to the paper.

I came to stand next to him, peering over his shoulder at the straggling words that covered the torn and dirtied scrap. The writing was in pencil, and almost illegible, the letters shaky and ill formed.

But looking more closely, I made them out.

Victoria Embankment. Six o'clock. Come alone.

I looked from the message up to Holmes. "You were expecting this, you said. Do you know who sent it, then?"

Holmes's eyes were still moving rapidly over the message. "I've an inkling, yes."

I waited, but he said nothing more, only continued to stare at the note, his thoughts obviously far away.

I forced myself to hide my impatience, probably without much success. I said, "Whoever composed the note was right-handed. With little education—and I should say a slight tendency to near-sightedness, such that they will either wear glasses or have a squint. The writer is a woman—not old; I should say between the ages of eighteen and thirty-five. She was in considerable emotional distress when she wrote that note. Even as she was writing, she was still trying to make up her mind, debating with herself about whether she really meant to go through with it—look at how hard she's pressed with her pencil there." I pointed to a spot on the second 'a'. "Hard enough that the point snapped off entirely. She was able to keep writing, though—with a different pencil. You can see the quality of the lead has changed. Which leads me to believe that she most likely works in a place where pencils are not difficult to find. A bar maid in a public house, maybe—where she would need to write down drink tallies and things like that? Though I admit that last bit is partially cheating," I felt compelled to add. "Since I already knew that you had been making inquiries at the White Hart this evening."

Holmes's lips quirked up, his lean, hawk-like features breaking into one of his rare smiles. "Cheating or not, your observations are quite good—and quite correct. I believe it is just as you say, that this message comes from the barmaid at the White Hart. I do not know for certain, since barring my order for a half pint, I did not speak with her. But I made it known that anyone coming forward with information to share about Inspector Mallows would be well recompensed for their trouble. And I had the distinct impression that there was something that she wished to say to me—but dared not voice in the presence of so many others. It would have been more desirable had she chosen a more conventional method of communicating, but I expect she did not wish to linger."

Holmes tapped the note with the tip of one long, thin finger, his lips pursed. "The question is, what does she know?"

Alarm prickled across my skin. "You intend to go to the embankment, then? It could be a trap! And it only says six o'clock. Does that mean morning or evening?"

"As to the last, I shall simply have to put in an appearance at both times. If no one is there to meet me this morning, I shall come again at evening. As to the possibility that it could be a trap—" Holmes stopped, looking at me. There was an odd expression in his gray eyes—something in between rueful amusement and resignation. "You will I imagine be familiar with the old country saying, sauce for the goose is sauce for the gander? I am, against all better judgment, resigning myself to your performing at the gala ball tomorrow night. Despite the virtual certainty that our enemies will seize the first available opportunity to attack. However—"

"However, I cannot complain when you run risks in the name of information gathering," I finished for him. "I understand. But I want to come with you."

Holmes eyed me—and then, to my surprise, "Yes, very well."

"Really?"

Uncle John was obviously startled, too. He had been watching us in silence, and now broke in, "I say Holmes, do you think that's wise? I mean, the note says, *come alone*. I was going to offer to go with you, of course—remain somewhere in concealment with my army revolver handy, just in case it is a trap. But Lucy—"

"Lucy is a force to be reckoned with in her own right." Again the wry amusement flickered in Holmes's gaze as he looked at me. "However, our nameless correspondent does not know that. If, as I believe, she is the barmaid at the White Hart, what she will see in Lucy is a girl of approximately her own age, friendly and nonthreatening in her appearance—which may go a long way to making her feel more at ease in approaching. Now."

Holmes broke off, looking from me to Uncle John. "I suggest that both of you ought to get what rest you may. We shall need to leave by five o'clock, and that hour will be here all too soon."

Uncle John stumped wearily off upstairs to find his own bed—but I lingered just for a moment after the sitting room door had shut behind him.

Holmes was filling his pipe with tobacco, looking ready to settle in for one of his famous smoking and thinking sessions that would last the remainder of the night.

"You ought to sleep, too."

Holmes shook out the match he had just lighted from the flames on the hearth and glanced up at me.

"The child Becky and that enormous hound are currently occupying my bedroom."

That was true. I had thought to put Becky to bed downstairs, in my own room. But she had been frightened to stay down there alone, while Holmes, Uncle John and I were talking together up here—so Mrs. Hudson had hastily changed the sheets on Holmes's bed for her.

About half the time, Holmes slept in an armchair or sprawled out on the sofa in any case.

"There's the couch. Or you could go downstairs. There's a spare bed in 221A."

Holmes smiled faintly. "You are quite determined to shape me into some semblance of a normal human being."

His manner was more amused than irritated—but all the same, I stopped short. *Was* that what I was doing?

When I was small, and had no idea of who my parents really were, I used to create fantasies for myself—all built around the basic script of my mother or father or sometimes both sweeping into my boarding school dormitory.

The stories varied: sometimes I was the daughter of an exiled king and queen—though their country of origin was always somewhat hazy in my mind—who had been forced to give me up for my own protection, for fear of nameless assassins.

Other times, I was the natural daughter of an opera singer or a famous actress on the stage. Or the child of a powerful duke or nobleman, whose enemies had stolen me away to be raised in secret.

But the stories always ended in roughly the same way: with my newly-discovered parents clasping me in their arms and declaring their devoted love.

Never once had my child's imagination conjured a man like Sherlock Holmes—who was approximately as likely to clasp me in his arms and call me his beloved daughter as he was to don pink ballet tights and turn pirouettes across the sitting room.

I opened my mouth, but before I could speak, Holmes went on, speaking around the stem of his pipe.

"Tomorrow morning—or I suppose I should properly say this morning—after our appointment on the embankment, I had planned to make a visit to Holloway Prison. I wish to speak with Constable Kelly for myself. I assume that you will wish to accompany me, as well?"

Instantly, all other thoughts fled out of my mind. I was not even tired anymore. "Yes, of course I'll come."

"You might see whether you can assist the child Becky in writing some little note or message for her brother when she wakes. It will give her something concrete to accomplish, and help her to feel that her brother is not lost to her."

I nodded again—startled by Holmes's perceptiveness, as well as his thinking of Becky's feelings. "Yes, I will. If she's not awake by the time we leave for the embankment, maybe we can stop back here on our way to Holloway."

Holmes nodded absently, and I went out, thinking of Becky—and of Jack.

The hot, angry feeling crawled up the back of my throat again when I thought of him being transferred to Holloway. They would probably have his hands manacled together in heavy irons, and make him ride in the back of a police wagon.

I was lying down in bed, trying to will myself into closing my eyes and snatching a few hours of rest—when I realized that if Holmes had intended to distract me, he had completely succeeded.

Regardless of my admonitions, he was probably sitting up right now, smoking his pipe and cogitating on the problems before us, with no intention whatsoever of sleeping tonight.

31. A Reluctant Ally

The Victoria Embankment had—according to my London guidebooks—once been a stretch of mud, ramshackle huts, and tumbled-down wharves. The engineer Sir Joseph Bazalgette had undertaken to improve the area: narrowing the river and creating a river walk that ran from Westminster all the way to Blackfriars.

That made for a total distance of roughly a mile and a quarter—a fact that weariness and distraction had evidently led me to overlook the night before.

Now I shivered in the chill morning mist that drifted off the river, clamping my teeth together to keep them from chattering.

"How are we to know *where* on the Embankment we are to meet her?"

If Holmes had stayed up the whole of last night, he showed no sign of it today.

I had dragged myself out of bed feeling as though my eyes were filled with sand and my head was too heavy for my neck. Holmes looked as fresh and well rested as though he had just spent a relaxing day at the seaside.

He wore his black Inverness coat, a deerstalker cap, and a woolen muffler wrapped around his neck and chin.

He peered along the row of dolphin-columned lampposts that ran along the edge of the river walk. Their golden glow winked out like fireflies in the mist and pre-dawn darkness.

"I should say that we have no other alternative but to begin walking, and hope that our correspondent approaches us."

Despite the early hour, there were already pedestrians, wrapped in cloaks and scarves and hunched against the cold as they hurried on their way.

In the streets behind us, I could see the knockers-up making their way from door to door—rapping at the doors and windows of those who were too poor to afford a clock, but needed some way of waking up in time for their shift at work.

"What does the barmaid from the White Hart look like?" I asked Holmes.

"She has myopic vision, exactly as you surmised last night. She has a habit of biting her fingernails. Also, she possesses a white cat."

"Oh, good. That ought to help."

I had had no time to eat anything before coming out—and already my fingertips were frozen. Though that was nothing compared to the uneasiness that was currently twisting my insides into a cold, painful knot.

Despite the presence of other pedestrians, this lonely river walk felt much too exposed and isolated to be secure—especially when we had no way of knowing who was a friend or foe, or who might even now be spying on us.

I gave Holmes a look. "All I have to do is accost passersby and demand to inspect their fingernails for evidence of biting and the hems of their coats for stray white cat hairs."

As usual, sarcasm bounced off Holmes like dry peas off a shovel. He gave me a serene glance. "She also has a quantity of copper-colored hair and blue eyes."

"Noted."

I glanced behind us to where Uncle John was lingering at a discreet distance. I did feel marginally safer with him here.

Becky was back in Baker Street, with luck still asleep—though if she woke, Mrs. Hudson would be there to look after her.

I straightened up and tried to rub some warmth back into my hands. "All right. Shall we get started?"

Half an hour later, I could see the graceful curves of Blackfriars Bridge up ahead. My fingers felt as though they ought to be turning blue with cold, and I was seriously contemplating the possibility that the note was an elaborate prank.

Then, beside me, Holmes suddenly stiffened—just the barest check of his movements, the slightest intake of his breath—but I still felt a jolt of anticipation.

"What is it?" I lowered my voice, taking care to keep up with our slow and stately progress along the walkway—even though every part of me wanted to stop dead and stare all around.

"Straight ahead. There, to the right."

I turned my head and saw a woman's figure, wrapped in shawls and standing on the edge of the path. Unlike the other pedestrians, she was not hurrying anywhere but was merely standing, staring out at the misty, dark expanse of river.

I curled my fingers into my palms. This girl was our lone potential informant—and I knew that we had to go slowly and carefully, for fear of scaring her off.

But all the same, it took all my self-restraint not to tackle her, seize her by the shoulders, and demand that she tell us everything that she knew.

Holmes—not terribly surprisingly—seemed to have far less trouble in being patient. His expression calm, he strolled forward, coming to a halt about five feet away from the shawl-wrapped girl.

For a second, she was too absorbed in her own thoughts to notice him—but then she gave a gasp and started, whirling to face him.

Holmes held up both hands palms-out in a gesture of peace. "Pray do not distress yourself. We have come at your invitation—but as you see, we have no connection to the police. And you are free to leave at any time."

The girl's face was a pale smudge in the glow cast by the nearest lamp. Though as I moved closer, I could see the coppery curls peeking out from beneath the shawl that covered her head.

Her attention whipped from Holmes to me and back again. Her eyes reminded me of a panicked horse's—darting back and forth, and so wide that I could see the whites. "*We*?" Her voice came out whispery, hoarse.

"May I introduce you to … to Lucy James."

I stepped closer. The girl looked to be about my own age—maybe a year or two younger—with a round, full-cheeked face and a snub nose scattered with freckles. Her eyes were pale blue—and though she still looked nervous, she did seem a little less frightened as her gaze swept over me.

Proof—not that I in fact needed it—of Holmes's abilities to correctly gauge a potential witness.

The girl turned back to Holmes. "You said there was money in it, if anyone could tell you about that policeman?"

"Inspector Mallows, yes. You have some information for us?"

"How *much* money?" The girl's voice sharpened. Then she seemed to recollect herself, because she went on in pious tones. "Not that it's for me. I've got a … a younger sister who's sick. Terrible sick, she is. I need the money to pay the doctor's bills."

Holmes did not bat an eyelash—or question the lie so bald-faced that a child of three could have seen through it.

"This is for you now." He handed across a gold sovereign. "With twice as much more for you if you tell us something of value."

The girl's eyes dropped to the coin in her hand, and I saw her bite her lip.

She was frightened, I realized—badly frightened. She might not actually have a sick younger sister at home, but *something* was preying on her mind.

"You're saying you'll give me two pounds more if I tell you what I know?"

"If the information is useful to us, certainly."

The girl stared down at the gold sovereign and seemed to debate with herself. Her eyes were downcast, but I could still see the greedy, hungry expression on her face.

Holmes's gold sovereign was probably the most money she had ever held at one time in her entire life.

Finally, she exhaled shakily and looked up at Holmes. "All right. I'll tell you. The name's Gl—" she stopped herself.

"I mean, Alice. I'm been barmaid at the White Hart for more than a year."

My skin crawled with impatience. I could not fault the girl for not wanting to tell us her real name. But I did wish that she would get on with it.

"That man—Mallows—he started coming into the pub maybe a month ago."

"He only started coming a month ago? You had never seen him before?"

"Never clapped eyes on him." Alice shook her head. "But he started coming a month ago, same as I said—regular as clockwork, he was. Every night, there he'd be at the bar. Nasty piece of goods he was, too." The edges of her mouth turned down. "I spilled a drop of his drink once, and you'd have thought I'd set him on fire, all the shouting and the cursing he did. *And* he was a mean tipper. Never got so much as a copper out of him, even when everything was just how he liked it. Some of the other girls said he'd tried to get rough with them, too."

I nodded, and Alice's gaze landed on me. "You'd met him?" she asked.

"Only once. But what you say about him does not surprise me at all."

"Well, then." Alice stopped, moistening her lips with the tip of her tongue.

Both Holmes and I waited. From somewhere out on the river, a boat blew its horn.

Finally, Alice said, her voice jerky, "Can I have my money now?"

Holmes's eyebrows rose. "Unfortunately if you expect to be paid in more gold sovereigns, you will have to give us something of more value that the unhappy sergeant's stinginess as a tipper or his propensity for mistreating bar girls."

Alice scowled at him—and for a second, I thought she was going to bolt. Her shoulders tensed, and she darted a look past Holmes, towards the streets beyond the embankment.

I held my breath, wondering whether I would do more harm than good if I tried to persuade her to stay.

Holmes was probably wiser. He did not bother to speak, but casually—almost carelessly—drew out another coin from his pocket, holding it between his forefinger and thumb.

The overhead glow of lamplight caught the sovereign's golden sheen.

Alice licked her lips again. "He played cards."

She spoke the words so quickly that for a second, I was not sure whether I had heard correctly.

"Cards?"

Alice bobbed her head. "Sat with some other regulars and played cards—or dice, sometimes." Her throat contracted visibly as she swallowed. "Thing was, he always won. *Always*. Used to come away from the table with a roll of banknotes that could choke a horse."

Holmes studied her, seeming to consider his next question.

When he said nothing, I asked, "The other men that he gambled with—you said they were regulars? What did they look like?"

Alice gave me a quick, scared look, followed by a shrug. "Just—you know, regular. Ordinary men, nothing special about them."

I opened my mouth, but she hurried on. Her eyes were darting back and forth again, anxious and hunted-looking.

"Right, can I have the money, now? I've got to be getting along."

She practically snatched the coin out of Holmes's hand—nor did she even wait to demand the promised third gold sovereign. Clutching her shawl more tightly around her, she plunged past us, moving back towards Westminster Bridge.

Holmes let her get several steps distant. Then he raised his voice, calling out after her, "*Éire go Brách*!"

At least, that was what it sounded like. I could not remember ever having heard the language or the words before.

The effect on Alice, though, was as if she had been shocked by a jolt of electricity. She whirled around and stared at Holmes, her mouth opening and closing and her hands clasped at her throat.

Then, without another word, she turned and ran blindly away.

I opened my mouth, about to apologize for having frightened her off. But Holmes—evidently reading my intention—spoke first. "It was not your fault. She had merely reached a crisis point in the internal struggle that brought her here: her own greed waging a war against loyalty to whoever it is that she betrayed by speaking with us."

I stared. "You think that she is *part* of this? You honestly think that girl is a German spy?"

Holmes gave me a look that he usually reserved for Uncle John—when he was too slow-witted to reach the same conclusion as Holmes.

"She need not know the whole of the organization's business. But she is linked to it somehow. A lover, perhaps? Or a brother?"

"I suppose." That would explain the girl's nervousness.

"The card games must have been a ruse," I said. "A means of passing extortion payments over to Inspector Mallows. But why go to the trouble? Surely it would have been easier to just hand him the money somewhere in secret?"

"Mallows was a policeman—which means that he had to exercise care. Corruption amongst our police force is all too common. Commissioner Bradford has of late been at some pains to stamp it out. Suddenly betraying evidence of having come into unexpected wealth might have brought Inspector Mallows under uncomfortable scrutiny. He might have been questioned, or followed and spied on—as in fact, he was, by Constable Kelly. The ruse of the card games was a simple yet effective one. If questioned by his superiors, he could truthfully claim that his sudden affluence was a result of being lucky at cards. A slightly unsavory pursuit for a police officer—but one that would have likely earned him no more than a reprimand, followed by an end to uncomfortable questions."

I could see the logic of what Holmes said. "But if they were going to kill him in the end, why bother with paying him at all? According to Alice, he had been coming into the White Hart to play at cards for nearly a month now."

"One might reasonably hypothesize that our unfortunate inspector was in some way making himself useful to the organization, such that they allowed him to remain alive."

"And then his usefulness ran out?"

Holmes made a vague gesture. "Presumably." His eyes were far distant, his thoughts seemingly miles away from the embankment and the wakening city of London all around us.

"What did you say to Alice there at the end?" I asked him. "Ere go—"

I had sung songs in everything from German to Italian to Latin and French. But I tripped over the unaccustomed syllables I had heard Holmes utter.

"Merely verifying a theory. And now, I am afraid that I must leave you—in pursuit of verification of another line of thought."

"But—"

Holmes paid no attention whatsoever to my half-uttered protest. He was already striding rapidly away, following the same direction that Alice had taken.

"Meet me at Holloway Prison at ten o'clock," he called back over his shoulder. "But if I am not there, do not wait. I shall leave word at the guard house that you are to be admitted to see Constable Kelly."

"Wait!" I called after him.

Holmes did not turn this time—only raised his hand in a wave and strode off, with the deceptively casual gate of his that could cover ground far more quickly than a run.

I bit my lip in frustration. Short of tearing after my father, tackling him, wrestling him to the ground and demanding that he answer my questions—an admittedly tempting prospect—there was nothing to do but let him go.

Though as I watched his tall figure disappear around a bend in the river, the folds of his cloak flapping about his legs, it occurred to me that by the time this case was over, I might have a whole new sense of sympathy for how Uncle John must have felt all these years.

32. Ireland Forever

"Mary, what does—"

I broke off speaking abruptly as I entered the front door of the flat and realized that Mary was not alone.

Not only was she not alone, she was with a young *man*. They were sitting in the flat's outer room, Mary on the sofa and the young man on a nearby chair. Their heads were together, and they had plainly been deep in conversation until I interrupted.

"Oh, I'm sorry. I—" I was not usually so tongue-tied.

In all the time Mary had shared the flat with me, I had never known her to bring a friend home. Certainly not a sweetheart.

Beyond deploring the bad manners and poor acting of the young men in the opera company, I had never seen her express interest in *any* member of the opposite sex.

Though on second glance, I had to revise my initial impression: her current caller could not be a sweetheart after all.

The man jumped to his feet, turning to face me, and I saw he was wearing the white collar and the long black cassock of a Catholic priest.

"You must be Miss James."

He was somewhere around thirty, or a year or two more, with a similar coloring to Mary's: black hair and blue eyes. He had a deep voice, with an Irish accent that was stronger than Mary's. "I have heard so much about you that I feel as though we are acquainted already. But of course we have never met. Let me introduce myself. I am Keenan Mulloy. Mary's brother."

I stared at him—even more astonished. He did *look* like Mary. Even without him saying anything, I would have guessed at some family relationship between them. But sister and brother?

I had never heard Mary mention any siblings.

"Mary never told me—" I began.

Mary interrupted, jumping up off the sofa and crossing to stand beside Keenan. "I never told her that you were coming today. Of course, I didn't know it myself."

Mary's voice was hard, clipped-sounding, and she looked upset—even for someone whose habitual expression was one of vexed discontent. Her lips were pinched tight, and bright spots of color burned in both her cheeks.

"Unfortunately, Keenan has to be *going* now." She landed even harder than usual on the emphasized word.

Keenan's face was not angry, like Mary's. His expression was more pained as he turned to his sister. "Mary, I must—"

Mary did not let him finish. "I have to go, Keenan. I'll be late for the theater. And anyway, you've already said what you came here to say."

I had the impression that if they had been alone, Keenan might have argued. I actually opened my mouth, about to offer to leave and give them privacy to finish whatever talk I had interrupted.

But before I could, Keenan bowed his head. "I shall pray for you, Mary."

His voice was soft. Then, without another word, he moved to the door.

He stopped, though, with one hand on the doorknob. His fingers tightened, as though he were struggling with himself, or debating. Then he swung back around—to me, though, not to his sister.

"I beg your pardon, Miss James."

I almost drew back at the look in Keenan's intense gaze. His eyes were hollow and bitter, completely devoid of the peace one usually associates with a man of the cloth.

"I hope that you will not think me forward in asking. But you occasionally stay elsewhere, with relatives, do you not?"

I had not told Mary of my connection to Sherlock Holmes—but I had to offer her some explanation for where I slept on the nights when I did not come back to the Exeter Street flat.

"Yes, that's right." I had no idea why Keenan Mulloy should care where I slept.

"An admirable idea. To spend time with your family, that is. Family"—his gaze flicked briefly to his sister, the edges of his mouth twisting—"family is all any of us have in this sad world of ours."

The door closed behind him, and neither Mary nor I spoke for what felt like quite a length of time. The awkwardness of the silence was almost enough to make me forget the reason I had come back to the flat in the first place.

Finally, I said, "I'm sorry to have interrupted—"

My words collided in mid-air with Mary's as she began, "Keenan—"

We both stopped short, and I gestured for Mary to keep going.

Her eyes were on the area rug on the floor, her hands knotted in a fold of her skirt. "I was just going to say that Keenan came over to discuss some family business. He says—that is, he doesn't like my being on the stage. That's why I've never talked about him before."

Mary finally dragged her gaze up to meet mine. "You know how priests are—well, maybe you don't." Mary sped up, the words coming more and more rapidly now that she'd begun. "But where I come from, theater is the work of the devil, and if you're an actress on the stage, you're thought to be no better than a common *doxy*. Keenan thinks that I'm shaming our *family* by singing in operettas. He's always after me to leave the whole business behind and come and keep house for him. *He* thinks I should spend my time embroidering altar cloths for the church and bringing soup to a lot of cripples and *invalids*."

Her voice twisted scornfully on the last word.

"I'm sorry." I was not sure what else I ought to say.

To me, Keenan Mulloy had not seemed like the sort of man to consider his sister a harlot for entertaining on the stage. But that particular attitude certainly was not unheard of.

Since Roman times, actresses had been branded as one of the less respectable professions.

"Families can be difficult."

I had a sudden memory of Holmes striding off and leaving me with absolutely no idea of where he was going or what his next step in our investigations was going to be.

"I know." Mary's voice broke with emotion. But then she shook her head and asked, "What was it you were saying, just when you came in? Was it something about the show for tonight?"

"Oh—no, nothing like that."

After Holmes had abandoned me on the Embankment, I had been left at something of a loose end. Uncle John—having lost sight of Holmes, too—had approached me and asked whether I wished to return to 221B.

But I told him that no, I would go back to Exeter Street. I had two reasons for being here: the first was that I wanted to question Mary further about the man who had arranged our performance at tonight's gala. The second reason had to do with the strange words that Holmes had called out to Alice at the last.

"Do you know what"—I tried to remember the exact syllables that Holmes had used—"what *Éire go Brách* means?" I asked Mary.

In thinking about it further, I had realized that the words sounded as though they might—possibly—be Gaelic. Or Irish, as I supposed it was properly called.

Now the effect on Mary was every bit as dramatic as the effect on Alice had been. Her eyes flared wide, her face went white to the lips—and then she lunged forward, seizing hold of my wrist.

"What do you know?" Her voice was a whispered hiss. "What have you heard? Were you *eavesdropping* on Keenan and me?"

Her fingers bit painfully into my skin, and the look in her eyes was almost wild. For a half-second, I was too shocked to move—then I clamped firmly down on a flicker of fear.

Harriet, my last close friend, had turned out to be a German spy. I tried not to think about her often—and I usually even succeeded. I was also trying my hardest not to let her betrayal color my view of human nature. Just because Harriet had proved a traitor did not necessarily mean that Mary was hiding anything catastrophic or criminal.

She was hiding *something*, though.

I said, slowly, "I wasn't eavesdropping. I have no idea what you and Keenan said to one another, except for what I heard when I came in through the door."

I met Mary's gaze, ignoring the pain where her fingernails were digging in. "If you let go of me, I'll explain."

Mary did not move. I was not even sure whether she had heard a word that I said.

I kept my voice calm. "If you *don't* let go, you're not going to like me very much."

Mary was not un-athletic, exactly. But I had been learning the finer points of combat since I was a schoolgirl in braided pigtails.

That—finally—seemed to register. With a gulp and a shuddering rush of breath, Mary finally let go—though her hands remained clenched at her sides. Her whole body was rigid with what looked like barely-contained panic.

"That's better." I nodded. "Those words were just something I happened to hear someone say in the street." That much was true. "It sounded like Irish—so I thought I would ask you what they meant."

"Where in the street?" Mary's eyes narrowed.

"The Embankment."

I had learned a long time ago that when lying, it was important to tell the truth as much as possible. The principle had saved me from getting into trouble with our school headmistress dozens of times.

Mary gave me a hard look as though trying to decide whether she believed me or not. But then, finally, she relaxed a little, seeming to take me at my word.

"Oh. I'm sorry if I hurt you." She gave me a weak smile. "It's just those words—*Éire go Brách*—they're a ... a kind of slogan. A motto for ... some dangerous people. It doesn't do to be saying them out loud."

At least three-dozen questions crowded into my mind all at once—but I said nothing.

That was *not* one of my own personal principles. I was not particularly good at silent waiting. But I had learned through observing Holmes that sometimes saying nothing at all was the most effective interrogation technique.

The other person, uncomfortable with silence, would feel compelled to fill in the void.

In this case, Mary seemed to struggle for a moment, but then went on, "There's some that are fighting for independent rule for Ireland. Some that think the English have stolen the food from our mouths and killed our children and taken our lands—and it's time we threw them out of the country that's rightfully ours, not theirs. Keenan and I were just talking about it because we know—*knew*—someone who ... someone who felt that way."

Her voice wavered, her hands tightening into fists all over again.

"I'm sorry," I said quietly. My classes at school had not included very extensive information on the history of English rule in Ireland. But I did know enough to be certain that what Mary said was true. "I'm not Irish, but I grew up in America—where they were willing to fight a war to win their freedom. So I understand a little."

"Yes, well, maybe it's time for another war." Mary's eyes kindled briefly. But then she stopped and looked away. "Not that it's any of *my* fight. It's not like I'm a Fenian. It's just that you won't find many born in Ireland who welcome English rule."

"Fenian?"

Mary only shook her head, though, looking scared all over again. "Best not to say that out loud, either. I shouldn't have said it myself. That's the kind of thing that can get you killed back home where I'm from. My brother—"

She stopped abruptly and did not go on.

"Keenan?"

"No. My other—" her voice cut off again, her chin bobbing up and down as though she was fighting tears. The undercurrent of pain or sorrow that I always sensed in her was so much nearer to the surface, now—naked and raw. Even her voice was different; the Irish accent more plain, the notes of complaint and affectation completely gone.

"I'm sorry," I said again. Impulsively, I touched her hand. "I'm sorry for whoever you lost, or for whatever happened to hurt you."

Mary's hand was rigid under mine, like a block of wood. But finally she jerked her head, blinking rapidly.

"I'd better be getting down to the Savoy," she said. "I promised I'd help with packing some of the costumes for tonight."

"One other thing." I hated to ask Mary anything more, but I had to know. "I wanted to ask whether there was anything else you could tell me about the man from the British Museum who spoke to you the other night."

"What? Oh." Mary's eyes widened again, but then she stopped, giving me an odd look. "What do you mean?"

I was sorry for Mary. But I also wasn't being as successful as I'd like in suppressing the memory of Harriet. If Mary was involved in something criminal—or even shady—I needed to know.

"I just wondered whether he might have said anything else?"

"I—" Mary stopped speaking and stared at me intently, a look I could not at all read in her pale blue eyes.

When she went on, it was all in a rush—the words spoken so quickly that they almost ran together. "It was nothing important—not really. But he said that if I was one of the players chosen to perform, that I"—Mary's throat bobbed as she swallowed—"what he said to me was, *You might not wish to stay till the final dance of the ball.*"

33. Holloway

I stared up at the crenelated roofline of Holloway Prison, counting the chimes of a nearby church clock.

It played the twelve notes that signaled the third quarter of the hour.

Fifteen minutes left until ten, and there was still no sign of Holmes.

Beside me, Becky tugged on my hand. "Should we just go in?"

I had debated with myself about bringing her. But when I returned to Baker Street to ask for any messages she might wish me to bring to her brother, she had begged me to let her come along.

Seeing her small, teary-eyed face and tense shoulders—braced in anticipation of my refusal—I had not had the heart to say no.

What if something happened to Jack? What if Holmes couldn't save him?

I was trying hard to trample on that thought whenever it reared its ugly head. But I could not quite stamp it out.

If the worst did happen, Becky needed this chance to see her brother—

I stopped myself before I could add, *one last time.* She deserved the chance to see Jack, that was all.

Now I hesitated, debating. Holmes had told me ten o'clock; Becky and I were early. But on the other hand, he had said to go in without him if I did not appear—

"No." I shook my head before I could give way to the impulse to march straight up to the prison's main gates. "We need to wait until ten—just in case Holmes comes."

He had another fifteen minutes—and however much my nerves were twitching with the urgent need to make sure that Jack had survived his transfer to Holloway, I would wait.

Holmes had also said that he would leave word at the gatehouse to ensure that I would be admitted. But he would have said nothing, of course, about Becky, since he hadn't known she would be with me.

Becky's odds of getting in to see her brother would be much greater if Holmes himself were here.

Becky's shoulders slumped a little, but she nodded. Her small, freckled face was set with an almost adult look of weary endurance.

I felt a renewed flicker of anger. Whoever was behind her brother's arrest had a great deal to answer for.

Pedestrians passed by us on either side: corn chandlers with their seedbags, and dustmen with their fan-tail hats and wicker baskets—as well as men and women who walked with slow, plodding steps in the direction of the gaol. They must have friends or family inside, and be here to visit.

As the traffic rumbled past, and Becky held tight to my hand, I silently replayed Mary's final words to me.

You might not wish to stay till the final dance of the ball.

What did that mean?

I knew what it sounded as though it *might* mean. It sounded as though something were scheduled to happen at the ball. Something dangerous—something that Ferrars had felt obliged to warn Mary away from, for her own safety.

Although that was where my suppositions broke down.

Frances Ferrars—or whatever his real name was—had struck me as a young man utterly without conscience, the kind of man who would dig the gold fillings out of his dead grandmother's teeth for the sake of a few shillings.

However I looked at it, I could not imagine him caring enough about Mary one way or the other to bother with warning her away from potential danger.

But then why else had he said it?

I pushed a loosened tendril of hair back beneath the brim of my hat. The few hours of sleep I had managed to snatch last night had done little to banish my fatigue.

Maybe Ferrars had hidden depths of compassion.

Though that left me with the uncomfortable awareness that something was indeed going to happen at tonight's Guy Fawkes ball.

A bomb?

Another death-ray?

The most recent investigation I had shared with Holmes and Uncle John made either of those possibilities all too real.

Another chime of the church clock made me jump, snapping off my train of thought. Ten o'clock. Ten o'clock, and Holmes *still* was not here.

Becky's hand tightened around mine. She said nothing, but she tilted her head to look up at me with a look of entreaty.

"Yes, we'll go in now."

We had waited long enough. I had no idea what Holmes was planning, but whatever it was would have to happen with myself and Becky already inside the prison.

* * *

As it turned out, the guard on duty barely glanced at Becky. He was a middle-aged, stolid man, with a square-jawed face and a soldier's bearing—and apparently Holmes really had prepared a way for our arrival here, because once I had given my name, he merely grunted, "Follow me."

The guard led the way through a seemingly endless procession of narrow hallways, and past a countless number of locked and barred gates.

If I had had any thought of enabling Jack to escape from Holloway, that idea died as we made our way deeper into the heart of the gaol. Each gate had its own lock, its own key, and its own separate guard. Even if you somehow managed to get past one, the guard at the next gate would catch you before you made it anywhere within sight of the outside world.

I shivered.

Holloway was not as terrible as I had been imagining. The air was chilly, but not dank, and the glimpses I had into cells as we passed showed them small and Spartan, but clean. What troubled me more was the claustrophobia of the place: the sense of being buried alive, trapped inside these massive stone walls.

"Women's wing," the guard grunted over his shoulder.

He jerked his head to the right, and I glimpsed through another gateway a room where maybe two dozen women were seated on cots and stools, most engaged in sewing or knitting.

"Juvenile offenders through there." The guard nodded towards another gated doorway—but this one led only to a bend in the passage, so that I could not see through into the juvenile offenders' wing.

"What will happen to them?" I asked.

The guard shrugged. "Depends what sentence they get from the judge. Most that come here are waiting to be tried in court."

Like Jack.

Becky must have had the same thought. She clung a little more tightly onto my hand, but kept her head up, her posture defiant rather than afraid.

Finally, the guard drew up in front of yet another gate, this one fitted with a kind of iron grill on the top half. Maybe five or six feet away, I could see a second gate, with another grill—and through *that* gate, I could see an open air, square-shaped courtyard.

Men were milling around the yard, walking or talking together or slouching against the walls.

"That's where the prisoners take their daily exercise," the guard said. "Stay here, and I'll get Kelly to come and talk to you."

"Talk to us? Here?"

I looked at the arrangement of the two gates and pictured calling out a conversation across the distance between them.

The guard looked mildly apologetic. "Stops any visitors from trying to pass things to the prisoners. Wait here."

He departed, vanishing through a locked door at the side of the passage, and I squeezed Becky's hand.

She was on tiptoe, peering through the gateway and into the open prison yard. "Can you see him?"

I had been trying to pick Jack out from the crowds of prisoners, but without any success so far. I shook my head. "No, I—"

I stopped as a uniformed guard strolled across the courtyard. Not the same guard who had led us here; this man was taller and thinner. His face was shadowed by the brim of his cap, and he carried a heavy wooden truncheon in his hand.

He walked over to a group of prisoners standing against the far wall of the courtyard, said something—and then one of the prisoners at the back detached himself from the main group and started towards us.

My breath caught, and Becky let go of my hand to stand on her toes, pressing herself up against the iron grill.

"Jack! It's Jack!"

My heart sped up. Becky was right. I recognized Jack's dark hair and tall, broad-shouldered form as he came towards us.

Becky bounced on her toes. "Jack!"

He must have heard his sister's voice, because he stopped walking, and I saw a frown cross his face as he looked towards our gateway.

Until this second, it had not occurred to me that Jack might not want Becky to see him this way. I would have to—

Another prisoner came racing towards Jack across the pavement.

Jack's head snapped up, as though sensing a threat even before the second man reached him. But it was too late; everything happened so fast that Jack had no time to react, much less fight back.

I saw the glitter of a blade—a knife or some other sharp weapon in the second prisoner's hand. He thrust savagely at Jack's heart—

And the rest I seemed to see in disjointed fragments, time bending and slowing down like the images in a fun house mirror.

Jack's blank, astonished face.

Jack's body, pitching forwards, crumpling to the ground.

The uniformed guard sprinting towards him—

Becky's scream of horror snapped me back into the present moment, time resuming its normal course with a sickening lurch.

I leapt forwards, wrapping my arms around Becky and trying to make her turn away—but she shook me off furiously.

"It's Jack! Jack!" She was screaming and crying, throwing herself forwards against the metal grill.

Chaos had broken out inside the yard, and I could no longer see where Jack had fallen. More uniformed guards had come—blowing shrill whistles and shouting for the prisoners to line up, stay back.

The prisoners were paying no attention. Some were running towards the spot where Jack had fallen. Others were brawling, throwing punches and cursing each other as they spat and rolled on the ground, the violence erupting shockingly fast.

Finally, straining to see past the kicking, roiling bodies, I caught a glimpse of just the toe of a boot.

Jack was not moving.

I hugged Becky more tightly. My heart beat sickeningly hard, and my chest squeezed so tightly that I could not seem to draw in enough air.

I realized that my lips were unconsciously shaping a word.

Please. Please. Please.

The word seemed to hammer through me like a second pulse.

The fighting ended almost as suddenly as it had begun. The guards waded into the chaos, hauling the brawlers apart, wielding their truncheons with brutal efficiency.

It could not have been more than a minute before the prisoners were lined up in a sullen, straggling row and being herded out through a gate at the back of the courtyard.

All except for one last remaining form still lying on the ground and shrouded in a blanket that one of the guards must have brought.

I could not see his face. But it didn't matter.

I squeezed my eyes shut. I had been here before: frozen in the moment when all you desperately want is to be able to rewind time—or to wake up out of the nightmare into which you've been plunged.

But there *is* no going back, and no waking up, either.

Becky had stopped screaming and started to cry—wracking, uncontrollable sobs that shook her whole body.

I hugged her against me, even as I clutched at the wave of anger that hissed and sizzled through my veins.

Any second now, I would feel pain. I could feel it rolling towards me like a boulder. But as long as I could stay angry, I could hold off the grief and loss a few seconds more.

If the man who had stabbed Jack had appeared before me right now, I would have shot him dead without a second's remorse.

I strained to look for him among the crowds, but could not see him. Not that I had gotten a good enough look at him to really be sure of what he looked like.

Maybe the guards had already dragged him away.

More guards appeared, carrying a stretcher between them, which they set down on the ground next to Jack.

I struggled against the wish that I could hide my eyes like Becky, or look away.

I knew I was probably being unfair, but I was furious with Holmes, too—for letting me think that Jack was not in imminent danger, and for failing to save him.

The guards—showing far more efficiency than feeling—briskly dumped Jack's body onto the stretcher. The blanket slipped a little, giving me a glimpse of one of Jack's strong, calloused hands—hanging limp, now.

My eyes burned, pressure building and building inside my chest.

Most of all, I was angry with *myself*. I was angry with myself for bringing Becky here. I was angry with myself for not doing anything—for just standing here, frozen, while Jack—

One of the guards—the tall one, the one who had summoned Jack in the first place—suddenly turned towards Becky's and my gate.

I froze.

No. Not possible.

Shock was making me hallucinate, desperately searching for a reason to hope.

But then the tall guard raised his hand. His gaze was still fixed on Becky and me as he pushed back the brim of his hat just slightly.

I bit back a gasp, the hope I had been trying to suppress bounding to life inside my chest.

The other guards hefted the stretcher up between them, one at the front, and one behind.

"No! Jack!" With a fresh sob, Becky flung herself out of my arms, pounding on the metal gate with both fists.

I shook off the moment's paralysis, moving quickly to crouch down in front of her.

"Becky, listen to me. It's all right. It's going to be all right."

Tears were streaming down Becky's face as out in the yard the guards carried the stretcher away.

"It's *not* all right!" Becky's voice was so choked with sobs the words were scarcely intelligible. Her hands were scratched from where she had pounded on the iron grating. "How can you say that? How—"

I took hold of her shoulders. "Becky, listen to me. You trust me, don't you? And you trust Mr. Holmes? Remember all the stories you've read about him? He always wins in the end—*always*."

I strongly suspected that Uncle John wrote through an idealized lens on some of the cases he recorded—but Becky did not need to hear that right now.

Becky stopped fighting to get free of me and stared, still choking back sobs. "What—"

I lowered my voice to a near-soundless whisper.

"I can't say any more here." I had no idea whether any of the prison guards were eavesdropping on us at the moment—but it seemed a virtual certainty that they could be. They would not allow prisoners to speak with visitors in complete privacy.

"But you need to trust Mr. Holmes now. Trust *me*, when I say that it's going to be all right."

Becky was too intelligent to miss what I was saying. I saw the sudden hope kindle in her tear-filled eyes, and took her hand. "Let's go, now."

I spoke out loud, adding for the benefit of anyone who might be listening, "There's nothing for us to do here."

Becky nodded, taking tight hold of the hand that I offered her. Her face was completely transformed—turned from anguished to radiant in the space of a breath.

I would have to tell her to keep her head down on our way out of the prison, lest she give this entire charade away.

If it *was* a charade.

Looking down at Becky's teary gaze and tremulous smile, I mentally resolved that if my father had just been instrumental in giving this child false hope, I might just murder him myself.

34. Resurrection

"Lucy, my dear." Uncle John's voice was commendably patient. "You are going to wear a permanent track in the floor if you go on pacing in that way."

"I know." I paused in the midst of what was very likely my seven-hundredth circuit of the Baker Street sitting room, forcing myself to drop into a chair before I could reach my ultimate goal of the window.

My self-restraint did not last long. Within barely a second of sitting down, my skin was crawling with the need for movement again.

"I can't help it, Uncle John."

I gave in and jumped back up again, crossing to the window in a few quick steps. "Don't you think that he ought to be back by now?"

After leaving Holloway Prison, Becky and I had hired a hansom cab and come straight back to Baker Street. I did not know where else to go.

Now Becky was showing far more patience—and trust in Holmes—than I was managing at the moment.

She was sitting on the hearth at the other side of the room, occupied with feeding Prince some of Mrs. Hudson's buttered muffins.

Prince would very carefully and deliberately take each muffin—and then inhale them whole, as though weeks had passed since he had last been fed.

Becky looked almost carefree, giggling at him.

I looked quickly away, my heart clenching as I peered out into street below.

I knew what I saw. What I *thought* I saw. But now, as each second dripped tortuously by, I could feel cold doubt creeping in. What if I was wrong? Maybe my mind really had been playing tricks, or—

A step sounded on the stairs: a heavy, masculine tread that definitely was not Mrs. Hudson's.

I jumped, and Becky sprang instantly to her feet, proving that she was not as distracted or carefree as she had appeared.

There were two sets of feet coming up the stairs, I realized.

My heart pounded. I *wanted* to cross the room and fling the door open—but somehow, I could not make myself move. I stood frozen, as though my feet had suddenly grown roots and anchored me to the ground.

Finally, the latch clicked and—

"*Jack*!" Becky launched herself at the figure in the doorway, throwing herself headlong into his arms.

Jack caught her—and the stabbing ache in my chest reminded me that I had not taken a breath in what must have been close to a minute.

"Jack! Jack!" Becky was laughing and crying, both at the same time. "You're *alive*!"

Prince, joining in on the excitement, bounded forward to leap up and try to plant his massive paws on Jack's chest.

"Down, boy." Laughing, Jack held Prince off, hugging his sister closely. "Of course I'm alive. I promised you I'd never leave you on your own, didn't I?"

Becky said nothing, burying her face against Jack's shoulder. Her small arms were wrapped tight around his neck as though she never meant to let go.

Over the top of Becky's blond head, Jack's dark eyes finally met mine. "Hello there, Trouble."

I realized that without being aware of it, I had taken several steps towards the doorway—as though I were going to embrace Jack, too.

But I caught myself. We were not on those terms.

Although if I had had any doubts about my own feelings for Jack Kelly, those doubts would have vanished the second he walked through the door.

I summoned up a smile. "You look quite healthy, for a man who's supposed to be newly deceased."

Becky raised her head at that. "How, Jack? How did you manage it? Lucy said that you were only fooling. But what about the guards—and that man who stabbed you and everything?"

"You'd better ask Mr. Holmes about that." Jack glanced over his shoulder, and I realized that Holmes had entered the room behind him.

I was so preoccupied with Jack that I had not even seen him before now.

Jack shifted Becky's weight in his arms. "He appeared out of nowhere—dressed as a prison guard—and said that one of the other prisoners was going to pretend to stab me, and I had to fake being dead. That it was the only way of getting me out of prison and saving my life."

Holmes's jawline still bristled with trace wisps of the mutton-chop whiskers he had worn as a prison guard. "Constable Kelly cooperated admirably, obeying my instructions without question."

Holmes gray-eyed gaze held a rare look of approbation. "Another man in your position might well have given the whole game away by arguing or asking for further explanation."

Jack's eyes met mine again. "He said that you and he were convinced there was a plot to kill me."

I swallowed. This all still felt almost too good to believe, as though Jack might vanish in a puff of smoke at any minute.

Uncle John seemed to have no such concerns. Of course, he had years of experience with these surprises of Holmes's.

He beamed paternally on Becky and Jack. "But you must sit down and take some refreshment after your ordeal. Mrs. Hudson has already provided us with a tea tray, but I am sure that she can be prevailed on to bring an extra two cups, and perhaps some sandwiches?"

There was a flurry of activity as Uncle John ushered both Jack and Becky to the couch, where they settled with Becky sitting curled up on Jack's lap.

At eight, she was almost too big to fit there comfortably—but for today, I doubted that she cared.

I edged nearer to Holmes, lowering my voice.

"You could have told me." I tried—not very hard, but I did try—to keep the note of accusation out of my tone.

"I could have. However, I judged it important that your reaction to Constable Kelly's death should be authentic, thus lending credibility to the pretense of his demise."

I opened my mouth, but Holmes went on.

"You are about to say that it was cruel to enact the performance in front of young Miss Kelly." His gaze landed on Becky. "But may I remind you that it was hardly my idea to bring an eight-year-old child to a prison this morning."

"True."

"Knowing that she was there, I deemed it best to go ahead with the plan regardless. The danger to Constable Kelly's life would only grow more acute as time passed, and all the pieces of the ruse were already set into motion. I did take pains to alleviate the child's distress as soon as possible."

He had. Holmes had not been obliged to reveal himself to me, in his guise of a prison guard.

"Thank you. I still don't understand how you managed it, though. How did you get inside the prison, much less succeed in impersonating one of the guards?"

"That was the least difficult part of the scheme." Holmes sketched a careless gesture with one hand. "I have a contact amongst the guards—a young man whose life I had once saved when he had fallen foul of a nasty group of cut-throats. He was perfectly willing to smuggle me into the prison by way of the coal service delivery—and happy to lend me his spare uniform, as well."

"But the prisoner—the one who stabbed Jack? Pretended to stab him."

I could not help a glance over to the couch where Jack sat. He was not at all wounded that I could see.

"Also an acquaintance of mine. An elderly safecracker who goes by the name of Bones amongst his various criminal contacts. He was readily persuaded to lend his assistance in exchange for a promise that I would serve as a character witness when his case comes to trial. He understands that my endorsement is conditional on him keeping silence about today's work. I am confident that he will not say anything to give us away."

"But won't this … Bones … get into trouble? He just killed a fellow prisoner! Or at least everyone must suppose that he did."

"My contact amongst the guards has ensured that Bones is now locked securely in a solitary confinement cell, where he will be perfectly safe for the next day or at the very most two, until we can secure his release. We cannot hope to maintain our deception any longer than that. The morgatory arrangements at Holloway are somewhat lax, but eventually someone in authority will go to look for Constable Kelly's body. At which point they will discover that said body is nowhere to be found."

"Of course." A chill ran though me as I realized how very little time that gave us. "We have a day—possibly two—then, to prove Jack's innocence?"

Holmes looked far less daunted than I felt. "That seems an accurate assessment."

Jack was eating a muffin with one hand, Becky still perched on his knee. I thought he looked tired, but he was smiling, answering some question that Uncle John had asked him.

"Have you any idea where to begin?"

"I believe that your instincts were quite correct. We must return to the place where this entire affair began: The British Museum."

"Oh!" A jolt of remembrance went thought me. "I haven't had a chance yet to tell you what Mary said to me this morning."

I repeated as well as I could remember my conversation with Mary, and Ferrars's warning about not staying for the final dance.

Holmes's brows drew together. "An odd warning for him to give her. It seems entirely out of character that the man you encountered should be troubled by an attack of conscience in regards to the life of a girl he had never met before a day or two ago."

"I know. I had the same thought." I could not at all imagine Ferrars walking across the street to save Mary Mulloy's life, much less caring whether she died in a planned attack on the Guy Fawkes ball. "Do you think he gave her the warning, knowing that she would sooner or later repeat it to me? It could be a false lead, making us think that the attack will happen late in the evening, when in reality, it's planned for earlier on?"

Holmes steepled his fingers. "It is possible."

"Do you think we ought to speak with whatever museum officials are organizing the ball? Give them a warning that there may be trouble?"

Holmes considered, his brows drawn and his gray eyes focused on some spot on the rug. "I do not believe that would be productive, no. Remember that we are unfortunately operating in large part in the dark, without any certainty as to whom we can trust. Issue our warning to the wrong person—or to someone who may inform the wrong person—and we shall have tipped our hand, alerting the enemy to the fact that we suspect their plans. I believe that our better option is to remain silent in hopes that we may draw our suspected spy ring out into the open."

"But all of those people who will be at the ball. Innocent bystanders could be killed."

Holmes's face was grave. Not unsympathetic, but with a stern look to his gaze.

"One of the most difficult aspects of this profession—as you will yourself discover should you continue to pursue it—is the frequency with which we are forced to play God."

He did not say so aloud, but I knew what he was thinking—that my taking part in his detective work had been all my own idea. Holmes would gladly have kept me out of it, if he could.

Before I could do more than feel the weight of that settle over me like a heavy cloak, Holmes kept going.

"I am sensible of the responsibility we bear to protect those innocent lives. But I also have great confidence, not just in my own abilities, but rather in *our* combined ones."

He did not smile—and yet his expression altered, softening in some indefinable way. "I believe I may say without vanity that the guests at tonight's Guy Fawkes ball could not be in more capable hands."

35. GUNPOWDER, TREASON, AND PLOT

"What can you tell us about Commissioner Bradford?" Holmes asked.

Jack considered, frowning.

He, Holmes, and I were gathered in a recessed alcove of the Vase Room at The British Museum.

The gala event itself was being held close by in the Refreshment Room—but the various exhibits of the museum had also been thrown open to the attending guests, who milled around, exclaiming over Egyptian scarabs and sarcophagi and marveling over sections of Greek marble friezes.

The Vase Room, however, with its rather dull array of terracotta pots, was attracting very little notice—making it the perfect place for us to meet without attracting attention.

"I don't know him personally," Jack said. "The Commissioner's way over the head of an ordinary detective constable. But I've heard he's a former military man. Served in India.

That's where he lost his arm. They say he was mauled by a tiger. Beyond that?" Jack shrugged. "He's respected. Well liked."

"Do you think it likely he could be induced to turn traitor?"

Holmes and Jack were both dressed as members of the wait staff, in white jackets and waistcoats. Both of them carried silver trays of champagne flutes. Holmes had set his down shamelessly on the top rim of a large Etruscan pot, while Jack's tray rested on the floor.

"I wouldn't want to think so."

Jack was not supposed to be here at all. Holmes had tried to insist that he remain safely behind in Baker Street, since he was after all supposed to be dead.

Jack, though, had been respectfully but grimly determined to come, and had refused to so much as consider the possibility that he should stay behind.

I had to credit his strength of purpose. Few managed to override Sherlock Holmes—but Jack had managed it without ever once raising his voice or uttering a combative word.

As a compromise, he had been outfitted by Holmes with a black beard that altered his appearance quite a bit.

Becky had giggled uncontrollably at the sight of him, until Jack picked her up and turned her upside down in his arms—which made her laugh even harder.

She was not entirely happy about her brother's having come out to the museum tonight. But she had agreed to stay back in Baker Street with Uncle John and Prince—and she hadn't seemed frightened about saying goodbye.

Maybe she wasn't aware of the possible dangers. Or maybe—since Holmes had already brought her brother back from the dead—she simply trusted him to manage anything up to and including miracles.

"I met the commissioner once," Jack went on. "He came to the station house and talked with everyone—shook all our hands. He's the first commissioner to have done that. He's pushed for more education among the officers, too."

Like Jack, Holmes was disguised—in a truly appalling ginger wig that looked rather as though a longhaired cat had perched on his head. He had also acquired an indolent slouch and a hunched posture that he maintained even here, with only Jack and me.

As always, I was struck by Holmes's genius at immersing himself in the roles that he played.

"We will put Commissioner Bradford down as a remote possibility for our role of traitor—but not likely. I believe it is far more likely that—as Lucy and I surmised earlier—he is a target in tonight's affair rather than a culprit."

"The Commissioner and Lucy," Jack put in. "We know whoever's behind this wanted her here."

"We do." Holmes fixed Jack with a stern eye. "And I am counting on you to ensure that our enemies do not succeed in inflicting whatever harm they have planned for her."

"Yes, sir."

I felt my grasp on my temper slip a little. "Would the two of you like to pound your chests and roar like gorillas? First of all, I am standing right here with you—there is no need to talk about me as though I were nowhere in the room. And in the second place, I can look after myself. I have done so for quite some time."

I had witnessed Jack stepping in front of a bullet for me once before. I was not at *all* anxious to repeat the experience.

Holmes looked perfectly sanguine, despite my outburst. "While I despise aphorisms in the general sense, there is a saying about two heads being better than one that I believe applies here. I believe that Lucy will be safe in your presence."

Holmes was lucky that I was already dressed in Pitti-Sing's kimono and did not wish to get the costume spattered with blood—otherwise, I might have thrown a punch at him.

What had gotten into him? He was not usually so heavy-handed or so protective.

Jack only smiled, though, a flash of white in the dark beard. "I reckon Lucy will be safe here in her own presence, sir. I'm just here for backup."

Holmes was apparently satisfied. "And now I must depart to circulate more amongst the guests."

Holmes had postulated that the guise of waiter would allow both him and Jack to move virtually unnoticed amidst the crowds, eavesdropping as they chose.

Hardly anyone bothers to stop what they are saying just because a waiter has appeared to offer them champagne.

"I have learned one significant fact. Commissioner Bradford will make a formal speech and presentation of the firangi sword to the museum towards the end of the evening. Just before the final dance."

The final dance. My annoyance with Holmes evaporated as the words hammered home.

"Then that must be—"

"It would be an opportune time to arrange for an assassination attempt, yes—whether that attempt involves a rifle bullet or some sort of explosive device. Do you know where you are expected to be during the Commissioner's speech?"

"I'm supposed to meet with Mr. Harris—and the rest of the performers—in just a few minutes so that he can give us our final instructions."

"Then unless circumstances alter greatly, our original arrangement holds."

In talking the matter over back in Baker Street, we had reached a balance, of sorts, between protecting the lives of the ball attendees here and drawing our enemies out into the open.

If we had not discovered the source of the danger by midnight, Holmes would approach Commissioner Bradford and tell him the whole, asking that the ball guests be evacuated for their own safety.

"The man whom Lucy knew as Frances Ferrars has already appeared once in this affair. It is possible that he may be present tonight, also." He glanced at Jack. "You would recognize him, if you saw him again?"

"I'd know him."

"The individual who until recently was passing himself off as Dr. Everett may also be involved. Constable Kelly and I are at somewhat of a disadvantage, never having met the man. However, Lucy has furnished us with an adequate description that should enable us to spot him, should he appear."

At the thought of Dr. Everett, an involuntary shiver prickled through me.

Ferrars was a bully and a coward—as so many bullies are—with a cruel streak to compensate for his innate lack of intelligence.

I did not doubt for a moment that he would relish the chance to make life thoroughly unpleasant for me if ever I had the misfortune to fall into his power again.

But Ferrars was nothing compared to Dr. William Everett.

I had a knife-edged memory of Dr. Everett's long, cheese-white fingers and his jolly, good-humored voice that was like a wrapping of beautiful paper around a parcel of rotting meat.

I had met with few truly evil men in my life—but I had known enough to recognize when I found one, and Dr. Everett struck me as evil, through and through.

"Or the agents tonight may be a person or persons entirely unknown to us," Holmes finished.

Jack was frowning. "As I understand it, you don't want the small fish at the bottom of this whole operation so much as you want the man—or woman—at the top. The one giving orders."

"Quite so. Thus far, we have only the vaguest knowledge of the individual who sits at the center of this ring of spies, pulling strings like a great spider adjusting the strands of his web." Holmes's expression was thoughtful. "It puts me in mind of another criminal mastermind with whom I have tangled."

"You don't think—"

"No, I do not suppose that Professor Moriarty has managed to resurrect himself from the dead in order to head a ring of German spies. I was merely reflecting on the similarities in criminal organization.

"To summarize, then: we may assume with virtual certainty that an attack is planned for tonight, likely directed against Commissioner Bradford, but possibly targeting Lucy as well. We may recognize the conspirators or they may be unknown quantities—which makes it all the more imperative that we keep alert and on guard throughout. Lucy will of course be most vulnerable, since her role as performer necessitates standing immobile on the stage area."

I had to bite my tongue to stop myself thanking Holmes so very much for having pointed that out.

I had not been unduly afraid until this moment. I think I had been pushing the personal component of tonight's threat out of my mind.

But now my whole body flashed hot and then cold again at the thought of doing exactly what Holmes had said: standing up on stage and singing the dainty and innocent lyrics of "Three Little Maids from School"—all the while just waiting for an assassin's bullet or bomb to end my performance with the proverbial *bang*.

I could not even muster up a smile over my own thoroughly terrible pun.

"I believe this goes without saying, but I shall say it none the less," Holmes finished. His gaze rested on mine, steady beneath his wig's absurd ginger fringe. "Be careful."

"And you."

"I shall return to the main reception room first." Holmes reached to retrieve his tray of champagne glasses from the Etruscan vase. "Wait five minutes before following, so that anyone watching will not automatically assume that we have been conversing out here."

Holmes slouched his way out, dropping effortlessly into his character's languid, indolent shuffle.

Watching him, it struck me for the first time that maybe my own love of acting and the theater actually came to me through my father.

"Lucy—"

I swung around. This was actually the first moment that Jack and I had had alone together since his escape from prison.

Back in Baker Street, we had been too busy theorizing and making plans with Uncle John and Holmes—and then, too, Becky had not wanted to leave his side.

"I'm so sorry that I brought Becky to Holloway this morning!" I interrupted whatever Jack had been about to say in a rush. "She was desperate to come and see you—and of course, I had no idea of what Holmes was planning. But I realize that you have every right to be angry with me for bringing her, all the same. A prison is no place for an eight-year-old girl—which I only realized once we were actually there. I'm afraid I'm still working at controlling my habit of acting first and thinking later."

"You don't say." Jack's stern face relaxed in a brief smile. "But it's all right about Becky. I know my sister. If you'd refused to bring her along, she'd only have climbed out of the window and tried to follow on her own—and got into who knows what trouble on the way."

That was unquestionably what I would have done in Becky's place at her age—and hearing Jack say it made me feel slightly less guilty.

I smiled. "Becky was right. That beard does make you look exactly like a pirate."

Jack laughed. "I'm pretty sure you're not allowed to make fun of a man who could be hauled back to prison at any moment. It's in the rulebook somewhere."

Actually, I had not intended it as a criticism. The beard made Jack look handsomer than ever, accentuating the lean, strong lines of his face and the graceful curve of his mouth.

And I clearly needed to stop, because I was beginning to sound just like one of the Twenty Lovesick Maidens in *Patience*.

"You're not going to be hauled back to prison!"

Though even as I said it, I was acutely aware that it wasn't a promise I could truthfully make.

Jack shrugged. "We've got a long way to go before I can even think about saying I'm out of the woods."

"You say that as though that means it can't be done."

Some of the grimness ebbed from Jack's expression. "You never give up, do you?"

"Never." I smiled faintly as I tilted my head to look up at him. "Impulsiveness and stubbornness—another two of my besetting sins."

Jack's smile faded. "Look. Tonight—your father's not wrong. It's going to be dangerous."

"Don't tell me that you're about to start lecturing me, too."

"No lectures. I just wanted to say that I'll be right there if you need me. Even if you can't see me, I'll be there."

There was only one thing that I could say to that. "Thank you."

"Thank *you*."

"For what? Holmes was the one who got you out of Holloway, not me."

And as Jack had just pointed out, smuggling him out of prison was a long way from declaring him actually vindicated and free.

"I know—and I told him thanks already." Jack's coffee-dark eyes were steady. "But while I was sitting in prison, I realized I needed to say something to you. Though I wasn't sure I'd ever get the chance."

My heart sped up as I waited, all the breath going out of me as though a vise had clamped around my ribs and squeezed.

"Thank you," Jack said. "For believing in me—for never thinking I was guilty."

"Oh." As declarations of undying passion went, *thank you for believing in me* was somewhat lacking.

I *would* have felt a wave of disappointment. Except that something in Jack's voice made me aware of how close we were standing. Close enough that I could see the tiny points of his eyelashes, the flecks of gold around the irises of his eyes.

I felt blood spilling up into my cheeks, and opened my mouth—but no words emerged.

Apparently I was no better at heartfelt declarations. Maybe it was not only acting abilities that I got from Holmes.

But only yesterday, when Jack was in prison, I had been kicking myself for not being able to tell him how I felt. Like Jack, I had thought I might never get the chance.

I swallowed. "You believed in me, when you first met me," I said. "And I'm sure I was a much more hopeless case than you. I couldn't even remember my own name."

Jack's hand moved, almost as though he were going to reach for me. "Lucy—"

"Lucy!"

The second voice to speak my name was considerably shriller and less warm than Jack's had been.

Jack and I leapt apart, and I spun to see Mary advancing on our alcove, the skirts of her kimono flapping about her ankles.

"Lucy, *there* you are! Mr. Harris sent me to find you. He wants you back in the reception room *at once*."

I felt my chest constrict for an entirely different reason as Mary's gaze fell on Jack. She, after all, had seen him in our flat, when he brought Becky for singing lessons. If anyone at tonight's gala were likely to recognize him, it would be Mary.

She barely glanced at him, though.

Jack had instantly and deftly retrieved his tray from the floor, snapping into a respectful, blank-faced waiter's pose. And Mary was simply not to the sort of girl to look twice at a member of the serving staff.

"Hurry." She tried to thread her arm through mine, pulling me back towards the reception room. "You *know* what Mr. Harris will say if we're late."

I did—only too well. Still, glancing back over my shoulder at Jack, I was tempted to pull away from Mary's grasp.

I *would* have done, but I could not think of a convincing excuse. Even Mary was unlikely to believe a vague murmur about a dropped handkerchief.

"I was looking *everywhere* for you." Mary's voice was naturally on the shrill side, and as she went on, I did not doubt that Jack overheard every word. "Why on *earth* were you wasting time speaking to one of the *waiters*? There are simply *throngs* of eligible men here—and Mr. Harris has given us permission to dance, in between our performances, if we are *asked*."

It would appear strange to turn and look back over my shoulder again—so with a herculean effort, I kept my gaze fixed straight ahead.

Inwardly, though, I ground my teeth at Mary's interruption. Just when Jack was about to say—what?

I still did not know what he might have said.

He could have been about to ask whether I knew the time. Or whether I could tell him how to get to the gallery of Grecian urns.

"Is that why you're here? For the sake of the eligible young men?"

The look on Mary's face was—almost—enough to make me feel guilty for asking the question. Something hard, bleak and bitter crossed her gaze.

"Don't be ridiculous. I was only telling you what Mr. Harris said. Come along." She tugged harder on my arm. "I'm going to be stuck right in the back of the chorus—as *usual*—unless we hurry."

"Mary?"

As we reached the entrance to the crowded reception room, I paused. The noise and the heat of hundreds of guests crammed into a single space washed over me.

"What is it?"

I hesitated, wondering whether I ought to remind her of Ferrars's warning that she might not wish to stay for the final dance. But either we would uncover the spy ring's plot—in which case Mary would be safe. Or else we might fail, in which case Mary would be evacuated along with all the other guests.

"Nothing."

Stepping forward, I moved towards the front of the room, where Mr. Harris waited on a small wooden stage.

36. THE PLAY'S THE THING

For that evening's performance in the reception room I had even less attention to spare for my parts than I had at the Savoy the night before.

We began with several songs from *The Mikado*, then moved on to *Patience* and finally to *The Gondoliers* while supper was being served. I sang the part of Pitti-Sing in "Three Little Maids," took part in a duet of "Prithee, Pretty Maiden"—and all the while felt as though my chest had been painted with the kind of giant bulls-eye target you would find on an archery range.

During the break in the performance I also had cause to silently curse Mr. Harris for ever saying that we were allowed to accept invitations to dance.

In theory, it should have given me a good excuse for circulating amongst the guests and trying to spot any familiar faces. Actually, it *did* give me the opportunity. It was just that I saw precisely no trace of either Ferrars, Dr. Everett, or anyone else that I recognized, and I overheard not a single helpfully whispered conversation about where a bomb had been planted or a sniper's rifle set up.

In fact, nothing whatsoever happened, except that I was besieged with requests to dance from both young men and men old enough to be my grandfather.

The after supper set of dances saw me fending off the advances of a black-mustached Frenchman who kept ogling me through his monocle and complimenting me on the color of my eyes.

They are so very green, chère mademoiselle. They make me think of the dewy green grass on a halcyon summer's day. Of priceless emeralds. Of the clear sea, near my home in—

I was tempted to let him keep going—mostly out of morbid curiosity to see whether he would eventually run out of extravagant compliments. But his breath was atrocious, he kept stepping on my feet—and I was horribly aware of the hour having just struck eleven o'clock.

One hour left. One *hour* until we evacuated the museum and gave up hope of proving Jack's innocence—or until violence struck, and an attempt was made on the police commissioner's life.

"Excuse me, *monsieur*." I curtsied briefly. "This has been delightful, but I am afraid that I must go to—"

My mind drew a blank, so I murmured something unintelligible and turned away.

The orchestra was playing loudly enough that it would be difficult for him to hear me in any case.

I edged my way around the ballroom, avoiding stately society matrons and slightly tipsy gentlemen who looked as though they might ask me for a dance.

Under any other circumstances, I might actually have enjoyed an evening such as this one. The chandeliers glowed with light, and the music sparkled; the ensemble played waltzes and schottisches, polkas and quadrilles. On the dance floor, men in black evening wear and ladies in jewel-bright ball gowns spun and twirled in time to the melodies.

I scanned the crowd, searching for Jack's dark head or Holmes's ginger wig. But I could find neither. I had seen them periodically throughout the evening, but somehow or other during my interlude with the amorous Frenchman, I had lost sight of both of them.

I had yet to see Commissioner Bradford, either, or to be introduced to him—but I assumed that he must be here. To the right of the stage area where the other players and I had been singing, there was a wooden podium, draped in red, blue, and white ribbons.

Presumably before the end of the evening, the commissioner would stand on that podium and give a speech in which he presented his antique sword to the museum.

I closed my eyes, willing away the traces of a headache that was beginning to beat at my temples. I devoutly hoped that Holmes and Jack were having better luck than I was.

As I opened my eyes again, a flicker of movement caught my eye in the doorway to one of the adjoining galleries—which was odd. Now that the dancing had begun, ball guests had stopped milling around the museum and congregated here.

I turned, in time to see a head of black hair and a white waiter's jacket vanishing into the shadows beyond the ballroom.

Jack? I only had time for a glimpse, but it looked like him.

I stood on tiptoe, trying to get a broad overview of the crowd and see whether I could spy Jack anywhere else in the room. I *did* spot Holmes this time—he was all the way over on the other side of the reception room, serving champagne to a very stout woman whose gown was encrusted with so many pearls and crystals that she looked rather as though she had been doused in glue and then rolled through a trough of gems.

More importantly, Holmes was too far away for me to signal or attract his attention. Crossing to him would involve circling the entire dance floor—which would take too much time. Already the man who might have been Jack was entirely out of sight.

I hesitated for another long moment. I was due to sing again in fifteen minutes. Mr. Harris would doubtless burst a blood vessel if I were not back by then.

But Jack had promised that he would be with me one way or another, throughout the whole course of the evening. If he had left to go into some other part of the museum, he must have had a good reason for it.

My pulse quickened, beating all the way out to the tips of my fingers as I moved swiftly to the gallery entrance where the male figure had vanished.

I hesitated in the doorway, peering into the gloom within. The museum lights had been turned down—probably when the ball had begun—and the gallery was in shadow.

Display cases loomed up, black in the darkness. Huge statues lined the walls like some sort of demonic stone army.

I stood uncertainly, unsure of which way I ought to go—then realized that a doorway at the far end of the gallery was partly ajar.

Nothing ventured, nothing gained.

Holmes would probably despise that aphorism, too.

I had been singing the part of Patience most recently, and still wore my dairy-maid's apron and ruffled muslin gown.

I gathered up my skirt in one hand and moved swiftly down the gallery, trying to step as softly as I could.

When I reached the door at the opposite end of the room, I pulled it open, and found that it led to a flight of steps that went downwards.

At a guess, this was a set of stairs leading down to the basement storage areas, where artifacts and antiquities not on display in the galleries were stored.

I swallowed. Despite what I had told Jack, I was trying very hard *not* to simply follow my impulses tonight. The stakes were too high for me to make any errors through lack of care.

I had also been down in the museum basement before. That particular adventure had ended in a confrontation from which I had barely escaped alive.

I was carrying my evening bag—the small purse I used to hold my gloves and other odds and ends. I edged my way onto the top stair and then turned, using the bag to wedge open the door so that it would not swing shut behind me.

The stairwell was entirely dark. I had to proceed through touch alone, keeping one hand on the wall to guide me. Though after I had gone perhaps ten or fifteen steps, I realized that there was a faint glow of light coming from down below.

I quickened my pace, emerging into one of the storage areas I remembered from my last visit to the museum's basement floor: row upon row of wooden and metal shelves, all stacked with crates, boxes, and baskets—some labeled, others simply crammed in and caked with what looked like years' worth of dust.

A dark-haired man in a white waiter's coat was just disappearing down the end of one of the aisles.

"Jack?" I kept my voice low—too low, apparently, for him to hear me, because he didn't turn or come back into view.

I ignored the creeping, crawling sensation across the back of my neck.

The first time I had sung before an audience, I had been terrified before the performance—so petrified that I had nearly been unable to make myself walk out onto the stage.

My head was crowded with all the possible disasters that might occur, all the ways that the performance might go wrong.

Maybe it is simply human nature to fear the unknown.

However, in this case, I knew exactly where I was: in a dusty, crowded storage area beneath The British Museum.

I knew exactly what awaited me here, too. Jack was—must be—somewhere up ahead.

I tried to breathe from the bottom of my lungs, the way I had been trained to when I sang. I always found that it calmed me. Although tonight, it was helping less than usual with slowing my galloping heart.

I slid my hand into the pocket of my skirt, tightening my fingers into a fist—then before I could change my mind, sped down the long aisle of shelves, turned right—

And came face to face with Frances Ferrars, holding a gun.

37. TRAPPED

I stood motionless, afraid even to draw breath as I stared at the barrel of the gun.

Ferrars's thin lips curved in a smile. "I knew you'd follow me down here."

His voice was the one I remembered: slightly high for a man, and—since he was not bothering to be charming—with cockney undertones.

"Your father's not the only one who can put on a wig."

A jolt of shock went through me, moving inch by inch down my spine.

Ferrars was still wearing the white waiter's uniform jacket—and the head of dark hair that had made him look like Jack from behind. Though as he spoke, he pulled the wig off, letting it fall carelessly to the ground.

His own golden-fair curls sprang out, released from their confinement—and I studied his face.

Jack was handsome, with carved, masculine features and a hard, sometimes dangerous edge.

Ferrars, on the other hand, was beautiful. There was no other word. His eyes were large and blue, his features so finely drawn that they might almost have belonged to a lady. At first glance, at least, he looked like a painting of a Botticelli angel.

It was only on second glance that one noticed the shallowness in his blue gaze—the spoiled, petulant set to his mouth.

I moistened my lips. "Very well. You have gotten me down here—I assume for some purpose. What do you want?"

A flicker of something like disappointment crossed Ferrars's gaze. He would probably have enjoyed this far more if I had swooned in proper maidenly fashion, or at the very least shrieked.

But he recovered, gesturing with the gun.

"Turn around."

"So that you can shoot me in the back? I don't think so. I would much prefer that if you are going to kill me, you do it face to face."

Ferrars's mouth twisted. "I'm not going to kill you, you stupid cow. Not yet, anyway. I want you to turn around and *walk*."

There was a tightly strung edge to his voice. His brow was beaded with sweat, and his jaw was clenched so hard that I could see a muscle ticking in one cheek.

There was a limit to how far I could push him before he snapped.

I held up my hands in a pacifying gesture and turned around. "All right."

"Now go straight ahead."

On edge or not, he had enough sense not to come close enough to jab the barrel of the pistol against my spine. If he had, I might have tried to get the gun away from him.

The gun might not have been physically touching me, but I could still *feel* it, like a weight pressing coldly between my shoulder blades.

"Move!" Ferrars snapped.

I quickened my pace, walking past rows of pottery jars and baskets filled with what looked like chips of white marble. My mind was racing, rifling through my available options. But as far as I could see, I had only one truly viable one: to stay quiet, do as Ferrars asked, and wait for any chance that might come my way.

"That door," Ferrars said behind me. "Open it."

We had come to a plain metal door, set in the wall at the end of the aisle. A brass key was in the lock. My skin prickled at sight of how closely the metal panel fitted its frame. The room inside must be nearly soundproof.

I pulled on the handle and the door swung silently open. The hinges had been oiled so as to make no sound.

Light spilled out from a camping lantern hung on a hook on the far wall. The rest of the room was small, windowless, and extremely dirty.

And sitting slumped against the wall, with his hands bound behind him, sat Jack.

His head had fallen forward onto his chest, so that for one horrible moment, I thought that he might be unconscious—or worse.

But then his head lifted at the sound of my footstep in the doorway. His dark eyes met mine.

"Hello, Trouble."

His words came out slightly blurred. His lower lip was bloodied, as though he'd been struck in the jaw.

I dug my nails hard into my palms, and mentally added another item to the already lengthy list of reasons I had to dislike Frances Ferrars.

"Are you all right?"

Jack shrugged—as well as he could, with his arms immobilized behind him. "Might be tempted to stab myself, out of boredom. But otherwise I'm fine."

"Get in!" Ferrars shoved me forwards into the room—though when I recovered my balance, he was still in the doorway. Still too far out of my reach to safely try for the gun.

"Back"—he gestured with the pistol. "Get back against that wall. And don't try anything," he added, narrowing his eyes.

I would not have credited Ferrars with remotely acute powers of observation, but right now it was as though he was reading my mind.

"Or I'll shoot yer pet bluebottle over there in the gut." He waved the gun in Jack's direction. "I saw a man shot there, once." Ferrars's lips pulled in a thoroughly unpleasant smile. "Took him a whole week to die."

"What is it you want?" I tried to keep my voice calm, steady, as I moved to do as Ferrars had ordered—standing over against the left hand wall of the narrow little room, the one opposite Jack.

Now that I had more time to observe, I could see that the room seemed to be a supply room of some kind, or maybe a disused janitor's closet.

A bundle of mops and brooms stood propped up in one corner, and an assortment of pails and buckets lay in a haphazard pile next to me.

It looked as though the janitor had once been in the habit of making tea here, too. There was a low wooden counter that ran along part of the wall above Jack's head, with a rusty-looking gas ring, a battered tin kettle, and a biscuit tin that, to judge by the droppings around it, had clearly provided meals for several happy mice.

Only when I was standing safely against the wall, several feet away from the doorway, did Ferrars edge his way into the room.

I had grappled hand-to-hand with him once before, and succeeded in not only escaping from him, but also knocking him to the ground.

In a way, it was gratifying that he had gained enough respect for my abilities to be so careful. But it also left me with a disturbingly narrow window of opportunity—particularly with Jack here, bound and immobile.

How quickly could Ferrars get off a shot in Jack's direction? Too fast. Too fast for me to risk it.

"All right." Ferrars's voice was still tense. But his gun hand was absolutely steady as he kept the barrel of the pistol aimed at me. "I'll tell you what's going to happen next."

I risked just a quick glance across at Jack—but then kept my expression neutral, my gaze fixed on Ferrars's face.

"This"—with a flourish, Ferrars stepped aside, revealing a black box with a plunger on top. Wires traveled from it upwards into a vent in the ceiling—"is the detonator for a bomb."

I held myself tight in check to keep from recoiling. Not that I had anywhere to go, with my back pressed up against the mortared wall. "A bomb?"

"That's right. You press that there"—Ferrars waved a hand at the plunger—"And then—bang!"

His lips curved again in a smile of genuine pleasure that almost made me shiver.

I risked another quick glance at Jack. But even if his hands were free, he was too far away to safely make a grab for Ferrars's gun.

Jack was watching Ferrars with a completely flat expression, his jaw set.

"Whom are you planning to blow up?" I asked. Ferrars laughed—a sound like knives scraping across rock. "Not me, luv. You."

I felt my eyebrows rocket up. "Me?"

"Yeah, that's right." Ferrars's gun hand still remained perfectly steady.

Drat.

"You're going to blow up the police commissioner for us." He seemed slightly less nervous, now. Calm enough that I could safely push him for more information?

It did not matter what I thought—I had to risk it. I needed time, above anything else. Time to gain myself and Jack an opportunity to escape. Time for a miracle to occur.

I swallowed against the dryness in my mouth. "Why would you want to blow up Commissioner Bradford? He seems like a good man."

"A *good man*?" Ferrars's face twisted in an ugly sneer as he mocked my tone. "He's a pig. A filthy pig sitting on top of a whole *sty* of pigs."

On the last word, he hauled back, driving a hard kick into Jack's outstretched leg.

Jack grunted, but made no other sound. I bit my tongue and tasted blood.

I needed time. But not if it came at the cost of getting Jack's bones broken.

"I've just been upstairs. There aren't any wires connecting to a bomb in the ballroom." Holmes, in his guise of waiter, had made a search of the room.

Ferrars frowned.

That's right. Look at me. Pay attention to me. Definitely don't bother with looking at Jack.

"'Course there ain't. The wires down here are just for show," Ferrars said. "Once the bomb goes off upstairs, everything'll be blown to smithereens. No one'll be able to tell that the detonator down here wasn't connected."

My heart dropped. There went any hope I had of getting past Ferrars and yanking out the wires.

"Why bother with the arrangement down here, then?"

"Because, like I said, you're going to blow up the police commissioner for us. Or that's how it's going to look." Ferrars laughed gratingly again. "I'm just waiting for the bomb upstairs to blow. Then I'll shoot the both of you. He's already wanted for murder of the fat inspector." He jerked his head in Jack's direction. "It'll look like he shot you, set off the bomb, then killed himself."

My heart pounded. "How long?"

Ferrars shrugged. "Ten minutes."

Ten minutes. Ten minutes until Jack was as good as dead—we were *both* as good as dead—and countless people upstairs died.

I widened my eyes, trying to look both shocked and frightened. Which was unfortunately all too easy. "Do you mean to say that it was *you* who killed Inspector Mallows?"

I held my breath as I waited for Ferrars's reply. *Come along, take the bait. Don't pass up this opportunity to crow about how clever you are.*

Every second that passed brought us nearer to the bomb exploding. But I also needed to buy us time.

Ferrars's chest swelled. "That's right. The fat slob had it coming. Thought he could blackmail us, didn't he?"

"Blackmail?"

I was hoping that Ferrars might give away what, exactly, Inspector Mallows had known that had got him killed.

But Ferrars went on as though he had not heard me, his eyes darkening with memory, his lips curving in a small, eerie smile. "I got him when he was on his way home. Never even heard me coming."

He was describing a murder—the end of a fellow human being's *life.* True, Inspector Mallows had not been a very likable man or a good one. But my stomach still clenched.

"How did you get Jack's truncheon?" I asked. "And his fingerprints on it?"

"That part was easy. We just asked—" Ferrars broke off, a suddenly cagey look flashing across his face. "Never mind. You're talking too much!" His voice rose and he took a menacing step towards me. "I didn't bring you down here so that you could jabber the night away. I brought you here so that you could do as you're told!"

Moistening my lips, I looked over Ferrars's shoulder. His step towards me had brought him in front of Jack.

I smiled a bright, apologetic smile. "I'm afraid that there is just one crucial problem with your plans."

"What?" Ferrars's face darkened, the beginnings of a snarl trembling on his upper lip. "What the 'ell are you talking about?"

He was on the verge of snapping; pushing him any farther would be taking a risk.

A coward with a gun in his hands is often more dangerous than a brave man. I had heard Uncle John say that once. *The coward wants above all else to prove to you—and himself—that he is not afraid.*

"There's something that you don't yet know."

"What?" Ferrars was still angry—but puzzled. Clearly the script for this conversation had gone differently inside his own mind. Probably his version had included me dissolving into a weeping puddle of fear by now.

In a single smooth motion, I brought out the Ladysmith pistol that I had carried all night in the pocket of whatever costume I happened to wear.

"I'm an actress." I aimed the pistol at Ferrars's heart. "I'm trained to notice the way that people move—the way that they walk. You can put on a wig and a waiter's jacket, but you still move nothing at all like Jack does. I knew the entire time that I was following you down here that it was a trap."

For a brief second, Ferrars looked as though I had smacked him across the face with a dead fish. Then his expression darkened with fury, and he made a brief, convulsive movement as though to spring for me.

"I wouldn't do that if I were you." I flicked the safety off the pistol with my thumb. "In addition to being an actress, I am an excellent shot. You may also have a gun, but the safety catch on yours is still on."

Ferrars's lips drew back. "You think I'm afraid? You'd need more than a little pea-shooter to do any real damage."

That unfortunately was all too true. The small, pearl-handled Ladysmith I carried was the only weapon that I could reasonably conceal while wearing a theatrical costume. A great heavy gun like Uncle John's army revolver, for example, would create something of a stir if it tumbled out onto the stage during one of my songs.

But the Ladysmith's bullets were small enough caliber that a single shot very likely would not incapacitate.

Unless I shot Ferrars straight through the eye, which I was unwilling to do unless I had absolutely no other choice. Ferrars was not worth having a murder on my conscience.

I kept my voice calm, conversational. "I might not be able to cause you serious injury. But what I can do is provide a distraction."

"Distraction?" It was almost comical to watch the look of confusion pass across Ferrars's too-handsome face. "What are you talking about?"

"That."

As I spoke the last word, Jack surged to his feet, wrapping one arm around Ferrars's chest and yanking him backwards. Ferrars's gun clattered to the floor as Jack laid the blade of his knife against Ferrars's throat.

"Easy, now," Jack murmured. "No need to get excited. Just stay quiet and maybe there's a chance you'll get to walk out of here."

Ferrars really was a coward. The knife blade had barely nicked him, but his face blanched, turning chalky white, and he went rigidly immobile in Jack's grasp.

"It didn't occur to you that it was rather too easy for you to grab Jack and drag him down here?" I asked. "We knew you would make a move like this. When Jack said he was tempted to stab himself from sheer boredom when we first came in here, that was him telling me that you hadn't found and taken away the knife he'd hidden in the top of his boot."

Jack looked up at me. "Sorry it took so long. I couldn't get the angle of the knife right."

He turned, showing me his wrist, which was still wrapped with the frayed remains of a rope. It was stained with blood; he must have cut himself while sawing through the bonds.

I let out a breath. Swooning with relief was out of the question; I still had standards. So I only steadied myself with one hand against the wall.

"Better late than never. We need to get upst—"

"Dear me, dear me."

The sound of the voice behind me made me feel as though my entire body had suddenly fallen through a crack in the surface of an icy pond.

Even before I turned, my pulse had already slammed into higher gear. But as I faced the doorway, I froze, my heart going momentarily dead in my chest.

Dr. William Everett—at least, that was the name by which I knew him—stood just outside the little storage room. With him, her back pressed to his front, was Mary.

And Everett was holding a revolver pressed firmly to her temple.

38. Shots in the Night

My own heartbeat pounded, reverberating in my ears. No plan survives first contact with the enemy.

That was another of Uncle John's sayings, one learned from his army days. That was why it was important always to formulate backup plans.

But *none* of our plans for this evening had involved Mary's being dragged into this confrontation.

Unlike mine, Dr. Everett's weapon was a .44 caliber British Bulldog revolver that would do fatal damage, especially fired at close range. One squeeze of his finger, and the doctor could end Mary's life.

Mary still wore her kimono from the *Mikado* number. Beneath the white stage makeup, her face was grayish pale, her eyes terrified and pleading.

"Lucy? Lucy, what's *happening*? What is all this about? Tell him to let me go!"

Her voice broke on the final words as Dr. Everett yanked her even harder against him. "Shut it."

His voice was indifferent, almost careless—and with equal indifference, he struck the butt of his revolver against the side of Mary's face.

Mary gasped in pain and then started to cry—though she was also obviously terrified of moving or making a sound. Tears rolled in silent tracks down her face, making trails in the face paint.

"Dear, dear." In a blink, Dr. Everett's usual jolly, unassuming persona was back—all the more sickening because I knew exactly what lay behind the mask.

At least he had dropped the pretense of a nervous stutter that he had assumed at our last meeting.

He wore a gentleman's evening dress of black tie and white waistcoat. He had not been among the guests at the ball, I was certain. I would have seen him. But maybe he had blended with the arriving guests in order to get into the museum, then remained in concealment until now.

His long thin face was fixed in an affable half-smile. Only his eyes remained chillingly, soullessly cold.

"Our present circumstances are lamentably melodramatic." His glance swiveled from me, still clutching my pistol, to Jack, whose grip on Ferrars hadn't faltered.

"I believe that this conversation would go more smoothly if you would put the gun down, Miss James?"

I did *not* do as he asked. I doubted that he expected I would. Instead, I forced a breath past the tightness in my chest.

"Let her go. Mary doesn't have any part of this."

"On the contrary." Dr. Everett's thin mouth creased in a smile. "She is currently serving as hostage to your good behavior—which means that she has a very *important* part in this. Now,

Miss James. I really must insist that you set the weapon on the floor. Unless you wish your friend's brains to be spattered all over those rather uninspired examples of ancient Assyrian pots."

He nodded towards the nearest storage shelf.

Mary almost choked, trying to hold back a fresh sob.

"All right!" I held my hands up, bending down to set the Ladysmith at my feet. I felt horribly naked without the weapon, but could not see any other choice. I did not for a single moment doubt that Dr. Everett would make good on his threat.

I felt as though I were watching the sands of an invisible hourglass slip steadily away. Ten minutes, Ferrars had said. How much longer did we have now? Eight minutes? Less.

Dr. Everett nodded. "Very good, very good. Now you." His gaze fixed on Jack. "You let my associate go and step away. Slowly, if you please."

"Yeah, I don't think so." Jack's expression was grimly set, but his voice was even. "You'll just shoot her anyway and then move on to the rest of us."

"Perhaps, perhaps." The doctor's tone held a slightly more biting edge than usual. "But I shall certainly shoot her if you do *not* comply."

"Try it," Jack said. "Your friend here will be dead before her body even hits the ground."

"Dear me." Dr. Everett's voice was still pleasant, genteel. But he was sufficiently irritated that he omitted adding a second *dear me*. "I do so abhor an impasse. Perhaps I have not found quite the right bargaining point for you."

Keeping his hold on Mary, he abruptly took the revolver away from her temple and pointed it at me, instead.

"If you do not do as I ask, I will shoot *Miss James* first." Dr. Everett's voice was now laced with steel.

Jack's grip on Ferrars did not slacken, but I saw his expression shift, almost imperceptibly.

He was gauging the distance between himself and Doctor Everett—calculating whether he could tackle the doctor and wrestle the gun away before Dr. Everett managed to get off a shot.

But that was impossible. Jack was hampered by holding Ferrars. He would have to shove Ferrars away first—or kill him—and *then* launch himself at the doctor. By which point, Dr. Everett would already have shot me.

My heart thundered in my ears, the beats seeming unnaturally stretched and lengthened. Even the sights and colors of this dingy little basement storage room seemed unnaturally clear and bright.

This would be an excellent time for that miracle I had been hoping for to arrive.

However, since no miracle was forthcoming, I would just have to make my own.

I saw Dr. Everett's finger move on the revolver's trigger—and I threw myself forward, diving down low, so that I crashed into first Mary's legs and then Everett's.

A roar of a gunshot tore through the room, hammering my eardrums. A burning flash of pain shot through my upper arm. But Mary and Dr. Everett toppled over, landing on the floor with me.

I scrambled to untangle myself, searching frantically for the doctor's weapon, which had fallen—I thought it had fallen—

when I knocked him over. I barely heard the voice calling my name.

"Lucy!" Jack's voice finally cut through the ringing in my ears. I turned to realize that he had come to crouch beside me, his expression more shaken than I had ever seen it.

"Lucy, how badly are you hurt?"

"Hurt?" I felt oddly light-headed, but I looked down at the red stain that had blossomed on the sleeve of my dairy-maid's gown. That explained the burning pain in my arm; the bullet must have grazed me.

I looked up and saw that both Ferrars and Dr. Everett lay unmoving on the ground. Mary was huddled in a corner, still sobbing.

"Are they dead?"

"Not unless Goldilocks there died from sheer terror. I knocked them out, that's all."

Which left us free—but it also meant we couldn't question them as to the location of the bomb.

"We need to get upstairs."

Jack looked down at my arm.

Before he could speak I said, "I will *not* let you go alone!"

Jack opened his mouth, then closed it again. "All right, then. Come on."

We locked the still-unconscious Everett and Ferrars in the storage room. Jack took the key. I managed to get to the top of the basement stairs without stopping, though dizziness kept coming at me in waves. Behind me, I could hear Mary stumbling along more slowly. But I didn't have any attention to spare for her just now.

"Where would they have hidden a bomb?" Jack was not out of breath in the slightest.

I pressed my eyes shut, ordering myself to *think*. Where would—

Jack and I both spoke at the same time. "The podium!"

The podium in the ballroom, where Commissioner Bradford would give his speech.

Jack opened his mouth.

"Go," I told him. I would only slow him down.

Jack started forwards—and nearly collided with two men who were just leaving the ballroom.

Holmes, still wearing his ginger wig. And an older man, with a crest of white hair, a white mustache, and a tanned, square-cut face. This second man wore a military uniform, the chest arrayed with ribbons and medals—and one of his sleeves was empty, pinned up at the elbow. Police Commissioner Bradford.

"Lucy!" A flash of relief crossed Holmes's face at sight of me. "What—"

"There's a bomb! It will go off in five minutes or less if we can't stop it!"

The Police Commissioner straightened, giving me a long look. His eyes were steady and grave—and even though my dizziness, I could see why Jack thought him an honorable man. There was something about him that I liked at once.

"How sure of that are you, young lady?"

"Positive, sir." It was Jack who spoke. "The criminals who set the bomb are unconscious in the basement. You'll want to send a couple of constables down there to take charge of them."

Commissioner Bradford transferred his attention to Jack. He looked as though he were trying to make up his mind about something. Jack held the older man's gaze.

"This is the detective constable you were telling me about?" Commissioner Bradford asked Holmes.

"Yes, quite correct."

The police commissioner seemed to come to a rapid decision. "You get to work on clearing the ballroom. Try to keep people calm. Say the word *bomb* or *explosion*, and there'll be all the makings of a riot in here."

"Yes, sir."

Holmes was already halfway across the ballroom, heading straight towards the podium. Plainly he had the same thought as to the bomb's location as I. Now I just had to hope that we were right.

By the time I managed to push my way across the ballroom, Holmes and Commissioner Bradford were working together to tilt the podium over onto its side.

Behind me, Jack had stopped the orchestra from playing and was directing the guests to file out. But there were still far too many people in the ballroom—and as the commissioner had said, if word got out about a bomb, there would be an instant stampede. People would be trampled and hurt or even killed.

Holmes succeeded in moving the podium and sucked in a breath. "There we are. Quite a clever apparatus, really."

My vision had started to shiver oddly, but I saw Holmes point to a complicated-looking arrangement of tubes and glass vials. "As you can see, the acid in this vial here would in a few more minutes have eroded through the barrier to mix with—"

"We don't need a lecture right now!" Commissioner Bradford barked. "What we need to know is whether it can be disarmed!"

Holmes's lips pursed as he studied the apparatus. "I believe … yes."

Reaching into the mechanism with one deft, delicate motion, he withdrew a small glass vial of some clear liquid. "The device is now harmless."

39. Epilogue

Police Commissioner Bradford took out a handkerchief and mopped his brow. "I—and your country—thank you."

His glance included the three of us: Holmes, myself, and Jack.

We were standing on the steps outside the museum. The ball was over, and the guests were gone—most of them with no idea of how narrowly they had escaped death tonight. Mary had departed, too, saying that she was going back to our flat.

At some point, I was going to have to give her a severely edited version of tonight's events, one that kept Sherlock Holmes's name entirely out of it. But that shouldn't be too hard. She had never seen Holmes—and she already knew that Jack was a policeman. I could say that the criminals who had taken her captive had been trying to frame Jack, out of a desire for revenge.

Below us in the street, I could see Ferrars and Dr. Everett being led, in handcuffs, to a waiting police wagon. Dr. Everett's face was stony. Ferrars looked torn between anger and terror.

My arm burned as though it had been dipped in boiling oil, but I blinked hard, trying to clear shreds of fog from my sight. I still needed to speak with Commissioner Bradford, urgently.

"That man is the one who killed Inspector Mallows." I gestured to Ferrars. "*Not* Constable Kelly. I don't doubt that Dr. Everett gave the orders. But Ferrars fully admitted to carrying out the murder in my hearing. I will testify to it, if need be."

"Thank you, Miss James. Though it may not be necessary. I myself heard those two berating one another before I unlocked the caretaker's room. Mr. Holmes has also testified on behalf of Constable Kelly's good character. And it is possible a confession may be wrung from our long-haired prisoner." Commissioner Bradford's eyes were trained appraisingly on Ferrars. "He looks the type to break under pressure."

The commissioner glanced at Jack. "At any rate, I believe a formal pardon and apology to you are in order, Constable Kelly. As well as a commendation for your bravery and quick thinking tonight."

"Thank you, sir." Jack said something else—I thought—but the words deconstructed into a meaningless jumble as a roaring filled my ears.

Through the darkening tunnel of my vision, I saw Holmes's eyes widen in entirely uncharacteristic alarm. "Catch her! She's going to faint!"

I drew myself up—or tried to. My muscles refused to obey. "That is ridiculous. I never faint—"

I did not get any further, though. A great wave of darkness seemed to rise up, swallowing me whole.

* * *

Jack's face was the first thing I saw when I opened my eyes.

He was sitting on a hard wooden chair beside my bed, and we appeared to be ... back in Baker Street.

That's right. I tried to push my hair back before wincing as I remembered my injured arm.

I had a vague memory of the journey back here from the museum. Mrs. Hudson's shocked, frightened face when we appeared on her doorstep. Uncle John, examining and bandaging my arm.

"I'm going to have to come up with a new name for you," Jack said.

Weak morning sunlight filtered through the curtains. He was smiling faintly, but I could still see the lingering signs of worry in his dark eyes. "I think you've moved past *Trouble* right on into *Mad as a Hatter*."

I struggled to sit up, finally accepting the hand that Jack offered. "I'm eminently sensible!"

"You dove straight *towards* a loaded weapon."

"True. But everything worked out all right in the end."

"Except for the part where you got shot."

"Not very badly. If we are competing for heroic injuries received in the line of duty, you're still ahead of me. You were shot. Mine was only a graze."

Uncle John had studied the wound and proclaimed it not even the sort of injury that could be stitched. My arm was heavily bandaged from my shoulder down to my elbow—and it throbbed sourly at the moment—but it would heal in a few weeks' time.

I touched the bandages, mentally calculating how close my upper arm was to my heart. "It could have been much worse."

"Trust me, I know."

Jack leaned forward, taking my hand. The touch seemed to run all through me, sparking through my veins.

Jack's eyes fell to our joined fingers, then he seemed to drag his gaze back to mine. "Lucy, I—"

The door behind him swung open, admitting my father.

Holmes still wore the waiter's jacket, but he had at least discarded the ginger wig. He looked at Jack. "You are due at New Scotland Yard in half an hour. Watson has summoned you a cab."

"Thank you, sir." Jack straightened quickly, returning to his place on the chair.

"Scotland Yard!" I looked from Holmes to Jack. "You're not being arrested after all, are you?"

"No, Commissioner Bradford's taken care of all that. They just want me to make a formal statement."

I exhaled with relief. "Good."

"Is it all right if Becky stays here for the morning, sir? I'm not sure how long I'll be."

Holmes's face relaxed into what for him was practically a smile. "The child shows a high degree of promise as a critical thinker. Some of her answers to the puzzles I have set her are decidedly original, even."

I smiled. Knowing Becky, that did not surprise me at all.

Jack looked down at me, seeming to hesitate. But then he stood up, moving away from the bed. "See you soon, Batty."

I made a face. "That's even worse than Trouble."

Jack winked at me. The earnest, intent look in his gaze—if it had ever been there at all—was gone now. "How about Crazy?"

Holmes stood scowling down at me until Jack had gone out.

"Would you like some … what is the proper thing to offer in these circumstances? Some calves' foot jelly?"

"Ugh." I made a face. "No thank you. And I think you're mixing up remedies for gunshots with recipes for invalids."

"Perhaps." Holmes continued to frown. "You at least ought to rest."

"I've just slept all night!" I raised my eyebrows. "Is this your notion of parental guidance?"

"Perhaps." Holmes grimaced. "Although it is not an attitude that appears to come easily to me. I am at the least having serious doubts as to whether you should continue to be involved in this investigation."

"Dr. Everett and Ferrars are already in custody, though."

"For now. At least the case against them is far more likely to stick, with the police commissioner serving as witness for the prosecution. Even traitors amongst the police force can hardly ignore or combat his testimony. Still—"

A muscle ticked in Holmes's jawline as he looked down at me, and his gaze moved to my bandaged arm.

"My rational mind is at war with my emotional responses—a circumstance which I have spent much of my life taking great pains to avoid. As much of an asset as you undoubtedly are to my investigations—"

"An asset?"

Holmes's choice of words touched me almost as much as his concern. I was—*almost*—no longer sorry that he had come in and interrupted whatever Jack had been about to say.

"Really?"

Holmes's eyebrows climbed. "Was that ever in question? I realize that I am not given to effusions. But yes. You are quick-witted, insightful, courageous, and observant. In short, you are—exactly the daughter I would have wished for."

For a second, I could scarcely see my father, through the shimmering of tears that filled my vision. "Thank you."

"Yes—hmmm. However, the fact remains—"

"If you're going to question my involvement, I'm involved in the investigation already," I said quietly.

The memory of those minutes in the museum basement came back to me.

"Ferrars said *your father*, to me—meaning you. *Your father's not the only one who can put on a wig*. He knows that we are related. He knows how we are related. Which means that the rest of his organization clearly does, too."

I studied Holmes's face as I finished speaking. "You're not surprised." His expression was grim, but not in the least shocked.

"No. I am afraid that I suspected that such might be the case."

"Why?"

Holmes did not answer at once, but his eyes flicked just briefly upwards, towards the upper floor where Uncle John had his room. Then he looked down at me. "Perhaps we ought to postpone this discussion until you are feeling more restored."

Despite what I had told Holmes about having slept, I was feeling tired. My eyelids seemed to have been weighted with lead.

"Will you at least tell me about *Éire go Brách*?" I asked. "Do you think the organization we are tracking has something to do with Ireland and not Germany after all?"

"Not necessarily. I merely believe the situation more complicated—and that there are more organizations than just the Kaiser's who would revel in Britain's downfall and ruin."

I try not to let my eyes slide shut.

Holmes's expression softened. "I am hardly one to preach, given how often Watson has lectured me on the importance of proper rest. But I do admit that it has its place in restoring both mind and body after an injury. Sleep, and we can discuss all of this at further length later on."

I let myself drop back onto the pillows. I shut my eyes, feeling myself start to drift off.

A sudden realization flashed across my mind—the nagging memory that I had searched for in vain before.

My eyes snapped open again. "You told him!"

Holmes had moved to the door, his hand on the knob. He blinked. "I beg your pardon?"

"Jack. When we were talking before—at the start of all of this—you said that Jack might find it hard to voice his feelings, knowing that I had once been courted by Johnny Rockefeller. But how would Jack have known that? I never said anything! *You* must have told him."

I sat up straighter, my fatigue all but gone. "That's the only way that you could have known about Jack's knowing. You must have spoken to Jack in private, sometime when I wasn't there, and—"

I stopped, staring at Holmes as another memory seemed to slot into place in my mind.

"Last night—at the museum. All of that rubbish about believing me to be safe in Jack's presence. You weren't being overprotective. You said it *deliberately*, as some sort of test, or—"

Holmes's face was the oddest mixture of culpability and pride that I had ever seen. He turned more fully around, releasing his hold on the door.

"I find myself even less prepared to cope with the possibility of a son-in-law than I was with a daughter. However, having observed you with Constable Kelly, I found myself once again prey to an almost overwhelming emotional impulse. In this case, to ensure that the young man was worthy of you."

"You saw ..."

"My dear Lucy. Just because I do not myself partake in affairs of the heart does not mean that I am blind to them. I have seen how the young man looks at you—particularly when he does not believe that he is being observed. As you and Watson know, I deplore poetic descriptions. However, I believe it would be accurate to say that Constable Kelly looks at you as though you were the sunrise on a dark winter morning."

I blinked again—this time against a fresh shimmer of tears.

"However, emotional infatuation is a notoriously unreliable foundation for marital happiness. I wished to ensure that Constable Kelly had the courage to overcome what he might see as a disparity in your relative stations. Hence my mention of the Rockefeller boy. Also, given your proclivities for ploughing headlong into danger with utter disregard for your personal safety—"

Holmes cleared his throat. "Yes, well. Given all of that, I doubt that you would find happiness with a man who insists on keeping his wife safely at home, out of harm's way. I wished there to be no doubt in my own mind that Constable Kelly could accept you for who you are—a free and independent agent, capable of making decisions and looking after yourself."

I wiped my cheek. Without my realizing it, a tear had slipped out from the corner of my eye.

Holmes was silent a moment. Then he smiled.

"I must say that the young man has so far not only passed every test I have set him but exceeded my expectations. All save one: I believe he still hesitates to speak, believing his station and family background make a marriage between you unthinkable. As of course, in the eyes of society at large, it does."

"Maybe I'll have to ask him to marry me instead."

Holmes's smile deepened. "As I say, I never thought to have a daughter, much less a son-in-law. Nor, I know, is it my place to influence your choosing, given the lack of a role I have played in your life to date. However, if Constable Kelly is your choice, then should you wish it—and only should you wish it—you have what I suppose one may term my blessing."

I stopped crying. I had been waiting to say these words a long while, and I was not going to spoil them with tears.

I smiled, looking up into the keen gray eyes of Sherlock Holmes.

Thank you, Father.

In my mind, the words were clear and resonant.

But what I heard myself say was, "Thank you, Mr. Holmes."

THE END

ACKNOWLEDGEMENTS

My first round of thanks goes to my father, Charles Veley, for reading me Sherlock Holmes books as bedtime stories before I could read them—or anything else of that level, for that matter—for myself. Also thank you to my mother for letting him read murder mysteries to a seven year old.

Secondly, I must thank my father again for creating the wonderful character of Lucy James and then being gracious enough to hand her over to me; I couldn't love writing her more.

Thank you to my husband, Nathan, for all the constant support and for being every bit as brilliantly intelligent as Sherlock Holmes.

Thank you to my daughters, for being my real-life inspiration for Becky's character; anyone who doubts the realism of Becky's spunkiness should meet my girls.

To my son who … well, honestly at three years old, you're not a tremendous help with the writing, but that's okay, you're still the literal cutest.

Thanks also to Laurence Bouvard and Edward Petherbridge for their wonderful audiobook performances in the Audible version of *Remember Remember*. I must confess that I am a lifelong fan of Mr. Petherbridge, and that hearing his voice reading my words is more or less a ridiculously over-the-top dream come true.

Lastly, to Holmes fans everywhere: thank you for your continued love of the Sherlock Holmes character that allows authors like myself the chance to write books like *Remember, Remember*, and imagine ourselves for a short while into Holmes's world.

A Note of Thanks to Our Readers, and Some News

Thank you for reading this third episode of the *Sherlock Holmes and Lucy James Mystery Series.*

If you've enjoyed the story, we would very much appreciate your going to the page where you bought the book and uploading a quick review. As you probably know, reviews make a big difference!

The other three adventures in the series are currently available in e-book, paperback and audiobook formats: *The Last Moriarty, The Wilhelm Conspiracy,* and the prequel to the series, *The Crown Jewel Mystery.*

Watch for more Sherlock and Lucy books to be released in 2017, including:

The Jubilee Problem (September)
Death at the Diogenes Club (November)

And next year, be sure to watch for *The Return of the Ripper* and a collection of Sherlock and Lucy short stories, coming in early 2018!

About the Author

Anna Elliott is the author of the *Twilight of Avalon* trilogy, and *The Pride and Prejudice Chronicles.* She was delighted to lend a hand in giving the character of Lucy James her own voice, firstly because she loves Sherlock Holmes as much as her father, Charles Veley, and second because it almost never happens that someone with a dilemma shouts, "Quick, we need an author of historical fiction!" She lives in Maryland with her husband and three children.

Contents

PART I
BACK IN TIME

PART II
FORWARD

Made in the USA
Middletown, DE
24 November 2017